ROBERT TRAVER is the pen name of a former Michigan Supreme Court justice. He is also the author of *Anatomy of a Murder*, *Hornstein's Boy*, and *Trout Madness*. He lives in the Upper Peninsula area of Michigan.

PEOPLE VERSUS KIRK

Also by Robert Traver

Anatomy of a Murder
Hornstein's Boy
Trout Madness

PEOPLE VERSUS KIRK

Robert Traver

St. Martin's Press
New York

For information, write: St. Martin's Press,
175 Fifth Avenue, New York, N.Y. 10010
Manufactured in the United States of America
Library of Congress Cataloging in Publication Data

Traver, Robert, 1903–
People versus Kirk.

I. Title.
PS3570.R339P4 813'.54 81–8885
ISBN 0–312–60006–2 AACR2

Design by Manuela Paul
10 9 8 7 6 5 4 3 2 1
First Edition

To Paul C. Young, American pioneer
in a neglected field of psychology.

When to the sessions of sweet silent thought
I summon up remembrance of things past,
I sigh the lack of many a thing I sought,
And with old woes new wail my dear time's waste.

Sonnet XXX
WILLIAM SHAKESPEARE

PART ONE

Before The Trial

Chapter 1

Shortly before nine o'clock the sheriff marched into court with my client, jaw resolutely jutting, one hand resting with casual vigilance on the butt of his pistol, following so closely behind his prisoner that I helplessly thought of an eye-rolling cigar-puffing Groucho avidly stalking a dame in one of his old movies, the scene conveying a memorable picture of law and order triumphant.

At least our scene-creating sheriff doesn't have the poor bastard clamped in handcuffs, I thought, noticing that Randall Kirk, still wearing the informal sweater, slacks and sneakers outfit he'd been arrested in, was nearly as tall as the bulky sheriff, who, naturally, was known throughout his bailiwick as "Tiny."

All of which, I reflected, tended to confirm a recently proclaimed theory of my ever-scoffing law partner, Jeremiah Dundee. "Though—or maybe because—our sheriffs are just about the only breed of cops left in the whole country that the voters still have any say in choosing," he had said, "most of those who win the jobs seem to get elected more for their resemblance to that Matt Dillon character on TV than for possessing even the slightest aptitude for law enforcement." He had shaken his head. "I swear, getting elected sheriff nowadays is mostly a matter of combined altitude and avoirdupois, damned if it ain't."

"Amen," I had said. "That and for owning the highest bowling average among the swarm of rival candidates."

Sheriff Matthew Wallenstein carefully paraded my client up the broad middle aisle between the twin rows of mahogany benches and around the court-dividing mahogany railing, finally delivering him beside me at the defense table with all the dramatic aplomb of a headwaiter.

"Mornin', Fritz," the sheriff greeted me, giving me a hearty thump on the back. "How's the Clarence Darrow of the Iron Cliffs County Bar doin' this fine July mornin'?"

"Hi, Matt," I said after recovering, marveling over the man's unappeasable appetite for corn. I wondered vaguely whether he campaigned in his sleep as I watched him stride over to the adjoining prosecution table and virtually hug my legal opponent in the case, Eugene Canda, the curly-headed young prosecuting attorney (Michigan's prosaic statutory label for what on television is invariably called the DA). The sheriff hitched around his leather holster—which housed a revolver ponderous enough to floor a charging rhino—and finally squeezed himself into a mahogany chair beside the prosecutor while whispering earnestly into his ear.

I turned toward my client and found him also observing Sheriff Matt's pantomime, smiling faintly.

"Good morning, Randy," I said.

"Ah, good mornin' to you, Mr. Darrow," he said, playing the sheriff's game, almost contriving to sound like the hearty-voiced guano-spreading sheriff himself.

"Have a good weekend?" I inquired, making what had become our increasingly feeble Monday morning joke all the more feeble because he'd been confined in the county jail without bail ever since his arrest for murder over a month before.

"Radiant," he said. "One meets such an absorbing variety of people in the sheriff's resort hotel." He gave me a wan smile. "Perhaps I should say 'last resort hotel.' "

"Especially when one is confined in an exclusive third-floor cell, commanding such a magnificent view of Lake Superior and its iron-ore loading docks from one's flyblown window."

"Positively aerates the soul," my client said, absently fingering his wispy blond mustache, a creation he'd grown while in jail. He had sheepishly explained that its cultivation just might help him retain a few lingering wisps of sanity.

"Some guys got it made," I murmured, reaching for my battered leather briefcase—salvaged from law school days—plopping my already bulky files on our polished mahogany counsel table, wondering what in hell was delaying our circuit judge, and flipping open a manila folder to sneak a quick review before the tardy judge showed up.

Instead I grabbed the wrong folder and opened it to confront the initial newspaper write-up of my case, which I compulsively reread. Once again I was struck by the amount of spicy scandal a clever reporter—in this instance young Miles Coffey of the *Mining Gazette*—could manage to imply in an apparently straightforward account of the sensational homicide that had recently stirred the area.

MINING HEIRESS FOUND SLAIN
NEAR LUXURIOUS ISLAND HOME,

the headline read. "*Socialite Bachelor Jailed for Suspected Strangulation-Murder*" followed underneath. The news account itself, datelined Chippewa, an iron-mining town lying some dozen miles inland from the county courthouse, was brutally brief:

> The body of Mrs. Jason (Constance) Spurrier, 32, prominent society matron and heiress to an iron-mining fortune, was found late last night lying on the beach near her island summer home known as Treasure Island, located on exclusive Treasure Island Lake several miles north of this iron-mining town.
>
> The body of the dead woman was discovered around midnight wearing a bikini and lying face down in shallow water, by her housekeeper, Ms. Viola Axholm. Ms. Axholm dragged the body from the water and immediately summoned police.
>
> State police and the Iron Cliffs County Sheriff's Department joined in the investigation, following which State Police Detective Sergeant Harlow Maxim issued a brief statement to the effect that it appeared that the dead woman may have been strangled and that Randall Kirk, 28, a resident of Long Island and a

> frequent summer visitor in the area, was being held in the county jail at Iron Bay without bail on an open charge of first degree murder, adding that Kirk had signed a voluntary police statement.
>
> The dead woman is the former Constance Farrow, daughter of the late Mr. and Mrs. Borden Farrow, a pioneer iron-mining family in the Lake Superior area. She is survived by her husband, Jason Spurrier, and by a son by a former marriage, Marius Blair, age 11, presently attending school in the East. Funeral arrangements are incomplete, pending conclusion of the official autopsy and the return of the surviving husband from an eastern trip.

There it was, naked as a weather report, I mused, and yet the clever young *Gazette* reporter had not only managed to convey an impression of sybaritic goings-on in high places but had also posed some ever so titillating questions. What, for one thing, was the lovely, scantily clad Constance Spurrier doing out on her darkened beach at midnight? And how had my client, the personable young neighboring bachelor Randy Kirk, just happened to be on hand? And if a tryst hadn't been arranged, how else would he have known that Connie's husband was so conveniently out of town? What is the true story behind this enigmatic affair? Be sure to read all about it in future issues of the *Mining Gazette* . . .

Chapter 2

Court had been scheduled to open sharp at nine but Judge Brotherton, usually a stickler for punctuality, was already nearly a quarter-hour late. Just as I began toying with the heretical notion that this model of judicial punctilio might for once have forgotten a slated court hearing I was punished for my sins: a tall mahogany door breathed open and His Honor himself entered at full stride, his black robe billowing behind him, the heavy door closing after his passage with a pneumatic hiss reminiscent of that accompanying the entrance of an old-time stage villain.

He was carrying a legal-size manila folder, half-hidden in the rippling folds of his robe, which electrically swished and crackled with each new billow. As he gained and mounted the short steps leading up to his high mahogany bench he stumbled a little, and I wondered how many of the others present knew how nearsighted the poor man was and how proudly he disdained showing it. Finally he stood, flushed and glaring, between his bench and high-backed chair, his eyes owlishly magnified by the thick, horn-rimmed glasses he wore.

"Held up at a railroad crossing by a stalled ore train," he murmured to no one in particular, not by way of apology—as any of us courthouse regulars well knew—but rather so that we groundlings might marvel along with him over one of those unpredictable tricks of fortune that could occasionally conspire even to make *him* late. As we sat there duly marveling, Judge Brotherton nodded curtly at the bailiff, who rose and gaveled the sparsely filled courtroom to its feet.

"Hear ye, hear ye, hear!" he bawled with the ardor of a prize-fight announcer. "This honorable circuit court for the County of Iron Cliffs is now in session!" He then dealt his battered butcher block a final whack, whereupon all present plumped back to their seats with a communal sigh.

"The law cagily copies the early churches," my law partner had recently announced during one of his declamatory seizures, "awing the peasantry into submission with a mixture of baffling ritual, high-flown rhetoric, and just plain hogwash."

"All our courtrooms lack are pipe organs two stories high," I had ventured.

"Mortgaged pipe organs," the old boy had corrected me, quick as a wink.

"Yes, sir," I had answered, meekly giving up, sensibly realizing that in an informal verbal tennis match with the old boy one simply couldn't ever win.

Judge Brotherton flipped open his manila folder and, bowing his head, leaned forward so long and intently that the initiated might have suspected he was deep in prayer. We older courtroom hands knew better. His bowed concentration was merely his sly way of making a final review of his notes without having to raise them to eye level and thus expose his nearsightedness.

The judge looked up, took a sip of water, cleared his throat, nodded at the court reporter to alert him that hostilities were imminent, adjusted his glasses by jiggling one of the bows, drilled his right ear with his little finger, rubbed his palm across the bristly margin of his nearly bald head (reminding me with a pang of my own thinning hair), and emitted a final trumpet clearing of his throat—all familiar symptoms that court was about to open. Naturally my ever-observant law partner had recently delivered himself on *that* phenomenon, too.

"Judges opening their courts for the day," he had declared,

"tend to exhibit all of the preliminary tics, scratchings and twitches of a pitcher going into his wind-up."

"Are we ready to proceed, gentlemen?" Judge Brotherton leaned forward and inquired, glancing down at the prosecutor's table and then over at mine.

Eugene Canda and I sprang to our feet and, amid a cascade of obeisant Your Honors, assured our poor overworked judge that we were panting to begin.

Chapter 3

"Very well," the judge said, leaning forward and taking a final squint at his notes. "This special July term of the circuit court for Iron Cliffs County is convened for the purpose of hearing the petition of one Frederic Ludlow, a duly licensed attorney admitted to practice in this court."

At the mention of my name I wriggled myself upright in my chair, felt my face redden, and barely restrained myself from rising and taking a bow.

"By his petition," the judge continued, "Mr. Ludlow seeks an order of this court requiring the sheriff of this county to allow the petitioner access to his jail along with another qualified person for the purpose of examining one Randall Kirk, client of petitioner, presently confined there without bail, awaiting trial on a charge of first degree murder of one Constance Spurrier, and for the further purpose of attempting to stimulate the recall of his client's claimed lapsed memory."

I glanced at my client, sitting next to me, head bowed, one hand over his eyes, his body seeming to sink lower as the judge continued, and I wondered if he could weather the storm. For by now I knew a number of things about both my client and his case that made his plight more baffling than even my petition disclosed; things that few people in the courtroom or elsewhere could possibly have known; a few things that puzzled even me, his lawyer; startling things I had only recently dredged out of him by threatening to quit his case if he didn't speak out.

One thing I had learned, but only after close and repeated questioning, sometimes to the point of open quarreling, was that Randall Kirk had long been in love with Constance Spurrier, dating back to the days he first began summering on the wooded shores of the lake where Connie lived.

During my almost-daily probing I had also learned in bits and snatches that in recent years he had spent most of the year at the Michigan cottage. He had inherited the cottage from his parents following a tragic automobile accident in which both were killed while returning to their permanent home in Long Island. My client still maintained that home as his "winter" as well as his legal residence.

My almost-daily drilling was not done out of morbid curiosity—heaven knows, defenders of forgetful murder clients scarcely have time for such luxuries—but in the waning hope of stimulating his memory as well as learning some of the other things he should rather obviously be able to recall, regardless of his claimed lost memory of what had happened on the fatal night. This constant probing had created a growing tension between us, aggravated by my increasingly impatient questioning that followed his continual lack of response. In fact, I had only lately consulted my partner about my frustration.

"Despite Watergate," I concluded my lament, "during the heyday of which so many in our profession achieved the public stature of scampering mice, we lawyers still possess a low animal pride. If I gotta lose his goddamn case I prefer doing so knowing everything he knows, so we can at least share the loss."

"Absolutely," Jeremiah agreed. "Tell the bastard plain out that if he doesn't come clean, and fast, you'll up and quit his case. You have my blessing, lad." He thought a moment. "And if he does talk I'll bet you a five you'll learn he's been laying the lass for years."

"It's a bet," I said, fleetingly recalling my own lone encounter with the disturbing Connie.

The showdown with Randy had come abruptly one drizzly afternoon up in my client's lonely third-floor cell. I'd even worked up a little mollifying speech, which I'd delivered while he sat on his narrow jail cot and I on his lone wooden stool.

"Look, Randy," I began, "while there is no law that a lawyer must fall in love with his client in order to decently represent him, it does help some if his client trusts him even just a little instead of clamming up about *some* things he's simply bound to know despite his claimed lack of memory about other things."

"Like what things?" my client said, giving me an amused smile.

"I'm not through yet," I said, doggedly pushing on. "Your continued combination of no talk and no recall is driving me up a tree. Now, let's grant you can't help your lack of memory about the fatal night, but frankly I'm getting fed up with your continued failure to tell me other things you're simply bound to know"—I paused—"that's unless you've completely lost your mind, which is something a groping defense attorney also needs to know."

"I hadn't realized I'd been evasive," Randall Kirk said, giving me a searching look. "What precisely do you think I've been holding out on you?"

"Damn near everything," I said, warming up. "And especially about the real relationship between you and Connie Spurrier, which could prove vital."

"I've already told you I've known and been fond of Connie since we were teen-agers," he said. "What more could you possibly need to know?"

"Plenty," I answered, pushing on. "And since you won't volunteer I've simply got to ask you. That's unless you expect me to blindly go into court to defend both you and Connie's memory—something, I may as well tell you now, I don't propose to do."

"Let's have it," he said quietly, half-shutting his eyes.

"Did you and Connie ever sleep together?"

His whole body seemed to tense and his fists clenched. For a moment I thought he was going to swing at me. But he just kept staring at me, not so much reproachfully as uncomprehendingly, staring in wonder at the crude country lawyer he had retained who could so boldly invade his privacy and, even worse, so crassly violate his personal code.

"Well?" I said, feeling my own hackles rising, reaching for my briefcase as though to take off.

"How could you dare ask such a thing?"

"Easy," I said, basking in the full glare of his scorn and barely conquering an impulse to hang my head. "All I got to do is remember how goddamn frustrated and stumped I feel trying to find a possible legal defense for a closemouthed guy accused of murder who only keeps telling me over and over that he can't recall a thing."

"What's that got to do with it?" he said.

"Plenty," I said, deciding finally to level with him all the way, whatever the cost. "During the umpteen times I've visited you up in this crummy cell you keep telling me the same old story, over and over, only recently reluctantly revealing that you might also have been in love with Connie Spurrier."

"I still don't get the point," he said coldly.

"You will," I said, "because I now think it's past high time I told you, without boring you with the legalistic details, that in my opinion you so far haven't come within a country mile of showing me a possible legal defense to your murder charge. Forgetting you killed a person is no defense to murder under any law I've been able to find, and, I may add, I've just about worn my ass off looking."

"Are you suggesting I plead guilty?" he said.

"Just lay off the sarcasm till I'm done," I said. "Now I cannot tell you how incurious I am about the love lives of the people I represent," I went on, "most of which either repel or bore the bejabbers out of me, except as their revelation just might help me to help them. Please get that clear."

"Go on," he said in a sort of resigned monotone.

"If I knew you had regularly been sleeping with Connie Spurrier, my sole reaction, aside from envy, would be for any possible clues that knowledge might lead to."

"Like what?"

"Like maybe somebody else killed her. Like maybe she

killed herself. Like maybe it was an accident or self-defense or something else. Are you still with me?"

"I'm still listening."

"Now you can choose to play it one of several ways," I said. "One, continue to clam up like a true gentleman stoicly taking his medicine to spare the memory and reputation of the woman he says he loved."

"Yes?"

"Another is to swallow your pride and help the baffled lawyer who's trying his damnedest to help you by telling him everything—and I mean *everything*—that just might possibly help him unravel what really happened." I paused to feed out some bait. "I'm only asking my client to confide a little in his own lawyer, not shout it to the world."

"Proceed," he said, for the first time seeming to untense a little.

"Now I'm going to ask you just once more one straight blunt question, all euphemism aside. If you prefer not to answer that question I promise I'll pick up my marbles and go, leaving you free to hire yourself a less prying and more genteel lawyer guaranteed to speaketh not in the idiom of the bowling alley. Are you ready?"

"I'm ready to listen," he answered quietly.

"Were you having sexual relations with Connie Spurrier?"

He sat staring coldly at me. As the silence continued, I arose from his wooden stool, stepped over to the narrow cell door, and stood facing him.

"Of course, if you still prefer to keep a stiff upper lip and let some other lawyer escort you from here to a new prison cell, then so be it," I said, glancing at my watch. "But two can play at feeling wounded, and I warn you that if you don't say something, and fast, I'll not only assume you've had it with me but I'll have had it permanently with you. Speak up, dammit, if only to tell me to get the hell on my way."

He glanced away, over at his seatless toilet, up at his barred cell window, then back at me before he spoke. "I'd—I'll have to ask you one question before I could possibly discuss yours," he said.

"Fire away."

"Would any answer I made to your question ever have to come out later in court?"

"Not necessarily," I said, failing to remind him that by asking his question he'd already pretty well answered mine—as well as just lost me a bet.

"But it might?"

"It could," I answered truthfully.

"How?" he pressed.

"In several ways. One, by the testimony of some third person." I paused and took a shot in the dark. "Like, say, by someone who maybe worked for Connie," I said, thinking of Connie's old housekeeper, Viola Axholm, who had discovered her body.

"But Axholm wouldn't ever—" he blurted, but caught himself and sat silently stroking his thin blond mustache.

"Nobody can predict the course of any jury trial," I went on, trying to help ease the pain of his revealing slip. "It might even happen that you'll finally have to tell the whole story yourself to stand a chance."

"You mean you might ask me about it in court?"

"Not if I could possibly help it. But the prosecutor might, that is unless he thought such a revelation might weaken his case by picturing Connie as a willing adultress. But the point is, he *could* ask you, whether or not you come clean with me here today. That's one big reason I need to know the true story now, not then. A lawyer rarely thrives on surprises in court, especially those bombshells his own client could have spared him."

"But if he did ask me couldn't I refuse to answer?"

"Well, if he asked you whether you had sexual relations with Connie on the night she died you could still honestly answer that you couldn't remember, couldn't you?"

"That's right," he agreed, nodding relievedly. "But how about on any other occasions?"

"I could object," I said.

"How come?"

"Well, for one thing I could object on the grounds that your answer might tend to incriminate you by imputing still another crime," I said, again failing to remind him that the very making of such an objection often itself tacitly conceded an affirmative answer to the question just asked, especially so in the minds of groping lay jurors unversed in more subtle constitutional niceties.

"I don't quite follow."

"Such an objection is often called 'pleading the Fifth,' especially by those carefree newspaper and other media lads and lassies often far more proficient in the art of draining one."

My labored pun had made him smile, however wanly. "But I still don't see what other crime I could be guilty of," he said.

"Adultery," I said, "that good old battered seventh commandment, remember?"

"But how could I ever be guilty of *that?*" he said. "I'm not even married."

"Under most modern statutory versions, including Michigan's, only one party to the collision need be married to make both guilty. Adultery's like the common cold—if one bedfellow contracts it his companion automatically does."

"I never knew that," he said thoughtfully.

"The law is like pregnancy," I ran on, "a little of either being a dangerous thing. You've been learning your law from the wrong almanacs." I glanced at my watch. "But you still haven't quite answered my question so I'd better repeat it. Were you laying Connie? Yes or no?"

"Yes," he answered quietly, almost resignedly, looking down at his hands lying open on his lap.

I restrained a sigh of relief and thought how right my discerning partner had been all along. "I think I'll run along now," I said, thinking about fishing and giving poor Randy a break, "and pester you for details later, probably tomorrow."

"Up to you, Counselor," he said, shrugging indifferently, "now that I've confessed to the one thing I never thought I'd reveal to another living soul."

Chapter 4

"How long had this been going on?" I asked him the next afternoon, back at my drilling.

He closed his eyes and breathed deeply before speaking, like a man steeling himself to face an unpleasant ordeal. "Intermittently, ever since our college days," he murmured, glancing away.

"Then what?" I pressed.

"Then she suddenly married Marius Blair, a summer guest staying on the same lake, and for a time naturally we saw very little of each other," he said, speaking now in a kind of resigned confessional monotone.

"Naturally," I said.

"This ran on until she and Dick—that was his nickname—broke up; then Connie and I again"—he paused, groping for words.

"Renewed your intimacy?" I suggested, cravenly glad, now that I'd gotten Connie safely laid, to go back on the euphemistic standard.

"Thank you, yes," he said, smiling faintly.

"Then what?" I said. He sat silent and unblinking, evidently dredging up a mixed bag of memories. "Then what?" I repeated.

"Oh yes," he murmured apologetically, sitting up straight on his cot. "Then several winters ago or possibly more, while I was out west skiing, Connie impulsively flew east and took off alone on a Caribbean cruise." He exhaled deeply, more like a sigh. "Probably it was my punishment for daring to desert her for skiing, though she'd never quite admit it." Again the swift exhalation. "In any case she richly succeeded in paying me back because she came home with a brand-new husband."

"Jason Spurrier, of course?" I said.

He nodded, his lips compressed.

"And you and she then resumed—ah—the old relationship?" I said, prodding gently, repeating the question when he failed to answer.

"Not right away," he murmured.

"When?" I said.

"When this marriage, too, started to cool and they separated. Along about midsummer, I'd say, about a year ago."

"But how did you and Connie ever manage?" I said, trying not to sound too voyeuristic. "I mean with the new husband around, however cooled his marriage?"

He smiled rather shamefacedly and half-shrugged. "He was often out of town—I mean back East—and when he was around he was usually out fishing. He was excellent at fishing."

"Fly fishing for trout?" I said, only dimly aware that there were curious people in the land who fished other ways for other underwater creatures.

"Of course," he answered.

"Ah, then we're all addled fellow fly fishermen together," I said, "since I too have long had the bug. Funny I haven't run across him on some trout stream or other."

"Probably because he usually fishes a private stretch he owns up on the Yellow Dog River near where it joins Lake Superior. Beautiful place where he's built a cabin, really a sumptuous lodge." He smiled. "Probably why you haven't run into me, either, since we both often sailed and fished together there."

When you weren't home romancing Connie, I thought. "You mean, then, that even after he and Connie actually separated you and he remained on good terms?"

"Oh, yes."

"And still fished together?"

"Yes. Rather more often, in fact."

"When was the last time?"

"Fairly recently," he said. "Let's see—about a week before he flew off to New York." Then a quick intake of breath. "Naturally we haven't since Connie's death."

"You mean, of course, because naturally you and he fell out?" I said.

"No," he said, uncorking a new surprise. "Only because I'm confined here in jail."

It was my turn to take a deep breath. "You mean that you and the bereaved husband *still* haven't fallen out?"

"That's right," he said, "though now during the trout season I don't see him quite so often."

Things were breaking pretty fast and I longed to whip out my notebook to jot them down but thought better of it, resolving instead to take careful mental notes, including his reply to my next question, which I still keep turning over in my mind.

"Tell me," I finally said, "did Jason Spurrier ever know about you and Connie?"

"No," he answered after a pause. "At least I'm pretty sure he didn't. If he suspected anything he surely never showed it. Naturally we never discussed the subject."

Naturally, I thought, for that would violate a gentlemen's code. "How long did you say he and Connie lived apart?" I said.

"About a year except for one fairly recent attempted reconciliation that apparently failed."

"Tell me about that?"

"This past spring, much to my surprise, Connie and he suddenly flew off to New York together, presumably to patch things up, but in a few days she flew back alone and refused even to discuss him or her trip."

"Who was the moving spirit in that attempt?"

"I think he was, but, as I say, Connie seemed only to want to blot him from her mind. All she ever told me about the whole thing was that he had left voluntarily when she earlier filed a divorce action and threatened to seek an injunction barring him from her place on the island."

"But to this day they never were actually divorced?"

"No, Connie kept putting it off, more from sheer inertia than anything, I guess. After their reconciliation attempt failed she told me she soon planned to see her lawyers and push her pending divorce case. Apparently she never did."

"She told you all this only quite recently, then?"

"Yes."

"While under Michigan's no-fault divorce law one can now get rid of a mate merely for eating crackers in bed, did she ever tell you her real reasons for wanting to get rid of him?" I asked.

"Only in a general way, because, as I say, Connie was always reluctant to discuss him, seeming only to want to banish him from her mind as well as from her life."

"Maybe," I said, weighing my words, "she found him—ah—rather inadequate—comparatively speaking, I mean."

He blushed prettily before speaking. "Well, he's considerably older than she is"—he bit his lip—"I mean was. Old enough, I suspect, to have been her father, as the saying goes. Are the reasons important?"

"Not really. The one big universal ground for divorce or separation in this enlightened era is that the parties can no longer endure each other—or think they can't. How come she ever married the old boy in the first place?"

He spread his hands. "I've often speculated about that myself, though I must say I always found him a delightful companion—urbane, cultured, awesomely erudite, with a passion to excel at whatever interests him." He frowned. "Apparently whatever it was she sought she didn't quite find in Jason Spurrier."

I nodded. "In my practice I've helped dissolve so many baffling matrimonial unions and battled so often over alimony, both pending and past due—'accrued acrimony,' my partner calls the latter—that I've ceased pondering why people ever marry," I said. "All I'm really sure of is that all manner of curious people do contrive officially to join hands and that one hell of a lot of them quickly repent and unhand each other." I shrugged. "Perhaps matrimony itself is becoming the biggest enemy of romance."

"You sound rather cynical," he said, smiling. "Are you by any chance married?"

"Married and the deathless knot dissolved," I said. "Divorced by my sensible bride so that I might continue to pursue the beckoning mermaids she evidently suspected I was wooing out on all the malarial bogs where it seems I fished far too often and tarried far too long."

"I know," he said, half-smiling. "Even Connie used to sulk over my own fishing."

"And since I've long suspected that masculine virtue is mostly confined to men in poor health," I ran on, "it follows as the day the night that any moderately healthy married male gives his wife fresh grounds for divorce at least once a day."

"You seem to have brooded over the subject," he said.

"I've seen so much matrimonial wreckage I've been forced to brood, I guess, just as I've also been forced to conclude that the bonds holding most marriages together are even more fragile than those holding friendship—which so damn many marriages seem to lack. People continue to gaily plunge into marriage, without bothering to learn whether they *like* each other —something fairly important to know, one might guess, before two strangers leap into a union so goddamn intimate."

"Love conquers all," he said, smiling wanly. "Isn't that the romantic sugar-coated pill we've all been taught to swallow ever since Shakespeare's day?"

"I guess so," I said, stretching and checking my watching. "But we're running late. Tell me, did I correctly understand you to say that you and the bereaved husband still remain friendly?"

"Oh yes," my client replied, nodding. "In fact he still visits me fairly regularly here in the jail. He's a most interesting man and I'd like to have you meet him. In fact he's told me he'd like to meet you."

Interesting indeed, I thought, both repelled and intrigued over what I was learning, suddenly growing weary of hearing any more about the lovely, restless Connie and the men in her life. But there was one question I still had to ask, a rather delicate one; so I mentally braced myself before letting fly with it.

"I've got one final question," I said. "Did you have a prior date to see Connie on the final night?"

He pondered a moment before replying. "I think not, because we rarely made advance plans to see each other."

"Surely you would remember if you had a date."

"Oh yes. As I've often told you, I remember everything that final day up until some time after darkness fell and I heard that little bell."

Here we go again, I thought. Several times during previous jail visits my client had mentioned hearing the ringing of a mysterious little bell while still home at his cottage, evidently one of his last memories on the fatal evening.

"So you had no formal date, then?" I pressed on, wanting to get away from *that* spooky subject, which was more and more giving me the creeps.

"No," he said. "After Jason moved off the island it was always understood between Connie and me that I'd come to her whenever"—he paused to find the words—"whenever the spirit moved."

"A sort of mutual telepathy, you mean?"

He nodded.

"And how often," I said, trying not to sound too much like a prying satyr, "did the spirit move?"

He flushed a little but answered steadily enough. "Most every night," he said. "Frequently I swam over, and she'd swim out to meet me on a sun raft she kept anchored there or else wait for me on the beach." He paused and then answered the natural question that would spring to the mind of any insect-plagued fisherman. "You see, she had one of those screened-in beach houses—really an elaborate open-air cottage. Sometimes we stayed on the sun raft."

"Then you probably also saw her the night before that final night?" I said, manfully quelling an unlawyerlike impulse to inquire how, after an evening spent with Connie in her sylvan bower, he ever managed to swim back.

"Oh yes. And the night before that."

"You clearly remember that?"

"Of course," he said, his voice fallen to a whisper. "Being with Connie was always an unforgettable experience."

"Except for that final night?"

"Except for that final night," he barely whispered, suddenly turning away.

"That's all for today," I said, rising and moving over to the cell door. "I'll go now, Randy, and ponder these new developments and see what I can come up with."

"Thank you and good-bye, Fritz," he said, calling me *that* for the first time, rising and holding out his hand. Then his face suddenly clouded and he turned away, and I left him standing staring out his narrow cell window. As I clattered down the two flights of circular iron jail stairs my head was full of speculations over the possible significance of this sudden rush of information revealed by my tormented client.

"The poor guy," I kept murmuring to myself while the key-rattling turnkey led me to freedom through a series of metal-shod doors. Suddenly I found myself out under the open sky breathing as deeply as a just-emerged diver. For a long time I stood by the side of my car catching my breath and watching a lone gull flying out over the harbor below. It was languidly wheeling high above the old hematite-stained ore-loading dock, now but a towering relic condemned as unsafe. The gull became a mere speck beyond the distant breakwater and then disappeared into the anonymous glitter of Lake Superior.

"Lucky bastard," I said out loud, climbing into my car.

Chapter 5

"Tell me more about Connie," I began as I launched my inquisition the following day, my client and I once again huddled in his cramped cell. This time I purposely began on a low key after the revelations of recent days, wanting to learn more about Connie mostly for the help it might give me in coming up with at least an arguable legal defense. I needed to gain more insight into the related puzzle of how my client could ever have brought himself to harm the woman he had so recently and reluctantly confessed he had loved so passionately and for so long. Moreover, I had to admit, the woman was beginning to intrigue me almost as much as she had him.

"Ah, Connie," he began, his eyes lighting. Leaning forward on his cot, he almost eagerly started to talk in a low, murmurous voice as though, once unlocked, he felt he somehow had to prove that their attraction was far more than mere lust. "Connie is really indescribable," he went on, as though she were still alive, "the most totally vibrant and complete woman I have ever known." He glanced my way and flashed a faint smile. "And I must say there were a few."

"Go on," I said, though, like a compulsive confessor, he needed no prompting.

"Yet some of our stormiest times together came when I

tried to tell her so—sometimes, I'm afraid, even in verse." He paused, searching for words. "Connie seemed especially to resent being put on any sort of pedestal, of being cast in the role of the irresistible female."

"Why?"

"I'm not quite sure I know. I think she simply preferred to be a total person rather than some kind of spotlighted femme fatale." He shrugged. "Anyway, I soon learned to soft-pedal my paeans of adoration."

"So she was a feminist?"

"No, no, no," he answered quickly. "At least not in the usual sense."

"Possibly because she could so richly afford not to give a damn," I could not resist saying.

"No, not that either. She did care, and deeply, and I've learned from others that she often gave money to help feminist causes."

"What, then?"

"It's hard to put into words. She seemed obsessed with the notion that the only true relationship between a man and a woman—indeed between people—had to be fifty-fifty, that anything less was a ritual waste of time, mere empty social and sexual posturing."

"Maybe she simply craved to *be* like a man," I said.

"The few times I ever heard Connie wish she'd been born a boy were almost invariably cries of resigned despair that things might never really change," he continued. "The one thing she most craved was an honest reciprocity between people; not having to play a role thrust upon her by society or by anyone, least of all by those fantasizing males who, as she once scathingly put it, 'prefer their women obscene but not heard, who feel their very manhood is threatened unless they can prolong the illusion of sweeping every woman off her feet by sheer masculine charm, and who have the ability to attribute any of their failures to their being either frigid neurotics or common whores.' "

"Connie must really have been *something,* " I said inanely, feeling this time not so much a twinge of envy as a guilty shock of recognition. "Tell me more."

He blinked in recollection. "Well, I especially recall one night when we were together, when suddenly she began pacing up and down her darkened bedroom, a shaft of moonlight gleaming on her slender body, all but shouting over the inequity and iniquity of it all."

"Do you recall what she said?"

"Not all, but one phrase still rings in my mind. Suddenly she paused in her pacing and grabbed up a partly filled wine glass from her night table, held it aloft, spilling some—I can still see its glistening course down her arm—and delivered herself."

"Yes?" I prompted him.

" 'Here's to the dubious future of a nation, a world, that continues to gloat and pride itself in stifling or ignoring over half its brains and talent.' "

I heard the distant clang of a slammed cell door, as though in benediction. "And Connie herself had brains and talent?" I asked.

"Loads of both," he said, swiftly telling me how through one of her visiting classmates he had learned that scholastically she was among the top of her class during all of her three years at college.

"Why only three?" I asked, puzzled.

"The summer following her third year was when she met and abruptly married Dick Blair," my client said, shrugging over the contradictory waste by Connie of her own brains and talent. He went on to tell how Connie loved music and had once played the piano not only well but brilliantly. "Yet during recent years she rarely played a note," he added, shaking his head.

"Poor, frustrated, paradoxical Connie," I murmured. "Maybe she was bedeviled by that form of poverty my law partner swears is one of the worst."

"I don't follow. She was quite wealthy, you know."

"That's the very point my partner made. 'While there are many kinds of poverty abroad in the land,' he recently declared, 'two of the very worst are either having too little—or else too goddam much.' "

"Possibly so," he said, blinking thoughtfully. "I'd never thought of that. Somehow reminds me of Cyril Connolly's haunting title for one of his books, *Enemies of Promise.* Maybe having too much money *is* an enemy."

"Tell me," I said, glancing at my watch and pushing on. "Were all of your meetings with Connie quite—ah—so tumultuous?"

"Heavens no, especially after I learned to modulate my praise." He smiled in recollection. "After that, when I'd occasionally lapse she'd usually confine her outbursts to wistfully wishing she'd been born a boy, as I just said." His eyes lit up. "But most of our times together were simply indescribable"—he smiled—"a dreadful confession for an aspiring writer to make, perhaps also showing that some of the most memorable experiences people have are simply beyond words."

"Writer?" I said, surprised.

He smiled sheepishly. "Oh, I've written a few stories and poems."

"Any published?"

"A few, mostly in obscure magazines you've probably never heard of. Maybe some day I might even tackle a novel—that's if I ever get out of this place."

"Meanwhile what *do* you do for a living?" I asked him, suddenly curious. "Between those occasional stories and poems, that is?"

"I have no regular job," he said, shrugging, going on to explain that he lived on the income from a trust fund left by his dead parents. "All I really want to do, I guess, is to write." He smiled. "That and fish for trout between seizures. Maybe my own particular form of poverty is that I have a little too much to bother writing what I really feel, and a little too little to give up trying."

"As my partner said, there are many kinds of poverty lurking around, ready to stifle talent and ambition—though I must say I never could afford to explore Connie's or your own more modest variety. Guess my main ambition is not to make a Guinness record for writing the longest legal brief in the world but rather for getting on to and finally landing the biggest and boobiest speckled mermaid still at large."

"Maybe you're lucky, something like the poor fisherman

who scrimps to buy one coveted fly rod—which he treats like a fairy wand—over the rich one who can airily buy a dozen—and then often treats them like his wife's discarded curtain rods."

"So true. But getting back to Connie," I pushed on. "I still can't quite *see* her. Surely as a writer you can re-create more vividly how it was between you when things weren't so stormy." I paused, searching for words. "Tell me about your silences."

My question seemed to send him into a glow of remembrance as he stared up at the metal-plated ceiling of his cell. "Ah Connie, Connie," he murmured. "How can mere clumsy words ever tell the state of enchantment, of suspended ecstasy and bliss, that came over me when we two were together. Time itself seemed to halt and yet there was always the strange feeling that I was being with her for the first time."

"Try."

"Even when we were apart her spell seemed to linger, enveloping me like a mist." He smiled faintly. "And how can I say, without appearing a chauvinist monster, that after getting to know Connie I not so much forsook the other women I've known as forgot all about them?"

"Try," I repeated.

"Connie? Connie?" he went on, placing his open hand against his chest as the words came tumbling forth in a murmurous rush. "Connie was everything to me . . . at once my enchantress and mistress and yet my virgin sweetheart . . . my consoling friend and confidante . . . at times even my very mother."

"Mother?" I said, blinking.

"Yes, mother," he said, glancing toward me, "for with her I often felt an almost smothering sense of peace and security, as though I were both her lover and her child—sometimes mingled, I must admit, with a little-boy feeling of guilty naughtiness."

"Doesn't all this," I said, choosing my words, "make it all the more strange that she chose to marry Dick Blair and later Jason Spurrier rather than you?"

"I've often thought of that," he said, glancing about his cell. "I've had plenty of time to think, you know, hibernating in this iron sty. Sometimes I think we were too much alike, that our very dependence on each other, our sense of need, sometimes frightened her away." He smiled. "Or maybe my rebound theory is merely that of another wounded male massaging his ruffled ego."

"Go on," I said. "I think I'm beginning to see."

"Still other times I've wondered whether Connie wasn't essentially a lonely person endlessly searching for *someone*—friend, lover, what I'm not quite sure—whom she didn't feel either drawn or compelled to go to bed with in order to know and love."

"You may be veering close," I said, glancing at my watch. "All of which in a way makes things all the more confusing." I began gathering up my briefcase, making ready to leave.

"If you'd only known Connie you might better understand what I'm trying to say," he said, rising and elaborately stretching. "But then you must have known her," he went on, turning my way. "Born and raised in the same town and all. Surely you knew her, didn't you?"

"Only fleetingly," I answered, truthfully enough but still only a half-truth—which I guess can sometimes make by far the biggest lie. "And that usually when she was whirling past me in a cloud of dust in one or other of her latest sports cars."

"How odd you two never met," he continued musingly. "I've always thought you had because, as I told you the first time we ever talked here in jail, she once told me that if I ever really needed a lawyer I should call on you." He shrugged. "So I'd always assumed you knew each other."

"Not so odd when I tell you I'm nearly eight years older than she was," I evasively countered, wondering over my reluctance to tell him about our one memorable meeting—memorable to me, at least. "But perhaps you forget, not being a native, that despite its booster clubs and paved streets and indoor plumbing, our town is still nothing but a mining camp."

"Mining camp?" he repeated, puzzled. "I don't quite follow."

"In all mining camps," I continued, somewhat like my partner sounding off, "there are but two classes of people: those who own and run the mines and those who work in them—both classes being attended by a scattering of tradesmen and assorted commoners who feed, clothe, notarize, and finally, ever so graciously, bury them. Connie came from one class and I from the other and rarely the twain do mingle."

"Hard to believe," my client said, shaking his head. He moved over to the tap, drew a jet of water into a paper cup, and made a face as he drank it. "Seems the longer you run this stuff the warmer and lousier it gets—and looks," he said, adding, "Want some?"

"No, thanks," I said, recoiling as from a laboratory specimen. I was trying to recall my lone meeting with Connie—the one time she hadn't left me in a cloud of dust, for this time the cloud had been mostly compounded of sand pebbles. She must still have been in college, I mused, for I hadn't been long out of law school myself and had only recently acquired a second-hand set of mortgaged Michigan reports. I'd been returning from an afternoon of fishing and was rounding a slow, sandy bend in the road when suddenly I'd spotted a car stopped dead in the road just ahead of me.

"Damn," I said, sliding to a stop only inches from its rear bumper and slowly crawling out of my own bush car to go take a look. The stalled car was one of those big, low, pregnant-looking sports cars, quite the rage at the time, the kind that still occasionally goaded my law partner into melancholy declamations on the evils of conspicuous consumption and waste.

Both windows were reeled up, despite the warm day, so I peered in the passenger window, and saw a woman half-sitting and half-lying across the front seat, covered to her throat by a large towel held by a clasp. Only her tanned bar arms showed, both of which were folded mummylike across her breasts, I was relieved to note.

"Hello," I said, but she did not stir and I saw a glistening veil of perspiration on her face and arms, doubtless caused from being so cooped up. Peering closer I was struck by the strange, compelling beauty of this sleeping woman, if "beauty" is quite the word, for here was no conventional good-looker. Her gleaming black hair was almost defiantly straight, for one thing, while her prominent cheekbones, curving, slightly flared nose, and sharply protruding chin somehow reminded me of the angular, jutting quality, the hewn, carved expression, seen on the faces of certain American Indians. The moist, lacquered look from the perspiration only strengthened the impression. Even in slumbering repose her face possessed an aura of pent-up intensity, a luminous magnetic quality that held me staring like any slavering window-peeper, which I guess in a way I was.

"Hello," I repeated, louder this time, and she moved a little, dislodging the clasp that held her towel and exposing one of her breasts. I tried to look away, fumbled for a coin, which I found, and tapped discreetly against the window. Suddenly she awoke and looked out at me, steadily and unblinkingly, with eyes of an indeterminant shade that somehow reminded me of distant, tumbling clouds seen across an open expanse of sea. She continued to look at me with an expression that oddly combined one of wide-eyed wonder with one of an almost disconcertingly calm appraisal.

"Hello," she said at last, smiling, reaching across, and reeling down the window. This maneuver further dislodged her towel, this time exposing both breasts, which once again I valiantly tried to ignore. "My, my," she said in a low, throaty voice, following the path of my eyes and quickly regathering the towel about her, pinching it like a shawl until she found and restored the clasp. "And here it seems we've only just barely met. I'm Connie Farrow, from town. As you may have noticed admidst the distractions, I seem to be stuck in the sand."

"Oh," I said, surprised at hearing her name, for though I'd had many hurried glimpses of her in the past, sweeping in or out of the local stores but mostly in passing cars, this was our first close-up encounter and I had long carried the false impression of her as being one of the more familiar busty, bouncing, tennis-playing country-club types rather than this lean, darkly haunting creature wrapped in an over-sized towel. "My name is—"

"Frederic Ludlow," she broke in, brushing a strand of hair from her eyes, "the town's newest lawyer, with offices over the dime store, just returning from still another fishing trip and probably more than a little irked to find still another stupid woman driver blocking his way."

"But how could you know all that?" I said, both irked *and* intrigued. "And whatever brought you way out here in the boondocks?"

"I happen to know about you because I'm taking a census on the few attractive men left in town," she said with a throaty laugh, almost a chuckle. "And I'm stuck here because today, after a rather sleepless night, I woke up a little bored and went for a drive. I finally found myself on this road, and wondered where it ever went. The boredom has abated but the wonder remains."

"Oh," I inanely repeated, preening over being included in her latest census. I went on to explain that the road she was on branched off into two roads a mile or so farther on—"beyond which only careening logging trucks and crazy trout fishermen ever dare venture." I then inquired whether she'd just taken a bath or whether the towel she was wearing was the latest thing in feminine chic.

"Neither," she said, laughing, explaining that she had already found my forks in the road and had somehow managed to get turned around, finally getting stuck in the sand where I'd just found her. "The more I tried to get unstuck the more I got stuck. Then the motor died and simply wouldn't start. I waited and waited for help. Finally I decided to sun myself but the clouds of insects soon drove me running, and before I had a chance to get dressed I must have dozed off. How do you ever stand them out fishing?"

"Probably a natural immunity developed from overexposure," I said, "plus the ability to survive smoking Italian cigars." I glanced at my watch and saw I was running quite late for a date. "How about giving your motor a try?"

She tried, but there was only a metallic whir, so I motioned her to release the hood. I spotted a dangling wire which I quickly reattached to a nearby projection and, lo, the motor started. Back at her window I asked her to rock her car gently back and forth before moving forward, which she did, and slowly drew free.

"Thank you, kind Frederic," she said, pausing and reaching out her hand for mine, which I took. Suddenly she removed her hand and drew away, leaving me standing there staring down at the crisp new twenty-dollar bill I held in my hand.

"No, no, no," I shouted, scrambling after her, waving the bill, but she quickly reeled up the window. I crossed to the other side, just able to reach in and cram the money down between her breasts before she'd reeled up her window, narrowly missing my arm, and drove away. "I may be poor but I'm awfully proud," I called after her inanely. "And, anyway, didn't you know my goddamn mechanic's license has expired?"

I turned and trudged back to my car, slumping into my seat, when suddenly I saw her swiftly back up, narrowly miss ramming my car, and leap out and run up to me, her towel billowing and her tanned legs showing. She leaned against my open window, panting a little, before she spoke in her low, husky voice.

"Thank you, proud fisherman," she said, suddenly leaning in and kissing me long and hard on the mouth. "Just a little something you might remember me by," she said, breaking away, her towel again flying. The next thing I knew she was pulling away, leaving me sitting there beatifically observing the torrent of sand and pebbles pelting merrily against my windshield; also leaving me at least one hour late, I finally saw, for my all-but-forgotten date.

Poor Connie had guessed right: I *had* remembered. And now, small world, I found myself defending the man accused of her murder, ironically on her own recommendation. Perhaps he might even have been my rival if I hadn't been born on the wrong side of the tracks or, who knows, hadn't been quite so poky and shy one bygone day while driving home from fishing.

Chapter 6

But all that was in the realm of the past. The sound of the judge's voice brought me back to the grim business at hand. "Petitioner further avers," he was saying, "that he has made diligent effort both to account for his client's lapse of memory and to stimulate its recall, but without success; that he believes his client is ready and anxious to assist him in his defense but that for some reason unknown to petitioner, whether because of amnesia, shock, somnambulism, unconsciousness or some other reason, petitioner's client has been and remains totally unable to remember his whereabouts or actions during the critical period involved, namely, during the time of the alleged homicide."

I glanced across at the prosecutor's table and discovered the whispering sheriff still engaging the young prosecutor's ear. At least I found it refreshing for once to see the sheriff without his Matt Dillon cowboy hat, which, along with his silver sheriff's badge, I had long assumed he wore in bed.

Sheriff Matt glanced up, caught me looking, and gave me a quick hand-spreading shrug and little smile that conveyed a plea as eloquent as a shout. "Look," he seemed to be saying, "today we may be fightin', Fritzy boy, but please don't stay sore at your ol' pal Sheriff Matt, an' above all don't forget to slip him a vote this coming November."

"Petitioner further avers," the judge continued, "that he is advised that memory lost through amnesia, shock, somnambulism, unconsciousness or by the passage of time may sometimes be recovered by means of hypnosis"—here I heard a surprised gasp from the courtroom onlookers—"and that one Hugh Salter, a retired medical doctor with many years' experience in the study and application of hypnosis, has informed petitioner that he might by such means be able to induce such memory recall in the accused; and that petitioner further believes and avers that such an effort is essential to any intelligent appraisal or preparation of a possible defense to the pending murder charge."

The judge paused, absently reached for his water glass, raised it to his lips, and found it empty, causing a faint titter to ripple across the back court. Frowning, the judge grabbed for and uncapped his gleaming Thermos jug and held it over his glass, but no water came and the titters increased. The judge glared down at his erring bailiff, who doubled as waterboy, who in turn quickly deserted his own gavel, grabbed up the empty jug, and fled water-bound out the same hissing mahogany door. Meanwhile the judge, whether too parched or too piqued to proceed, ducked his head over his notes, so I, taking advantage of this undeclared recess, craned around to size up the spectators behind me.

In the very front row I saw my nodding and smiling silvery-haired law partner, Jeremiah Dundee—who gave me a discreet, two-fingered salute—sitting alongside his old friend (and, I hoped, my star witness at today's hearing), lanky, bespectacled Dr. Hugh Salter, as usual sitting with his legs crossed and, again as usual, his long legs looking less crossed than entwined. He reminded me of an old sitting photo I'd recently seen of the similarly lean and gangling English writer Lytton Strachey, even to the tiny-lensed wire-rimmed spectacles he wore.

Looking beyond them I was glad to note how few people there were in court, despite the notoriety of our case. And these were mostly singles and twosomes, mostly hooky-playing courthouse employees, I guessed, seeking some titillating respite from their daily chores. Then, almost with relief, I spotted the inevitable trio of busily whispering blue-haired women, present at every spicy courtroom clash, it seemed, dressed to the teeth and fairly clanking with jewelry, and yet, oddly enough, still wearing their plastic hair curlers, like aging belles forever preparing for a ball never to be held.

Jeremiah had a theory that these omnipresent ladies were really a special breed of modern witches who haunt every courtroom in the land, lurking behind the paneling and emerging, presto, only when sensational courtroom doings were afoot. Since they or their identical twins seemed indeed to haunt virtually every criminal trial I ever engaged in, I was inclined to agree, though sometimes I wondered how they managed to survive between acts, especially behind the acres of heavy mahogany paneling that adorned this particular courtroom.

Gazing across the wide expanse of all but empty mahogany benches, it again swept over me, as it often had in the past, that, in addition to the inevitable ladies in curlers, a depressing prevalence of mahogany pervaded my courtroom life. In fact the phenomenon had so often puzzled me that I'd recently sought enlightenment from my partner, Jeremiah, who after all had been but a growing lad back in the days when the "new" county courthouse was being built. Surely he would have an explanation of the riddle, I felt, and, sure enough, the old boy had.

"How come, pard," I had one day asked him during a courtroom lull in another case, gesturing at the vast sea of mahogany all about us, "how come all the goddamn mahogany, especially way up here on the remote shores of Lake Superior in a heavily wooded area long noted for the excellence of its own native hardwood and pine?"

"Easy, pard," he had scornfully answered. "Only by importing the most exotic and expensive timber from halfway round the goddamn world could the preening local political gnomes and dwarfs who had the say back then hope to adequately and forever impress upon us poor bastards who pay the taxes the immortal quality of their own exquisite good taste."

Musing in a kind of mahogany fog, I recalled also that I'd

played a rather big hand myself in the paucity of spectators at today's hearing: this by the simple expedient of failing to tell the one county-wide newspaper anything about it. This meant that for days I'd been ducking the *Gazette*'s eager young reporter, Miles Coffey, and failing to return his phone calls. I'd finally solved the problem by taking off on a prolonged trout safari—for once with the blessing of my office-bound partner.

All this maneuvering was part of our strategy to keep a low public profile in the case, a strategy virtually forced upon us when Randall Kirk, only a day or so after the surprising revelations he'd made about Connie and himself, had equally surprisingly flatly rejected my recommendation that he continue to demand and go ahead with a scheduled preliminary examination to be held in his case. I had earlier demanded such an examination upon his initial lower-court arraignment, which had since been postponed at my request in the vain hope that he might recover his memory. The postponed examination was now imminent and I had stopped by to discuss it with him.

"Will this examination have to be held in public?" he suddenly demanded. "With reporters and everybody able to attend?"

Yes, such a hearing would be open to the public and doubtless held before the same lower-court judge before whom he'd first been arraigned following his arrest, I explained. No, it would probably not end the case—in fact that was quite unlikely—for such hearings were in no sense trials but rather the surviving offspring of ancient legal procedures designed mostly to prevent the once-prevalent practice of arresting and indefinitely confining people to await future trials on charges that—if any trial were ever held—often proved groundless.

"Seems there's a spreading modern revival of that ancient custom," my client said with a faint smile.

"Alas, yes," I ran on, wondering how accurately I would plagiarize the words I'd first heard as a student from the lips of my old criminal law professor, J. B. "Jabby" Waite: "In a murder case all the prosecution need show at such a preliminary hearing is that the victim is indeed dead and that there is probable cause to believe that the accused may have feloniously caused it."

"Then why bother?" my client asked, gently stroking his silken mustache with one finger.

"Because such a preliminary hearing would almost surely furnish us with at least *some* clues as to the nature and strengths of the prosecution's proofs." I went on, my voice rising. "Clues that might in turn furnish your groping lawyer with some sort of clue to building a possible defense, if there is one."

"Clues such as what, Counselor?" he asked, as I noted his sudden forsaking of the more pal-sy Fritz of our recent encounters.

"Clues as to whether the prosecution's proofs are largely circumstantial or whether there might have been any eyewitnesses," I ran on. "Clues as to possible physical evidence such as fingerprints and the like. Clues of what you may really have told the cops. Clues as to the precise cause of death, which must be shown, and which would almost surely require medical testimony subject to cross-examination. After all, all we really so far know about your case is contained in one cryptic newspaper account—that and what is locked up in your own recalcitrant memory."

"But all this would have to come out in public and still wouldn't stop any later trial?" he said, as much to himself as to me.

"I just *told* you that," I half-shouted, rising and pacing his narrow cell. "But from such a hearing we *might* learn a little more about your goddamn case so that with luck I *might* come up with some sort of"—I paused, teetering on the brink of "viable," but recovering in the nick of time—"half-decent defense." I glanced at my watch and moved to his cell door. "How about it?" I said. "Do we go ahead with a preliminary examination, as I urgently recommend, or don't we; yes or no?"

"Very well, Ludlow," he said with a half-smile. "The answer is no. Stopping any further cryptic newspaper accounts, as you call them, is the very least I can do for poor Connie. And, too, I just might recover my memory before what you've just said was my inevitable trial."

"And then again you might not," I said, staring at him for

a moment before curtly saying "I'll be seeing you" and retreating toward the circular iron stairway. I wondered whether our next encounter would be to confer with him further or simply to announce my withdrawal from his case, something I'd just been at the point of doing.

"Have a nice, viable day," I heard him calling after me as I reached the top of the winding stairs.

From the jail I'd hurried back to our office to try to persuade my law partner to himself go visit the jail and try to talk our stubborn client out of waiving an examination. "It's either that, pard, or I'm just about ready to quit the case," I added. "How about it?"

"No way, pard," he replied.

"But why?"

"Because, as I told you back when we formed our historic partnership, I'm allergic to certain smells, sometimes so much so that I can scarcely breathe when I run into them, remember?"

"Yes, but—"

"And years ago I discovered that all jails stink of the very worst combination of those smells, so much so I daren't ever enter 'em."

"What kind of smells?"

"All jails stink," he said loftily as if chanting a locker-room limerick, "of stale sweat, urine, and disinfectant. Guess you can't blame 'em when we keep herding scared men into overcrowded iron coops. Guess also my fear of it has kept me fairly virtuous, comforting thought."

"Please go see Kirk," I pleaded.

"No way, lad," he said, gesturing at me and then himself. "I'll honor your allergies if you'll honor mine. You take care of our aromatic, jailed clients and I'll stay home and roll the legal spitballs." He held out his hand. "Is it a deal, pard?"

"Yes," I finally said, taking his hand. "But however able I am to stand the reek of your caged men, I must tell you that I'm growing goddamn allergic to our latest client. Making us waive examination could not only badly hurt him but make you and me look like a couple of freshman lawyers who don't know a bail bond from a bale of hay. Fact is, I'm still ready to walk out on the stubborn bastard."

All that this had prompted from my partner was an eloquent lecture on the duties of a lawyer to his client when the going got roughest, and a further dividend lecture on the dangers of false pride.

"Also the bastard just might agree to your pulling out," he said, winding up his argument, "not only leaving us holding the bag with all the work we've already done, but losing a golden chance to partake in the possible solving of surely the goddamnedest legal puzzle we've ever met. Let's waive the examination and play it cool, lad. Remember it's our waiving client who'll have to serve the time if we lose his case, not us. What do you say?"

"All right, all right," I had finally agreed.

"Mr. Sheriff," I heard the judge saying in a pained voice. "If it wouldn't too much discommode you, I'd be mighty pleased if you'd bestir yourself long enough to go find what's happened to your vanished bailiff and, even more important, to my own strayed water jug."

"Yes, Your Honor," the blushing sheriff mumbled, almost knocking over his tight-fitting mahogany chair as he jumped up, hitched his sagging pistol belt around and lumbered off in search of the judge's water jug. Lunging against the big mahogany door he nearly collided with the missing bailiff, who performed an impromptu balancing act to keep the judge's jug atop the new, matching tray he'd found.

"Had to send out for ice," the bailiff apologetically explained to the judge, miraculously delivering both jug and tray intact. The judge's thirst was then appeased, a gathering courtroom storm was averted, and, almost before one could say "allergy," hostilities once again got underway.

Chapter 7

"The respondent sheriff, by his counsel, Prosecuting Attorney Eugene Canda, answers that the requested order should be denied for the following reasons, which I quote," the judge said, again ducking his head to hide his nearsightedness as he read: " 'Because the so-called art or science of hypnotism has no standing in our courts; because its results would be inadmissible in any event, akin to those obtained by use of a polygraph, also known as a lie detector, or by so-called truth serum; that furthermore the results of any such examination would be misleading and untrustworthy; that in any case Dr. Hugh Salter is not qualified to attempt to stimulate any such memory recall; and, finally, that after diligent search and inquiry the respondent sheriff has been unable to find any legal authority for such a procedure as presently sought by petitioner and therefore prays that his petition be denied.' "

"Typical response by our fighting young DA," I had earlier remarked to my partner when our copy of the young prosecutor's answer to my petition had arrived in the morning mail. "Fighting, that is, to build a point-with-pride record so he can next run for Congress."

"Goddam place is already too crowded with spouting ex-DA's," Jeremiah said. "What's the lad's answer like?"

"Terse and acidly caustic," I said, tossing the answer across to him. "See for yourself."

"Hm," the old boy hummed to himself as he read, rubbing his chin, finally looking up, twinkly-eyed. "One might even say it's full of pith and vinegar," he said, winking at our secretary and tossing the paper back.

"*You* men!" murmured our long-suffering secretary, Monica Moynihan, with her tired, intellectual, Irish look, her pale face dependably reddening as she blushed like a girl, all the while patiently waiting for us to quit our bantering and get on with the morning's dictation.

This was the same Monica who, shortly after Jeremiah and I became partners, one morning during a similar session had put down her pencil, folded her hands in her lap, and made a disturbing announcement. Jeremiah had just been dictating something or other and was, as usual, goddaming away at a great clip when the blow fell.

"Mr. Dundee," she said, blushing to the roots of her soft, graying hair. "While I'm scarcely a girl anymore and have long been familiar with most of the swear words you use, sad to say, I must tell you that your repeated taking of God's name in vain is causing me great discomfort—doubly so when I later have to weed them out of my shorthand notes—and I'm afraid I must ask you to desist or I maybe compelled to leave."

My partner, visibly startled, sat pondering his answer while I silently prayed it would be a good one, for sweet Monica had been with me almost from the start and I was shocked over the prospect of ever losing her. Then I heard the preliminary rumblings of Jeremiah clearing his throat and I knew that the spigots of rebuttal were about to flow.

"Dear Miss Moynihan," he began. "First of all let me apologize for causing you any pain, which I swear was unintentional. Let me also try to explain. First, far from being a profanity of your capitalized God, mine always comes modestly robed in lower case, being merely the first syllable of a single word, and the appended 'dam' in my goddams being spelled like the traditional water barrier rather than any blasphemous curse."

"But it *sounds* so much like the other," she murmured, anxiously glancing my way.

"Ah, but the guilty intent is lacking, my dear," he ran on, gathering speed and volume and pointing one finger in the air, "without which there can *be* no blasphemy. For not only do I fail to spell my goddams the bad way but I use them only for occasional emphasis or as jocular epithet or mild expletive or mere slang intensive, but *never* intentionally to profane your or anyone's God, that I swear."

"Oh," she said, seeming on the verge of tears.

"The solemn truth is that my goddams are every bit as innocuous as the goldarns and goshdangs I've sometimes heard even from you; as doggone far from the real thing, say, as jumping Christopher, jeepers creepers and jiminy cricket are from *that* real thing, can't you see? Mencken and Partridge and the other burrowing wordsmiths are awash with similar examples."

"I—I simply hadn't realized."

"Moreover I've found that an occasional goddam can lend a certain beat and rhythm to a sentence or phrase sadly lacking without it and I'll gladly give you a small example if you'd like."

"Please do, Mr. Dundee."

"Has it never occurred to you, my dear, that calling a man simply a liar, naked and unadorned, never achieves quite the stature of calling him a *goddam* liar?"

"No, I'd never really thought of that, but it *does* sound far more—ah—resonant."

"Moreover, my dear, in our own work an occasional goddam can sometimes achieve wonders in relieving the sheer boredom of having daily to grapple with all our sedative legal rhetoric, with all those farty parties of the first part and all. Do you see?"

"You have opened my eyes, Mr. Dundee," she said with an apologetic smile. "And I'm sorry I brought up such a silly subject."

"Good, and thank you, dear Monica," my partner said, smiling over at me and rustling the papers he held, the spigots turned off. "And now, my enlightened child, may we proceed with the mundane chore at hand?"

"Yes, Jeremiah," she said with a wistful smile, retrieving her pencil and holding it poised over her pad. "If I may employ a slang expression, get on with your goddam dictation."

After that, not only did a kind of dictatorial truce prevail, but, as I've long speculated, it may also have marked the day the two fell in love.

Judge Brotherton took a final sip of water and looked down at my table. "Call your first witness, Mr. Ludlow," he said.

"Dr. Hugh Salter," I arose and said.

"Just one moment, please, Your Honor," Eugene Canda said, rising quickly and standing before his table.

"Yes, Mr. Prosecutor?" the judge said, peering owlishly down through his thick lenses, not quite hiding his annoyance over this further delay. "What is it you want to say?"

"Just this, Your Honor," the prosecutor said. "Since the whole basis of Mr. Ludlow's petition here today is the claimed loss of his client's memory, I rise to inquire whether Your Honor doesn't share with my client and me the view that the defendant Randall Kirk should rather obviously be called as the first witness to prove that elementary claim."

"Hm," hummed the judge, reflectively rubbing his bald spot and the back of his neck, glancing up at the stained-glass courtroom skylight—"Kept ever so thoughtfully restained by swarms of panhandling courthouse pigeons," the observant Jeremiah had recently remarked—then down at me. "What do you say, Mr. Ludlow?"

"The simplest reason I can give for not calling my client as my first witness, Your Honor, is that I had not planned on calling him."

"Please elucidate," the judge said with a resigned look, leaning back in his high-backed mahogany chair.

"In the first place," I began, "this hearing does not arise on the petition of Randall Kirk but rather on that of his perplexed defense attorney, who is trying to establish communication with his client on a crucial phase of that client's case so that he might appraise and prepare a possible legal defense, if any. At issue is not whether my client has truly forgotten the events of that fatal night but rather what he has both told and failed to tell his lawyer, as I have set forth at length in my sworn petition."

"Mr. Canda?" the judge said, looking over at the prosecutor's table.

"I still insist, Your Honor please, that the man who so far tells us only through his lawyer that he has forgotten his crime should now be sworn and share that secret here in open court and also subject himself to cross-examination on that claim."

"Mr. Ludlow?" the judge said, again looking my way.

"The truth or falsity of my client's claimed lack of memory cannot be decided here today," I said. "That question can only be resolved by a jury at his full-dress trial."

"Mr. Canda?" the judge said, again looking over at the prosecutor's table. Despite my current preoccupations, I could not help but think of the back-and-forth head-wagging of a crowd watching a spirited volley at tennis.

"I can only repeat," Eugene Canda said, "that in a proceeding, the whole rationale of which is based upon a claimed loss of memory, there ought to be some sworn judicial proof of that basic claim."

"Mr. Ludlow?" the judge said, swiftly lobbing the ball back at me.

"We are not trying the case of Randall Kirk here today," I said, "but rather that of his lawyer, who says he needs to bring in outside assistance to help communicate with his client, and which needed assistance the sheriff has barred from his jail. In other words, Your Honor, if you'll please forgive me, one helpless lawyer seeks your timely help to help persuade our unhelpful sheriff to open his jail to the help he needs."

"You must have worked on that one," the judge said, smiling wearily. "Anything else from you, Mr. Canda?"

"Only that juvenile literature and especially the world of the jangling nursery rhyme were evidently denied an eloquent creator when my esteemed opponent turned to the law," Eugene Canda said with all the biting sarcasm at his command.

"Are you through, Mr. Ludlow?" the judge said. "Any more doggerel today?"

"I'm sorry to prolong this argument, Your Honor," I said, "but after all, I didn't start it. I would like to give an illustration of my plight if I may."

"Proceed," the judge said, reaching resignedly for his water jug.

"Suppose my client spoke only Chinese," I said, "and the sheriff refused to let me bring an interpreter into the jail so that we might talk. If I filed a similar petition here today, would I first be required to produce my client to prove he can't speak English?—and, if so, how?"

"What do you say to that, Mr. Prosecutor?" the judge said.

"The analogy is false and begs the question. Obviously, in such a situation outside help would be needed to establish basic communication, granted, as would be the case, say, were his client deaf and dumb, both classic situations of the law." The prosecutor paused and glanced over his shoulder at cross-legged Hugh Salter sitting in the front row. "But here the sheriff is asked to admit to his jail a retired country doctor to use a dubious technique not recognized by the law—hypnotism—to recover a claimed loss of memory not yet even shown."

"Mr. Ludlow?" the judge said.

"I had thought we began arguing whether my client needed to be called to testify today, but instead my resourceful opponent now turns his guns upon the qualifications of my 'interpreter,' so to speak, as well as upon the means he uses, both of which I propose to explore extensively once we can get this stalled hearing underway. Pending that, I'd like to give a final illustration. Suppose I'd pleaded my client's insantiy and our choosy sheriff had barred our psychiatrist because he thought his education was inadequate. Would I be expected today to instead first call my client to the stand to show his addled state of mind?"

The head-turning judge, evidently now growing both fatigued and speechless, this time merely nodded at my opponent's table.

"I repeat that my opponent's illustrations are inapt," Eugene Canda said. "Moreover they are situations long recognized and traditionally accepted in the law whereas here we are asked to admit an unproved person using dubious means to restore a loss of memory not yet shown."

"*Mister* Ludlow?" the judge said, a note of desperation now creeping in.

"Mr. Canda continues to attack my 'interpreter' and his means," I said, "which, I repeat, is not for him to decide. In effect the court is being asked to make the astonishing ruling that county sheriffs, whose main discernible qualification for seeking office is the ability to plunk down the modest filing fee, are now qualified to pass upon both the professional competence and means used by any and all specialists or experts any defense attorney may henceforth date ask to visit a client in his jail. Furthermore, calling my client here today to show his loss of memory would in any case be fetching coals to Newcastle."

"What do you mean?" the judge said, leaning forward.

"I mean that in any case both the prosecutor and sheriff have long known about my client's claimed loss of memory, since the police statement my client made within hours of his arrest—before his own attorney had even been retained, much less heard his story." I glanced at the prosecutor. "If I have mispoken I invite my opponent to show I'm wrong."

"Mr. Canda?" the judge said, hunching forward in his high-backed chair, his interest rekindled.

"One moment, Your Honor," the prosecutor said, busily leafing through the files on his desk and then whispering with the sheriff.

"Your moment is up," the judge said. "What have you to say to Mr. Ludlow's claim?"

"First that any such police statement, if made, wouldn't replace his client's sworn testimony to that fact," a flushed Eugene Canda at length arose and said. "Moreover I regard Mr. Ludlow's dramatic challenge as a clever defense stratagem to get a free advance look at what his client may have told the police. Moreover—"

"Challenge revised," I interrupted hotly, shouting across at my opponent. "I now instead challenge him to produce and show his precious police statement solely to His Honor, thus keeping this grandstanding defense lawyer still groping in the dark. Moreover if the police statement doesn't show what I say it shows I promise to call my client immediately to the stand and end this time-delaying argument."

"Please speak only when recognized, Mr. Ludlow," the

judge said, frowning over his glasses. "What do you say, Mr. Canda?"

"I don't readily put my hands on any police statement, if indeed I have it in my file," the prosecutor arose and said, still shuffling his papers like a distracted blackjack dealer. "In any case that statement has not yet been offered in evidence and I prefer to reserve any decision on that until the coming trial."

"Anything further, Mr. Ludlow?"

"Well, I could suggest that the sheriff, who was present when the police statement was taken, might himself take the stand and enlighten us on my client's claimed loss of memory," I said. "But to save time and embarrassment, I'll offer still a further reason for not calling my client to the stand, namely, because my main witness, Dr. Hugh Salter, has warned me against it."

"Why?" asked the judge.

"Because he feels that for my client to be subjected to a public courtroom wrangle over his claimed loss of memory and, further, over the utility of hypnosis to stimulate its recall might well prejudice and even ruin any chance of ultimate success by that means, even should Your Honor finally rule to let my doctor try."

I glanced across at Eugene Canda. "And that such a hassle does seem likely, I think Your Honor may deduce not only from my opponent's formal answer but his argument and demeanor here today. In fact—"

It was now my bristling opponent's turn to leap up and talk out of turn. "Your Honor," he shouted, "I resent the implication that if I do not lie down and let my opponent have his way here today that my very resistance furnishes additional reason why his sensitive client need not take the stand. Moreover I invite my opponent to explain, if he can, why his client dare not risk witnessing any hassle—to borrow his elegant expression—from the witness chair but may safely do so now from the shelter of his own counsel table."

"What do you say?" the judge said, turning to me and barely suppressing a smile.

"One big difference, Mr. Canda," I said, smarting over the points he'd just scored, "is that if he remains sitting here and not up there"—I pointed up at the witness stand—"*you* won't get to maul him and work him over in your elegant, third-degree fashion. Furthermore, on the advice of Dr. Salter, and for kindred reasons, I didn't want my client even to be present in court today, much less testify, and he is here at all only at his own insistence."

I paused, reflecting rather guiltily that despite my show of candor the one big unspoken reason I didn't want my client even to be present in court, much less to testify, was his increasingly listless and indifferent attitude toward the possibility of recovering his memory, the prospect of which also lately seemed more and more to frighten him. Even more disturbing was his growing hostility toward the whole idea of using hypnosis to attempt recall. I didn't wish to risk unveiling either of these reasons before our perceptive judge or opposing counsel.

The latter was already on his feet, seeking the floor. "Your Honor," he began, but the weary judge quickly raised his hand and silenced him.

"Gentlemen, gentlemen," the judge said, "this endless wrangling has gone far enough. Both of you have made some interesting but inconclusive points and so I rule that calling the defendant as a witness is not necessary at this point. At the same time I reserve my ruling on whether he need be called at all, depending upon developments." He squinted out at the courtroom clock—the very face of which I knew he could scarcely see, much less tell the time from—and took a deep breath. "You may call your first witness, Mr. Ludlow"—he suppressed a smile—"after we take a five-minute recess."

I leaned over toward my client. "I suspect His Honor needs to pee," I whispered. "If you'd like to join him in that enterprise, if not quite in the same cubicle, I'll alert your armed shadow that nature must be served."

"Your intuition is sound," my client whispered back, giving me a grateful smile.

Chapter 8

The working area of the courtroom was divided from the rest by a low, ornate railing—really an elaborate mahogany fence—with a swinging gate at either end, also mahogany, for the passage to and fro of litigants, witnesses, prospective jurors, perjurers, and whomever else. I was going through one of these gates to join my partner and Hugh Salter in the back court when I was greeted by a familiar voice, the owner of which I'd been avoiding for days.

"Well, well," I heard the young *Gazette* reporter, Miles Coffey, saying, "at last I've tracked down the county's most elusive attorney. Where in hell, may I ask, have you been hiding out?"

"Sorry, Miles," I said, shrugging, at last fairly caught. "Been plenty busy lately, as you might guess, then took off for a few days fishing. At least you got here, which is the main thing, so I suppose some thoughtful soul must have tipped you off about today's hearing."

"Yes, but barely in time for the fireworks," Miles said, pouting. Miles was gotten up in what Jeremiah had recently called "the latest polyester uniform of the rising young conformist" and carrying the inevitable simulated-leather attaché case, the ensemble crowned by one of those eye-swooping haircuts that some wag had recently called "a thirty-five-dollar hairdo hiding a fifteen-cent brain"—except I knew that Miles was an unusually shrewd young reporter. "Wouldn't have made it here now," he said, "except for my new friend here, whom I'd like you to meet."

"Delighted, Miles," I said, curious to meet his last-minute tipster. Miles turned and motioned to an older man, seated in the second row of pewlike mahogany benches, who rose and quickly came forward.

"Jason Spurrier," Miles said, "meet Frederic Ludlow."

"I greatly enjoyed your spirited argument," Jason Spurrier said as we shook hands, "and I do wish you luck in recalling poor Randall's lost memory, a most curious thing."

"Thanks," I said, studying Connie's surviving husband and wondering vaguely where I'd seen him before. "But first I've got to win the right to try."

"It'll be an absorbing match to watch," he said in his cultured eastern-accented voice. The crisscross of minute wrinkles around his eyes lent them a faintly hooded aspect as they creased into a friendly smile. Ah, I thought, now I have it. . . . For this man bore a striking resemblance to an old-time movie actor I'd admired since boyhood, Adolphe Menjou, even to the same masklike expression, the ever so carefully trimmed and pointed mustaches, the aloof, faintly disdainful look of ironic amusement, and especially, I noted with an envious pang, the luxuriant head of iron-gray hair so immaculately arranged that it looked not so much combed as sculptured.

"I suppose Randy told you about today's hearing?" I said, mildly curious to learn how *he* knew. "Randy tells me you occasionally forsake your sailing and trout fishing long enough to visit him in the jail."

"Yes, he did tell me," he said, smiling, "and so, being a kind of old newspaper hand myself, I passed the news on to our young friend here, Miles, feeling he wouldn't want to miss such a dramatic courtroom duel." He moistened his lips and looked beyond me. "I see Randall's back at his table now, so I suppose that means you'll soon be back on the barricades." He again held out his hand. "Very good to meet you, Mr. Ludlow, and again the best of luck to you and Randall."

"Thank you," I said, turning to Miles. "See you soon, Miles, and the next time I hope I'll be easier to track down."

"Either I'll set out snares or consult my thoughtful friend here," Miles said, winking at me from under his contrived cowlick as I moved on to join Jeremiah and Hugh Salter.

"Nice going in your argument, boy," Jeremiah said as I sat down between them, lapsing, as he sometimes did—despite being born, raised, and duly altar-boyed in the upper-midwestern mining town of Chippewa—into a kind of local tavern talk with Dublinesque overtones. "Especially loved and envied your bit of doggerel, that I did. Sure an' you're after stealin' me own thunder, lad."

As I modestly blushed, Hugh Salter unfolded his long legs and leisurely recrossed them on the other side. "Glad you got in the part about the harm too much courtroom wrangling might do to our chances for any successful memory recall," he said in his deep, reverberant voice that sounded as though it was coming from a cistern. "In fact I'm a little concerned that our boy may have seen and heard too much already."

"I almost didn't mention it," I said, "feeling I already might have enough, and also so as not to encourage Eugene Canda to out-hassle even himself. But I changed my mind when I realized Gene would doubtless hassle away at top form whatever I said or did. Then, too, I particularly wanted the judge to know and realize that a ruling by him today that Randy had to take the stand might ruin any future chance for any successful memory recall."

"We'll see, we'll see," Hugh Salter musingly rumbled away, looking up at Jeremiah's pigeon-stained skylight. "Maybe it's already too late."

Jeremiah nodded over his shoulder. "Who's the distinguished-looking dude you were just gabbing with? Reminds me of that suave old movie actor, I forget his name."

"Adolphe Menjou," I said.

"*That's* him! Spittin' image. Who's the guy?"

"The bereaved husband, Jason Spurrier," I said, and I related the brief conversation we'd just had. "By the way, when did he get here today?"

"Shortly after the opening kick-off, along with the becowlicked newspaper lad. In fact nearly the whole trial cast seems to be assembled—at least the stars. Even my favorite witch, Viola Axholm, with all her profiles, is hovering back there somewhere."

I glanced around and spotted Constance Spurrier's frowning old housekeeper sitting alone in the last row, a study in black —like the lady in the old Charles Addams cartoons—her cleaver-sharp features reminding me that Jeremiah had recently sworn she looked like all of the Barrymores rolled into one—"all profile, viewed from whatever angle."

"Wonder how the old girl got here?" I said.

"Doubtless waited for a favorable breeze and swooped down here on her broom," Jeremiah said. "By the way, how about our finally meeting the young man we've all been workin' our asses off for?"

"By all means," I said. I leaned over the mahogany railing and whispered "Randy!" and shortly he joined us, met, and sat down between the man who'd dug up most of the law that was so far shaping our defense strategy and the man who hoped to retrieve his lost memory.

Both Jeremiah and Hugh Salter were aware of my growing concern over my client's increasingly indifferent attitude toward our efforts to help him, so we sat there and chatted about inconsequentials until the bailiff, court reporter, and clerk of the court quietly returned to their stations, heralding the imminent return of His Honor himself.

"Give 'em hell, lad," Jeremiah whispered as my client and I hurried back to our defense table. At the mahogany gate we were met by Jason Spurrier, who warmly grasped and shook my client's hand and said, "Best of luck, Randall, and I'll visit you soon and bring along those books I promised."

"Thank you, Jason," Randall said. Then the mahogany door hissed open, the judge swept in, the bailiff banged his gavel, and our recess was officially over.

Chapter 9

"The petitioner will call Dr. Hugh Salter," I arose and said for the second time that day, all but ducking as I awaited still another possible delaying objection from my opponent.

Hugh Salter seemed to share my apprehension, taking his time before arising, or rather unwinding, peering through his spectacles as he slowly picked his way up to the witness stand like some sort of wary, long-legged bird. First, there was the pause and investigative stoop to negotiate one of the swinging mahogany gates—which kept on swinging to a slow halt after his passage, like a fatigued metronome—then a leisurely amble past the empty jury box, then a tentative advance just beyond the court reporter's desk. There he was abruptly met by the skinny court clerk, Clovis Trepannier, who popped up suddenly in his mahogany cubicle just below the judge's bench, with his right hand already held aloft like an outraged traffic cop.

"Holt up you right hand to be swore!" he said, or rather shouted, with more than a trace of his boyhood French Canadian accent.

White-haired Clovis, whose wayward thatch of thinning silken hair seemed always to float a little above his head, like a wafted halo gone askew, had been county clerk almost as long as the "new" courthouse had been standing, a circumstance that had naturally not escaped the rhetorical net of my partner.

"Clovis single-handedly has raised the vagaries of political incumbency to a form of immortality," he had recently declared. Everyone agreed that Clovis did his most effective campaigning in the courtroom rather than on the hustings, people sometimes coming from miles around simply to watch him perform. "When Clovis swears a witness," one of his fans had bragged, "the sonofabitch bloody well *stays* sworn."

"You do solemnly swear," he now sang out with quavering evangelical neck-corded fervor, "dat you will tell the trut', the whole trut', and nossing bott the trut', so 'elp you God"—pointing at the mahogany witness box—"and please sit down dere!" Modulation had eluded Clovis from the cradle, and his invariably shouted injunction to the startled witness to please be seated seemed an integral part of the oath itself and often had to be repeated.

"I do," Hugh Salter said, making it on the first shout, easing his lanky frame down into the witness chair with an amused glint in his eye that plainly said that while the medical profession might have its own headaches, at least it didn't subscribe to any such medieval mumbo jumbo as the law's grotesque oath to witnesses.

"Your name, please?" I said.

"Hugh Salter," the witness said in his low, reverberant voice that seemed to create a rumbling echo throughout the all but empty chamber.

"Where do you live?"

"Town of Chippewa, this county."

"Your trade or profession, please?"

"Medical doctor," he said, adding with a smiling shrug, "finally turned out to pasture."

"Where have you practiced?"

"Always in this county and that mostly in and around Chippewa."

"For how long, Doctor?"

"Well now—good heavens—just short of a half a century."

"What schools did you attend?"

Eugene Canda was on his feet. "Respondent concedes the

eminent qualifications of the witness as a medical doctor," he said. "We question only his qualifications as a hypnotist able to stimulate memory recall."

"Thank you," I said, nodding, "so I will get on with that question." I consulted my notes. "Doctor," I continued, "are you familiar with the psychological phenomenon known as hypnotism or hypnosis?"

"Yes, rather extensively."

"For how long?"

"Ever since I've been in practice," he said, smiling. "In fact even in semisenile retirement I'm still at it."

"What first stimulated your interest in hypnosis, Doctor?"

"Well, while I was still in medical school I learned quite by accident through some outside reading that the eminent philosopher and psychologist William James had once called in a hypnotist to relieve the pain of his sister Alice, who was dying of cancer. Then when I discovered he had devoted a whole chapter to hypnosis in his classic *Principles of Psychology,* I was really hooked." He paused and looked up at the courtroom skylight. "I figured that if such a brilliant mind could believe in hypnosis—then scarcely even mentioned, much less taught, in our medical schools—it surely needed looking into. I looked and it was and remains a revelation."

"Doctor," I went on, "what continued your interest in hypnosis after medical school?"

"Primarily the possibility of alleviating pain in pregnant women who had reached term; that is, of easing the pangs of childbirth."

"Could you tell us a little more about that, Doctor?"

"Well," he said simply, "for years I used it on virtually all the expectant mothers I ever attended."

"And how many were there of those?"

"I've long ago lost track," he said, wagging his head. "Simply hundreds and hundreds—doubtless including your own mother at your birth, as nearly as I can recall."

"She never told me! Personally, I find that historic event a trifle hazy," I said, as the judge gave me a pained smile, and my opponent, a purse-lipped head-shaking scowl. "Did you have any failures?"

"Yes, there were a few women or their families who either failed to follow my explanation of its advantages or who openly scoffed at the whole notion of ever employing hypnosis on anyone for anything."

"How many of the women who consented to hypnosis were you unable to put under?"

"Well, there were perhaps a half-dozen women who simply failed to respond to my best attempts to hypnotize them either because of their low attention span or a language barrier and—oh yes—one poor romantic soul who thought she'd fallen in love with me."

"What happened?"

"I found her a new doctor." He blinked reminiscently. "Possibly that particular failure was less in her doctor's technique than in his nerve."

"Any other failures?"

"Then there were one or two cases where I simply failed, flubbed it, couldn't make the grade." He widened his hands. "For them there were and are no excuses."

"Considering all the cases you successfully handled, Doctor, was this such a bad average?"

"Rather high, I've since learned from my reading, but perhaps that's scarcely for me to say."

"Doctor," I said, pushing on, "with all the steady advances in modern anesthesia, what, if any, advantages are there in using such an off-beat and controversial technique—in the popular mind, I mean—as hypnosis? Why bother?"

Hugh Salter reflected a moment before he spoke. "In the often grim business of getting a child safely out of its mother's womb the mother has to work harder than she will ever have to work again," he said. "That conventional anesthesia may equally numb her pain, I do not question. The problem is that many also numb her ability to work."

"Why need the mother 'work,' Doctor, as you put it?"

"Because her ability or failure to work may often mean the difference between having a normal, healthy child and a maimed or malformed child—or indeed having any child at all."

"But why can she work efficiently under hypnosis but not as well under many conventional anesthetics?"

"Because under hypnosis, although her pain is gone, she nevertheless retains sufficient awareness not only to continue naturally to work on her own but also to follow the sometimes crucial directions of her physician." He paused. "A further advantage is that her painlessness may be prolonged by what is called posthypnotic suggestion."

"In other words, Doctor, is it fair to say that hypnosis both reduces pain and increases the chances for a normal delivery for both the mother and child?"

"Exactly," he answered, "besides possessing still other advantages—"

"Your Honor," I heard Eugene Canda saying with oiled sarcasm, "while I find this dissertation on painless motherhood utterly beguiling, I am unaware that the defendant in this case is about to deliver a child or has even become pregnant. Maybe I should speak to our sheriff about such shenanigans in his jail. Meanwhile I wonder, when will Dr. Salter begin to enlighten us on just how hypnosis might recover lost memory or on his own qualification ever to attempt it?"

"Mr. Ludlow?" the judge prompted me, not quite stifling a smile.

"The prosecutor, in his formal answer, has denied not only the qualifications of Dr. Salter to induce hypnosis but also the utility of it to recover lost memory as well as its ultimate admissibility in evidence even if successful," I said. "And since the doctor's capacity to induce hypnosis in anyone has been so sharply questioned here, I have naturally had to cover his past field of expertise in order to show the likelihood that he can do the same for my client—which in fact I was just about to turn to when my opponent felt compelled to interrupt."

"Proceed, proceed," the judge said. "That is, *after* we take a five-minute recess."

Chapter 10

"Doctor," I pushed on, following the recess, "did I hear you say earlier that since your retirement you have kept up your interest in hypnosis?"

"You did and I have," he said. "In fact even more so, now that I have more time."

"Do you subscribe to any periodicals or belong to any organizations devoted to the research and development of hypnosis?"

"Quite a few," he answered, proceeding to tick off an imposing list of both, throwing in a brief guided tour of the many books on the subject in his own library. "One of my proudest possessions," he concluded, "is an original copy of Dr. James Esdaile's rare old book about his medical experiences with hypnosis in India, then still called mesmerism."

I was coming to the hard part and stared up at the courtroom skylight for inspiration. For the time had come to admit that my witness had never had any practical experience with memory recall; it would never do to wait for the acidulous Eugene Canda to lovingly bring that out.

"Moving now to memory recall, Doctor," I began, "have you studied the literature on the subject?"

"Extensively."

"And is the literature itself extensive?"

"Very," the witness answered, reaching for his notebook, "as you know from the many books I've loaned you to bone up for this case."

"No need to get into those now," I said, holding up my hand. "And have you seen memory recall attempted by others?"

"I have."

"Successfully?"

"Numerous times."

"In this particular area, Doctor?"

"Well no, but at the various symposiums I've attended elsewhere, especially since my retirement."

I paused before taking the plunge. "Now, Doctor, have you yourself ever attempted memory recall?"

"I have not."

"Why not?"

"Largely because I never had any occasion to. When I was still practicing medicine I used hypnosis for other purposes, as I've just said. I guess I was always too busy ever to try the memory thing." He smiled wryly. "Now that I've joined the geriatric set, with whole deserts of leisure on my hands, I don't have anybody to practice on—except possibly myself."

"Doctor," I said, "will you please tell the court whether or not you think you are qualified to attempt the hypnotic recall of memory?"

Hugh Salter turned to Judge Brotherton and spoke quietly. "I really think I am, Judge," he said, "though I would not want to guarantee the results. Few people familiar with the phenomenon would dare risk that."

"Doctor," I said, mentally sighing to be over this hurdle, "will you please briefly summarize for us the theory and practice behind such attempted recall?"

"Well, it's a large subject to reduce to capsule form," he said, "but I might begin by saying that the normal waking mind is sometimes known as the objective conscious mind, while that of a sleeping or hypnotized person more nearly approaches what is known as a subjective or unconscious state, which largely controls memory."

"Yes?" I said.

"Simple relaxation itself is often an aid to achieving the latter state," he went on. "Hence the famous couch of the psychoanalysts which, contrary to the popular notion, was not invented merely to furnish cartoon fodder for the *New Yorker* but rather to help relax and unlock the unconscious mind of its occupant."

"Can you give us an example?"

"Perhaps one of the commonest is the person who goes to bed puzzling over a name or face or date—anything at all—that had earlier just kept eluding him, poised on thc tip of his tongue. It happens to all of us. 'Eureka!' he cries out in the night, and, lo, he has the answer. What has happened is that the subjective mind has simply had a chance to take over."

"Why ever bother then with hypnosis?"

"To organize and concentrate the effort and, when successful, hasten the achievement of a favorable state for recall." He reflected a moment. "Memories are not so much lost as buried. All hypnosis does is aid in their disinterment. Hypnosis properly used never creates or suggests what is recalled; all it does is unlock what's already there, no more and no less."

"Doctor," I concluded swiftly, though there was much more I might have asked, "do you know of any qualified practitioner of hypnosis in this area who might attempt memory recall on Kirk should you be found disqualified?"

"None that I am aware of," he said. "The few practitioners around tend to keep out of the Yellow Pages."

"Your witness," I said, turning toward the champing young prosecutor.

"We'll adjourn for lunch," the judge said, looking down at the bailiff and signaling with one raised finger.

"Hear ye, hear ye, hear ye," bawled the latter after we were gaveled to our feet, "this honorable court is adjourned until one o'clock—*sharp!*"

Chapter 11

The lunch hour was over and nearly everyone was back in place, including the whispering trio of becurlered ladies as well as my client—who once again had been paraded the length of the courtroom and dramatically delivered at my table by the gun-toting sheriff. We awaited only the judge.

"Mr. Ludlow," I heard my client whispering at my side, he having lately abandoned calling me by the more pal-sy Fritz.

"Yes, Randy?" I said, looking into his unsmiling face and troubled eyes. "What's on your mind?"

"Do we have to go ahead with this childish nonsense?" he blurted in a sort of raspy whisper, rather like a small boy uncorking a grievance he'd long been nursing.

Here we go again, I thought, depressed by this new development. "Look, do I have to threaten to quit your goddamn case every time I make a move to help you?" I whispered back.

"That might be the simplest solution for all concerned," he whispered, looking almost grateful at my suggestion, and for the first time unmistakably showing a disposition to get me to hell off of his case.

Stung, I sat debating whether to repack my briefcase, tell him to go four-letter himself, and stomp out of court in high dudgeon. But walking out right then was a luxury that, aside from assuaging my pride, might also win me a swift contempt citation from the judge.

As I sat pondering this latest crisis in my case, I also found myself feeling more determined than ever to stick it out. For the truth was, it suddenly dawned on me, that I was already deeply hooked by it, as were my old friends Jeremiah and Hugh Salter. Already we had devoted far more time and cerebration to the case than any mere legal fees could ever repay. How could I possibly walk out on something that was more and more beginning to haunt my dreams?

My partner had recently rhapsodized on the subject in his usual colorful fashion. "A lawyer deep in his case is like a man fallen in love," he had said. "Whether shaving or bathing or plain old-fashioned knaving, in bed or out, always and forever he is obsessed by his goddam case."

"Randy," I whispered, pride successfully swallowed, "let's defer any decision until after this afternoon's session. By then I hope you'll see that what I'm trying to do may be your only chance—that's unless you want to commit a kind of legal suicide. What do you say?"

He sat looking down at his hands lying open on his lap, staring at them so fixedly that I wondered if he'd heard me. "What do you say, Randy?" I repeated.

The decision was taken out of our hands by the entrance of the judge, robe again billowing and crackling, and before I could dig out my notepad—"Hear ye, hear ye, hear ye!"—young Eugene Canda and old Doctor Hugh were locked in their own rhetorical tug-of-war.

"Doctor," Eugene Canda began, aiming at once for the groin, "what makes you think you can make a man recall what he's forgotten when you've never tried it before?"

"Young man," Hugh Salter answered softly, "all I said earlier, I believe, was that I think I may be qualified to give it an honest try—perhaps even the old college try, if you prefer."

"But how?"

"By hypnosis, of course, the thing I've just been running on about."

"I don't mean that. I mean what makes you think you are qualified to try?"

"Well, it's a long story, some of the highlights of which I've tried to give here this forenoon."

"Will you please try again?"

Eugene Canda, for all of his choirboy look of innocence, was a crafty and relentless cross-examiner who could lead an unwary witness into forests of hidden traps, as I ruefully knew from our own past courtroom clashes. So I sat there holding my breath and nervously wondering how this retired and occasionally forgetful old doctor would fare before such a crafty assault.

"Fair enough, young man," Hugh Salter began. "First I've read a lot on the subject, including scores of case histories. Then I've watched actual attempts at memory recall and age regression by others, largely at out-of-town psychology conferences and the like."

"Anything else?"

"Then, as I've earlier said, I'm a pretty old hand at inducing hypnotic trance myself." He paused. "Look, just suppose for a moment you were sitting here in this witness chair and I was down there in your shoes and I bluntly asked you why you thought you were ever qualified to run the first time as prosecutor of this county, having never prosecuted even one criminal case. Wouldn't *your* answer have to be pretty much the same as mine?"

"I'm asking the questions, Doctor," Eugene Canda said, his flushed face suddenly matched the color of his russet hair. He again consulted his notes as I breathed a bit easier.

"Doctor," he began again, taking a new tack, "Mr. Ludlow's petition speaks of, and I quote, 'amnesia, shock, somnambulism, unconsciousness or some other condition.' Am I correct in assuming that you helped draft that portion?"

"Naturally, young man."

"All right, Doctor, if you can so confidently conjure up all these possibilities, why can't you tell us *which* one might account for Kirk's claimed loss of memory?"

"Because I'm not able to."

"But why aren't you able to, Doctor?" Eugene Canda softly asked, triumphantly stepping back.

"Because your sheriff seems to share your own prejudice

against hypnosis, and won't let me have at Kirk so that I just might find out."

Judge Brotherton stifled a smile. Eugene Canda looked up from his notes and was again back at the witness, making me somehow think of a terrier worrying a bespectacled bear.

"Doctor, how could you possibly tell which condition caused his loss of memory, even if you should finally 'have at him,' as you so elegantly put it?"

"That idiom goes back at least to the first Queen Elizabeth, so don't make light of it. Now to answer your question, I'm not sure that I can isolate the precise cause but I still might make him remember, which I guess is the main thing we're after."

"But how could you recover his memory and still not account for its lapse?"

"Again it's a long story, but in many cases amnesia is simply the mind's retreat from what it dare not remember. Hypnosis may unlock it and, in doing so, may also account for the locking."

Eugene Canda again quickly stepped back, a telltale sign that he was about to hurl another fast ball. "Doctor," he all but purred, "are you suggesting that Kirk was so horrified by what he did to Constance Spurrier that he's blotted it from his mind?"

I half-rose to object, but eased back down in my chair, for this was one gnawing question that haunted all of us, and a losing objection on it now would only etch it deeper into the case.

"That is indeed one possibility." Hugh Salter answered with unruffled calm. "The answer to that question might save a long and expensive public trial if only I were allowed to have at him—begging your and Queen Elizabeth's pardon."

"But, Doctor—"

"Just a minute, please—I hadn't quite finished. At the same time I must add that there can be many cases of blocked memory without guilt."

I again sat marveling at the old boy for not only holding his own with a clever young witness-trapper but also for so subtly planting the seed that a future trial might be avoided if only we had our way. "Prosecutor Blocks Chance to Save County Long,

Expensive Trial," was one headline the politically ambitious Eugene Canda did not care to read about just then.

Eugene Canda doggedly pushed on. "Can you name some forms of guiltless amnesia?"

"Many, among the commonest being war veterans suffering from what, when I was a gangling young soldier in the medical corps swathed in yards of khaki leggings, we used to call shell shock. Then, in our own pastoral times, there are the many witnesses and victims of violent crime who similarly blot out the memory and can recall neither the crime nor its perpetrator. In fact, a recent newspaper article on the subject by Dr. Martin Reiser estimates that at least two hundred American police departments are now using hypnosis in such situations. Then not too long ago, Walter Cronkite himself, on the evening news, told about how those young men were caught—"

"What young men?"

"The ones who abducted and held that school bus full of children—twenty-six, I believe, besides the driver."

"Hypnosis, of course?"

"You're getting the hang of it, young man. Under hypnosis the bus driver sufficiently recalled the license number of a car the abductors drove—which led to their arrest and conviction. Then there was the even more recent case—"

"That's quite enough, Doctor," the prosecutor said. "Surely you are aware, are you not, that the few cases you speak of concern the victims and witnesses of crime and not, as here, using hypnosis on the accused criminal himself?"

"Oh, yes, and also that all kinds of prickly constitutional barriers stand in the way of its possible general use upon defendants charged with crime. But I am also aware, young man, that defendants can waive their constitutional rights and that here we have one seeking to arm his own lawyer with the tools to stimulate his own memory recall."

"One small correction, Doctor; it's the defendant's lawyer who's doing all the waiving here, with not a word from the silent defendant himself."

"We'll take a brief recess here," the judge said with a smile. "Must go make a phone call that this very examination reminds me I plumb clean forgot."

Chapter 12

"Doctor," Eugene Canda said, back again on the attack, "in your testimony this morning, recounting your early interest in hypnosis, did you not use the phrase, and I quote, 'then scarcely mentioned, much less taught, in our medical schools'?"

"Yes, I did."

"Are things any different today?"

"Alas, not vastly, young man," Hugh Salter answered with a melancholy shake of his head. "Even today only a comparative handful of medical schools give courses in hypnosis."

"Are you now saying that no physicians use hypnosis in their work, Doctor?"

"Not quite, young man, but the comparative few who do —and this, by the way, includes many nonphysicians—often do so almost stealthily, some even trying to escape the ancient stigma attached to its name by calling it something else."

"Doctor," the prosecutor pushed on, "I also note that you haven't mentioned any psychiatrists employing hypnosis, although you earlier conceded that many of them do engage in memory recall. Why so, if hypnosis is all that good?"

"Simply because most of the medical schools—where virtually all psychiatrists are spawned—still don't teach it. Consequently hypnosis remains pretty much in their doghouse, too. One big blow—or should I say psychiatric trauma?—occurred when Freud himself, once an ardent student of hypnosis, abruptly turned against it."

Eugene Canda joyously scribbled down this latest revelation and returned to the attack. "Why?" he almost sang.

"I don't really know, but the professional gossip of the time has it that he once put a concupiscent young woman into deep hypnotic trance on his office couch, and quickly repented both of her and hypnosis when she rather strenuously tried to get him to join her there." He blinked in recollection. "Freud, by the way, attended the first international congress for experimental and therapeutic hypnotism held in Paris in 1889, along with men like William James and Lombroso."

Eugene Canda took a quick step back, always a sign of trouble, as I anxiously awaited his next question. "Doctor," he said, "if, as you concede, virtually all workers in the medical, psychiatric, and psychoanalytic professions rigorously avoid hypnosis who, then, has anything good to say for it?"

"Most psychologists, bless them. Hypnosis has had a checkered, if not fantastic, career and has long been perhaps the most neglected Topsy of the whole psychic realm. After almost perishing around the turn of the century it was saved largely by our psychologists. One might say that hypnosis moved directly from the vaudeville stage to the psychology laboratory."

"Starting on the striptease and nightclub arenas, Doctor?" Eugene Canda all but purred.

"No, on the vaudeville stage, as I just said."

"How far back does hypnosis go, then?"

"Hypnosis is really as old as human history," Hugh Salter continued, "but Anton Mesmer, who died in 1815, may fairly be called the father of modern hypnosis."

"Who was he?"

"A young, immensely ambitious Viennese doctor who began applying his pet theories of planetary magnetism to his own patients, believing that he possessed an animal magnetism flowing directly from himself to his patients. If all this sounds rather like W.C. Fields attempting a heart transplant," Hugh Salter continued, "the fact is that this young man, however deluded, began making dramatic cures. Patients started flocking to him, particularly women, and presently his fellow doctors started turning quite green with envy. Despite his obsessive theories, the man was actually practicing hypnotic suggestion, though neither his patients nor he ever seemed to realize it."

"What happened?" Eugene Canda ventured.

"Predictably, his envious colleagues ganged up on him, circulating stories that he was practicing black magic and the like, finally driving him off to an even more lucrative practice in Paris. There he built an enormous clinic in which he could treat as many as thirty women patients at a crack, all squatting around a large, circular wooden vat or baquet filled with water and iron filings."

("Vat iss baquet?" I had asked Hugh Salter in a heavy Germanic accent when I'd first heard this same story from him only a few weeks before.

"Zee baquet ees a vat, yes?" the old boy had promptly answered in an ascending French accent.

"You can say Vatican," Jeremiah had put in, whereupon we declared a mutual cease-fire and took time out for a drink.)

"What happened to Mesmer in Paris?" Eugene Canda asked, glancing back at the courtroom clock.

"In a few years—1784 to be exact—Mesmer's new crop of equally jealous Parisian medical rivals wangled the French government into appointing a royal commission to probe his so-called animal magnetism. By then Mesmer—who frequently practiced while clad in one or the other of his many exotic silk robes—had grown so popular that the commission, instead of daring to investigate him, decided to concentrate on a lesser-known disciple who ran a rival vat. They probed away and, finding no physical explanation for the cures, since there was none, sagely concluded and announced that the Mesmer method was a fraud and a fake."

"And wasn't it, Doctor?" Eugene Canda said.

"Partly," Hugh Salter said, "but Mesmer was also, beyond any doubt, a magnificent practitioner of hypnotic therapy, though ironically he probably never knew it. He died in grumbling and opulent obscurity in 1815, still clinging to his theory of animal magnetism."

"And medical hypnosis died with him?" Eugene Canda suavely suggested.

"Almost, but not quite. After the era of Mesmer, hypnosis went underground, so to speak," he began. "Its next big milestone came with the incredible career of a young Scottish doctor called James Esdaile, during the early 1800s."

"What'd *he* do?"

"Esdaile went to India and practiced in two government-run charity hospitals. In these he performed hundreds of operations, over three hundred of them major, and—mark this—lost not a single patient on the operating table and only five out of a hundred from postoperative infection—truly a remarkable performance even today."

"All of course done with hypnotism?" Eugene Canda said, adding a dash of irony to his patience.

"Correct, young man. Solely by using hypnotic anesthesia, accomplishing all this, mind, before the advent of conventional anesthesia and aseptic surgery. At the same time, back in London, if a person didn't die first of surgical shock, as so many did, his chances were about one in three of expiring later, largely from postoperative infection."

"Maybe he picked his patients?" Eugene Canda said, fighting back.

"He did not. He took them as they came—major amputations, removal of gross elephantiasistic tumors, cataracts, ulcers, cancerous tissue, the whole gamut. Moreover, most of his patients were poor, many already woefully emaciated and weak, and he usually performed these prodigies amidst primitive surroundings and in a debilitating climate."

"But how could Esdaile do all this while the doctors back home in London and elsewhere couldn't?"

"By using hypnosis, of course, though the doctors back home not only ignored his successes but even tried to get him fired."

"So once again your own profession turned thumbs down on hypnotism, right, Doctor?"

"Quite true. Aldous Huxley tells the whole sad story in one of his essays, called 'A Case of Voluntary Ignorance,' and I cannot resist quoting his scorching opening line: 'That men do not learn much from the lessons of history is the most important of lessons history has to teach.' After that he really pours it on."

"After Esdaile, who was the next lone medical disciple of hypnosis to bite the dust?"

"Esdaile was only one in a long line of medical pioneers to brave the scorn of the medical establishment of his time—men like Liebault and Bernheim in France and Elliotson and Braid in the British Isles—the latter invented the modern term hypnotism, by the way—yes, and Vogt and Schultz, in Germany, were equally scorned and humiliated."

"Doctor, if hypnosis is all that good, how come one of the world's oldest and most respected professions—I mean the medical, of course—has so consistently ignored it?"

Hugh Salter wearily shook his head. "*That,* young man, is an enigma I have long pondered."

"Maybe hypnotism is too hard to learn?" Eugene Canda suggested softly, making me sit up, sensing another trap.

"Esdaile later thought that, too, guessing that his fellow doctors shunned hypnosis because they might have to go back to school. He was wrong there, as he himself picked up his own remarkable technique mostly from his reading."

Softly, in an ascending tone of voice: "Just as you did yourself, right, Doctor?"

"Correct, young man, and if the afternoon were not so far gone I could probably teach you at least the basic rudiments of hypnotic induction before we left this room."

"Doctor," Eugene Canda said after he'd delightedly scribbled down this latest revelation, "is this why hypnotism so soon found itself reduced to vaudeville?"

"Largely, but again that's the story of virtually everything having to do with probing the human psyche, and why we today have whole squads of cross-legged gurus—bald or bearded or both—squatting on beaches and busy street corners."

"Because hypnosis is so easy to fake, you mean?"

"Not so much fake as misuse, simply to make money, massage the ego, and to amuse—the triple gods of our era. Sometimes I wonder whether the very ease of learning hypnotic induction hasn't turned off many of my brother doctors. After all their years of savage study they probably hate to swallow the idea of adopting a technique they could start picking up in hours. Also, doctors are largely taught to rely only upon those symptoms they can measure and calibrate—see, touch, hear, smell—in turn perhaps making them naturally skeptical of all they can't."

"Any other reasons?"

"Many doctors fear being regarded as quacks if they dare use it, because of the low opinion it has among people in general. That same fear probably kept me a secret practitioner until I finally rebelled and said to hell with it—begging your pardon, Judge."

"I allow five hells per witness," the judge said. "You have four left."

"And why does the general public frown on it?" Eugene Canda pressed.

"Because I'm afraid we poor humans have a helpless tendency to be suspicious of and hate—and blithely lump together—anything and everything we don't understand," Hugh Salter said, wagging his head sadly. "That's why most people continue to equate hypnosis with such diverse things as spiritualism, reincarnation, faith-healing, extrasensory perception, hallucinatory drugs—let's see—astrology and the casting of horoscopes, yoga, gnosticism, alchemy; I could run on and on. Through a kind of blind, invincible ignorance, many of my fellow doctors and, I'm afraid, even some of our rising young lawyers, tend resolutely to lump hypnosis with all these other things without bothering to sift the good from the bad."

"What has miraculously saved our patient, Doctor?"

"The psychologists at places like UCLA, Stanford, Harvard, Washington State, Duke, Chicago, and my own old school, Michigan—to name but a few on the steadily growing list."

Eugene Canda picked a new note pad off his table and padded up toward the witness stand, pausing halfway to aim a question, and I thought of a hunter advancing for the kill.

"Doctor, why did you hide what you were doing from the general public, as you mentioned earlier. Were you ashamed of it?"

"Certainly not. Perhaps it was partly the pressure of that conformity I just spoke of. Perhaps there was some fear of ridicule. But mostly, I think it was a simple desire to help my patients the best way I could and at the same time spare both of us the ridicule that so inevitably attends all hostility based upon ignorance alone."

"Doctor," Eugene Canda pressed on, "you've just said, did you not, that psychology was just about the only profession that looks favorably upon hypnosis?"

"That is correct, alas."

"And are you perchance a psychologist?"

"I am not, as you already know, though I must say I've certainly read a lot in the field."

"And I believe you also said earlier that psychiatrists have their own ways of stimulating memory recall."

"I did say that and it is a fact."

"Are there any essential differences between their way and the hypnosis way, Doctor?"

"In technique, considerably, yes, but basically their goals remain the same: to relax the subject, probe his unconscious, and let the buried memories flow. One uses hypnosis; the other his art."

"Any major differences?"

"Essentially none, I'd say, aside from the technique."

Again the quick step back. "Doctor, wouldn't Kirk be far better off, then, if his attempted memory recall were entrusted to a trained local psychiatrist rather than to an untrained and retired country baby doctor?"

It was a savage, thrusting question, the kind which, if objected to, only drove the point home deeper, but Hugh Salter sat there taking it smilingly. "First, young man, I'm not and never was a baby doctor, though I think I know what you mean. Moreover, I'm already deep in this case, Kirk's trial swiftly approaches, early memory stimulation is vital, and I think, considering the circumstances, that hypnotic recall in this case just might be faster." His smile broadened. "Also, a switch to a professional psychiatrist would doubtless be far more costly."

"Why so, Doctor?"

"Because I propose doing the job for nothing."

As Eugene Canda stood probing his notes for new inspiration, Hugh Salter, still smiling, continued to speak. "And since

I've answered quite a few fairly probing questions here today, I'd now like to ask one of you," he said. "Are you by any chance suggesting, young fellow, that if I *were* a trained psychiatrist your engaging pseudo-cowpoke sheriff would cheerfully let me have at Kirk?"

The question was indeed a scorcher, as I saw by the rush of blood to Eugene Canda's face. If he said yes, he not only conceded the validity of memory recall itself but also of our chief analogy; if he said no, then he admitted he was not only dead set against hypnosis but against any help whatever for Kirk.

"Mr. Canda?" the judge prodded.

"Your Honor," Eugene Canda said, rallying gamely, "I thought I was the one asking the questions here."

"You're right, there, but since I rather fancy the question I'll ask it myself. Consider the question asked."

"I'd first have to consult my client, Your Honor."

"Consult away, then."

After a few minutes of whispered huddling, Eugene Canda was back on his feet, still a little flushed. "My client is not prepared to say what he'd do in the hypothetical situation suggested," he said. "He further suggests that since the witness isn't a psychiatrist he still opposes allowing any hypnotist into his jail, especially one who now himself concedes he has never before tried memory recall."

The judge frowned and sighed. "Any more questions, Mr. Canda?"

"No, Your Honor," he said, evidently grown wary of asking any further devastating questions.

The judge looked at me. "Any more witnesses, Mr. Ludlow?"

"No, Your Honor," I arose and said. "That's unless you insist upon my client taking the stand, and if so I'd like to argue that a little further, if I may."

"I've not quite decided that," the judge said, looking back at Eugene Canda. "Do you plan to call any witnesses?"

"No, Your Honor," the young prosecutor said.

"Then we'll recess for five minutes," the judge said. "*Mister* Bailiff!"

Chapter 13

During recess I reviewed some of the law we'd found on our case, not that I needed a refresher, heaven knows, but mostly to avoid having to talk with my unpredictable client and risk a possible renewal of hostilities.

We had often worked far into the night preparing our petition. But since that document was in turn based upon the law we'd found—and also not found—we'd first had to spend many hours and days wrestling with *that.* In fact it all began with the first interview I'd had with Randall Kirk at the county jail, when I realized I was about to be retained by a murder client who could not remember whether or not he had committed the crime.

Earlier that same day I'd played hooky from work—I guess a fugitive cloud had passed over during the lunch hour—and it was nearly dusk when I checked back at the office, as I usually did, and there found a terse note from my irate partner.

"The one good thing about your fishing, pardner," it read, "is how it stimulates business, for almost invariably a brand-new case will pop up while you're off in the brambles chasing mermaids. Call the goddam county jail. I'll be waiting for you back at the office, following a cribbage session I've got earlier this evening over at Doctor Hugh's."

So it had been almost midnight when, still supperless and in my fishing clothes, I'd once again returned to the office and found Jeremiah pacing the floor—a sure sign he'd lost at cribbage, which he shortly grudingly confirmed. "But enough of that," he added. "Tell me about our new case."

"Partner," I said, breaking the news gently, "we've got a case by the tail, I swear, the like of which I've never before seen or heard of, in law school or out."

"Is that so?" Jeremiah said testily, settling back into his chair. "Tell me about the goddam thing."

"Not much to tell, pard," I said, launching into the sketchy story as I'd just heard it from Kirk, the main feature of which revolved around the singular fact that he couldn't remember even being with Constance Spurrier the night before much less doing her any harm.

"Maybe the shock of what he did made the guy forget," Jeremiah suggested, his legal gears already churning.

"Possibly," I said, "except that his loss of memory seems to have occurred even before he got to Connie's island."

"What do you mean?"

"I mean his forgetting began from the time when, while he was still back in his own cottage on the mainland, he hard the ringing of some sort of bell."

"What kind of a ringing bell?" Jeremiah pressed. "Bells ring lots of ways: clang, knell, chime, peal, and sometimes jingle—especially at Christmas—some still tintinnabulate, thanks to ole Mr. Poe, cracked ones go bong and even clank, and—les'see now—one day they'll surely toll for thee and me, just wait and see."

"Just a faint ringing," I said, reaching for my notebook. "I wrote down his exact words. Here they are: 'I heard the faint tinkling of a bell.' "

"Did you think to ask him if he'd ever had any similar lapse of memory before?"

"Naturally, and his answer was a positive no," I said. "In fact it was one of the few things the poor guy seemed really sure of. That and the fact that he was neither drunk nor drugged nor had ever suffered from epilepsy or somnambulism nor had had any recent falls or injuries. In fact, I asked him just about everything I could think of. His answers seem to boil down to one monotonous thing—the man's memory blacked out for the first time in his life when he heard the faint tinkling of a bell."

"Do you believe the guy?" Jeremiah asked, stroking his chin. I'd scarcely had time to think about this in all the rush, so I applied myself to that task and found myself, rather to my surprise, answering almost at once. "Damned if I don't," I said.

"Then of course we take his case and try to find a possible defense, right?"

"Righto, pard," I said, yawning elaborately, "but it's getting real late. Fatigue stalks the land, so let's delay exploring all that till tomorrow, right?"

"Tonight!" Jeremiah said. "Aromatic, unwashed fishermen must pay for their sins."

"Yessir," I said meekly.

After that, we carried on like a couple of first-year law students cramming for their finals in criminal law, starting with the possible defense of insanity, not because we thought it might even faintly fit our case but rather because we had to start somewhere. Insanity, we agreed, was one of the fundamental criminal defenses because it was, when it worked, a total, no-strings-attached, all-or-nothing defense, akin to self-defense in the realm of homicide.

"The two defenses differ," Jeremiah ran on, "in that self-defense claims legal justification while insanity claims excuse. It's as though in the first case the accused comes into court saying, 'Yes, I killed the bastard but I had to in order to save my own life,' while in insanity he says, 'Yes, I guess I up and killed him all right but I really didn't know what I was doing or that it was wrong.' "

"Well said, partner," I said, putting in my oar. "Or, put another way, every major crime requires two things: a criminal act done with a criminal intent, and lacking either ingredient, there can be no criminal responsibility."

"Yes?" Jeremiah said musingly, nodding and spurring me on.

"And just as self-defense goes to the first element of any

crime—the act—so insanity goes to the second—the criminal intent."

"Hm . . ." Jeremiah mused. "How about irresistible impulse?"

Both of us recalled from law school days that this comparatively rare criminal defense—usually called "dissociative reaction" in modern psychiatric circles—had some case authority going for it in Michigan, presenting a situation where the accused in effect argued, "Yes, I know I killed him and that it was wrong, but in my jumpy, addled mental state I simply couldn't resist doing it."

We also knew that this rather offbeat defense was aimed at mitigating the claimed simplistic harshness of the old English M'Naghten's Case "right and wrong" rule, handed down back in 1843—our federal courts and some other states having their own mitigating variations. These stemmed from a growing but still not majority belief that the old English rule too much ignored modern psychological knowledge and progress in that it isolated and rewarded but one type or symptom of mental aberration—only that involving moral blackout—forcing all other mental abberants to make a narrow choice between either perjuring themselves or taking their punishment on the chin.

"Jeremiah," I said plaintively, yawning and glancing desperately at my watch, "all this elementary hornbook jabber is getting us nowhere. And anyway, how in hell can we possibly come into court claiming Kirk couldn't help what he was doing when he's alrady told me and the cops that his mind was a total blank."

"Hmm," Jeremiah hummed, ignoring my state of fatigue. "What you've just said, pardner, at least presents nicely one other possible legal issue we can look into."

"How so?"

"By suggesting that one of our big initial problems is to find out whether forgetting what one has done, that is, amnesia, is ever a defense to crime. For that contribution, however inadvertent, I must grade you B-plus."

"Thanks," I said, finding my mind still churning away despite my fatigue. "Which may in turn suggest that some form of sleepwalking was present."

"Why that?"

"Well, if Kirk really strangled this healthy outdoor gal, Connie, then he must not only have been ambulant but possessed of considerable muscular coordination, right?"

"Good try," Jeremiah agreed. "Which in turn suggests an ambulant unconsciousness—which by the way you seem to be lapsing into right now, pard, so I'll relent and call it a night. Anyway, I see I'm going to have to have a heart-to-heart talk real soon with Doctor Hugh."

"Doctor Hugh?" I said, mildly rallying.

"Right," Jeremiah replied. "I've never told you before, but the old boy is a kind of amateur bear cat at hypnosis and puzzling over unusual and offbeat psychological states. Has used it for years in his practice. And this situation may be right down his alley."

"What do you mean?"

"Because while gabbing about the stuff over cribbage I've often heard him claim that hypnosis can sometimes even be used to recover lost memory and the like."

"Old Doctor Hugh?" I said unbelievingly. "I thought that all he ever cared about was delivering babies, drinking sour-mash bourbon whiskey, and beating your ass at cribbage. Small world."

"You may have the order wrong," Jeremiah said. "Anyway I guess he felt that his world view was too restricted, simply delivering one new baby after the other."

"He probably had a point, there, pard," I managed to mumble, already half-asleep.

"Scat! Off to bed!" Jeremiah ordered, arising and waving me away with the back of his hand. "For tomorrow we hit the law books."

"Just one more thing before I take off," I yawned and said. "Out of curiosity I finally asked the guy how he happened to retain me as his lawyer and surprisingly he told me, small world, that Connie herself had once told him that if he ever needed one, to try me."

"How come she never brought you her own legal business, then? With all her dough and all, she must have had plenty."

"Damned if I know," I said, still wondering a little about

that myself. "Maybe she happened to notice in the *Gazette* that I often defended criminal cases and occasionally even beat our tough young prosecutor. Maybe, scary thought, she had a premonition of what was going to happen to her."

"My, my. Never knew you knew the gal."

"Didn't, really, pard. Only ran into her once, stuck out on a country road."

"Tell me about it?"

"Not now, pard, some other time," I said, yawning helplessly.

"Scat!" he repeated. "Be off with you."

The next day we spent rummaging through our own modest library, mostly devoted to Michigan law, but at day's end we had drawn a total blank.

"At least Michigan hasn't yet gone either way on what seems to be one of our prime issues," Jeremiah said philosophically, "so tomorrow we'll raid the bigger courthouse library and see what we can come up with there."

After not one but nearly two days of further searching there, crouching on our knees one minute, scaling creaking old wooden ladders the next, the results were both sparse and mixed. First I came up with a note in an old volume of the *Lawyers Reports Annotated* to the chilling effect that hypnotism and any testimony adduced by it were frowned upon in all American courts. Then late in the afternoon, Jeremiah let out a little yelp, and bustled over and showed me a rather cryptic digest note citing an old Kentucky case that seemed to suggest that sleepwalking might sometimes be a defense to crime.

"Well, let's dig out the case and see what it says," I said.

"No way," Jeremiah said, gloomily shaking his head. "The decision is so old it predates our national reporter system, so it just plain ain't here."

"Then let's send to an even bigger library and get a photocopy," I said.

"No use," Jeremiah said, still dolefully wagging his head. "We've simply got to go personally raid that bigger library."

"But why?" I said, thinking of my summer fishing plans, already sadly endangered by this very case.

"Because, as any old courtroom hand like you should long have known, getting and reading that one old case, even if it turns out a real winner, still won't begin to tell us all we need to know."

"What do you mean?"

"Because we still wouldn't know if the case is still the law or in what other and later cases it may be cited, for or against, or how good or bad those latter cases may be and, further, where in hell, in turn, *they* may be cited. We'd only wind up more puzzled and bedeviled than ever."

"I think you rather overstate the thing," I said.

"Look, partner," Jeremiah said, raising both his head and his voice, and I could feel a full-dress declamation coming on: "We lawyers, contrary to the popular myth, never ever learn the law in the sense of carrying all the answers around in our heads like some sort of walking computer. All any moderately sane or lucky lawyer ever learns is how to sift out the legal issues from the tangled jungle of facts that confront him in every new legal situation, and, then, where and how to go hit the books to discover what the goddam law might be." He heaved a sigh. "A lawyer lacking a flock of law books is like a carpenter run out of nails. He—he's simply—"

"Screwed?" I suggested, ever the helpful pal of a groping friend in need.

"Precisely," my partner agreed, thoughtfully stroking his chin. "But I can see your mind is wandering, so why don't you run along on your date or go fishing, and I'll fuss around here a bit."

The old boy had read my mind, so I left him musing amidst the stacks of dusty law books and took off on a fishing spree. Later, checking back at the office, I found a bombshell note from Jeremiah announcing he was taking off that very night for our old down-state law school library.

"You can tell how hooked I am by our goddam case," his note added, "when I tell you that I'm *flying* down to old Ann Arbor town." I glanced at my watch and saw that the evening plane had already left, so I sat there marveling, recalling my partner's past scorn for all air travel.

"Airplanes aren't here to stay," was one of his favorite

explanations for why he would never fly, "or if *they* are, then maybe *we* ain't."

His note had a postscript. "I plan to be back Saturday on the early evening plane, so please forsake chasing gals or gills long enough to meet me, and arrange also for a huddle later over at Doctor Hugh's."

So that Saturday evening I duly forsook my normal pursuits and met his plane. Dusk saw the three of us settled around a table in Hugh Salter's tall, book-lined library with a tiny fire glowing in the grate at the far end.

"Let's get going," Hugh Salter said, glancing at his watch. "Seems I've got an important cribbage match later this evening with one of my favorite pigeons."

Chapter 14

"Unconsciousness is the magic word for the day," Jeremiah arose and said, launching his seminar. "A week ago I could barely pronounce the word but tonight you are beholding one of the world's top authorities on unconsciousness as a defense to crime—though some of us insiders prefer calling it either impaired consciousness or automatism." He paused, coughed discreetly, and made a little bow. "I now know beyond a shadow of a doubt that there is such a defense, that it is as little known as it is rarely used, and that all the American reported cases on it could probably be accommodated nicely in an occupied phone booth."

He then went on to explain that most of the standard textual legal sources either ignored the defense entirely or barely mentioned it; either that or erroneously lumped it under a plea of insanity. "In fact," he went on, holding up a finger, "during my three days of dredging I came up with only one searching law review article squarely on the subject."

Next he grabbed and held aloft a thick sheaf of photo copy, brandishing it like an auctioneer as he spoke. "I hold in my hand—if that phrase hasn't yet been banished from our language—a copy of that brilliant law review article. It was researched and written for the *Columbia Law Review* by a gifted young law professor called Sanford Fox, helped by Howard Chasanow, bless them both, on a grant from the Ford Foundation. In it he either cites or comments on virtually every important English and American case on the little-known subject of impaired consciousness as a criminal defense, ranging from the old English Hadfield case decided back in 1800, on down to the time his article went to press."

"Who was Hadfield?" I dutifully inquired, getting my cue.

"A British soldier who'd received a grievous head wound, I gather, in our own Revolutionary War that left him so addled that he conceived it his sole mission in life to rid England and the world of King George the Third." Jeremiah paused and glanced at his old friend Hugh Salter, who himself bore a venerable English name. "Regrettably, he bungled the job and bagged a royal attendant instead."

"What happened?" I said.

"He was defended by the wily Lord Erskine, who based his defense solely on his client's impaired consciousness, caused by the old head wound, and got his man acquitted—the first such case on record anywhere."

"And of course the defendant was duly knighted for his poor marksmanship by a grateful king," Hugh Salter said, winking at me.

"No, Hugh, but the addled old soldier still remained such a danger to himself and others that the perplexed authorities simply kept him on in jail." He shook his head. "This probably accounts for the case still being wrongfully construed in many quarters as either an early insanity case or as one of insane delusion. Both views are dead wrong and it remains, in fact, the earliest reported case in Anglo-American law squarely involving the rare legal defense of impaired consciousness."

"How does all this help our man Kirk and his mere, unaddled loss of memory?" I said.

"We'll be coming to that," Jeremiah said. "After that, there were quite a flock of English cases involving successful criminal defenses based on the same grounds, and I could run on about them for hours. But since we happen to live not in fogbound London but instead in water-hemmed northern Michigan the beautiful—as the tourist ads continue to chant—I'd better get on with the American cases." He turned to me. "The first such case arose in Kentucky in 1879—the very same case, partner, we ran across in that brief mention down in the courthouse library earlier this week—if all that adds up to a sentence."

"I remember the case," I said. "What happened?"

"A man called Fain fell asleep in a chair in a hotel lobby. Hours later, when a porter tried to shake him awake, Fain pulled a gun and shot him dead. At his homicide trial Fain defended himself solely on the grounds of unconsciousness, claiming he was unaware of his actions because he had suffered from somnambulism ever since boyhood and sometimes had to be restrained."

"Then why was such an unstable character let out on the loose, packing a loaded gun?" I said.

"Claimed someone in town was out to get him."

"Hm. . . . Sounds like a scene out of old Dodge City to me. What happened?"

"Trial judge wouldn't allow his testimony on this and wouldn't instruct the jury on his theory, so Fain was convicted, and then appealed."

"Yes?"

"The Kentucky high court bought Fain's theory and reversed his conviction, thus making the Fain case America's first and still one of its leading and most cited cases on the criminal defense of impaired consciousness." He consulted his notes. "And though insanity was not even mentioned in Fain's case, some of our standard law-office textual sources still erroneously tend to confuse that case with an insanity defense."

"What real difference does it make?" Hugh Salter inquired.

"Most states, including Michigan, now provide that when a person is acquitted by reason of insanity he either *may* or *must* —Michigan says must—be further committed for mental treatment, for reasons of public safety."

"And if it's this other defense, the man goes scot-free?" Hugh Salter asked.

"Right, Hugh, but only in states, of course, where the defense of unconsciousness is already allowed," Jeremiah explained. "Michigan seems never to have ruled either way on the defense, so the question remains open here, which at least gives our man Kirk a fighting chance. And, who knows, maybe gives us a chance to become some sort of backwoods legal pioneers."

"Dreamer," I said. "What happened after Fain?"

"Ah yes, Fain. . . . Skipping quite a few interim cases, I'll now jump ahead to what may be for us the crucially important case, the California Freeman case, decided in 1943."

"Who'd he wake up and shoot?" I said.

"Nobody, pard, for Mr. Freeman had other troubles. One day he drove through a stop sign going over sixty and crashed into another car, maiming the driver and killing his passenger."

"Plastered, no doubt?"

"No, pard, gone suddenly unconscious from an attack of epilepsy, as he testified at his subsequent trial for negligent homicide."

"You mean all of a sudden he blanked out?"

"No, he got his first attack at a friend's house a few miles from the scene but somehow rallied and managed to drive away."

"First attack ever, you mean?"

"No, the latest in a series of several."

"Of course he was convicted?"

"Yes, on the trial level, but again, as in the Fain case, won a reversal on appeal for failure of the trial judge to instruct the jury on the claimed defense of unconsciousness. In fact, the court went sled-length, saying that epilepsy is only one of a number of causes of unconsciousness and also that the defense was distinct from that of insanity and need not be specially pleaded."

"Very interesting," I said.

"It says more, much more, approvingly citing our old Kentucky friend Fain and still later cases, and winds up with this exquisite gem, which I now quote: 'A person who cannot comprehend the nature and quality of his act is not responsible. An act done in the absence of will is not any more the behavior of the actor than an act done contrary to his will.' Now isn't that sublimely poetic and lovely?"

"As Kirk's lawyer it sounds dreamy," I said, "but if I weren't I'd be inclined to say that both it and the Fain case just plain stink."

"Pure heresy, pard. Don't even think such dark thoughts. And the Freeman case may be even better than we know."

"In what way?"

"By its express linkage with such old common-law 'unconscious' cases as Fain—since Michigan has no statute on the subject—plus its explicit affirmation that the defense is not to be confused with insanity and, finally, its express recognition that the accused need not be literally out like a light in order to invoke it—which our man rather obviously wasn't."

"I don't quite follow that last bit," I said.

"Look, besides the 'out cold' cases I've already mentioned, I've run across still others that involve twilight situations where, though the accused is not totally 'out cold,' as I keep saying, he's still not quite all there either—which fits our own client's case if he actually did what the People claim he did."

"Can you give an example?"

"Many of these foggy, twilight situations are largely physical in origin—I'll have to peek at my notes—caused by poor circulation, say, or arising from glandular or metabolic disorders, or failure of the body to supply sufficient glucose to the brain, or due to liver disorders or diabetic reactions short of outright passing out, to name only some."

"Any others?"

"Then, as still other cases show, there are conditions more directly involving or impinging on the brain itself, such as—where's my list?—head trauma, certain forms of epilepsy, cerebral tumor and"—he glanced at Hugh Salter—"atherosclerosis, if I pronounce that right, Hugh, and encephalitis, besides others I can't offhand recall, much less pronounce."

"You're doing fine, Jeremiah," Hugh Salter said, "and, the way your partner keeps staring at you, grand proof that people are never so impressed as when they can't quite get the drift of what they're seeing and hearing."

"So true, Hugh. In other words the various cases show that the symptoms of unconsciousness can range from total blackout to the most subtle twilight zones. In fact the modern American judicial trend has more and more been to hold that for any behavior to be branded criminal it must be conscious behavior, some state legislatures now expressly so provding by statute, California apparently being the first."

"Can you offhand recall the others?" I said, hoping to find an emancipated state at least bordering on Michigan.

"I'll check my notes—yes, Arizona, Idaho, Montana, Nevada, Oklahoma, South Dakota—hm—but none this far east."

"Covered wagon in reverse—at least unconsciousness is working back our way," I said. "Did you find any acquittals based simply upon lack of recall, I mean upon just plain amnesia?"

"No, I didn't. Many of the cases I've mentioned naturally involved some sort of memory failure, of course, but that loss in turn was invariably shown to be due to some specific and ascertainable medical factor such as head trauma, or epilepsy, or a heart attack and the like."

"Did you run into anything on the subject of amnesia alone as a possible criminal defense?"

"I sure did and I was just coming to that; a long, blockbusting article in the *Yale Law Journal* running to one hundred twenty-nine footnotes, believe it or not."

"But no cases where a guy was sprung simply because he couldn't remember?"

"None, not one single case."

"Does the article say why not?"

"Only obliquely, the very absence of any such acquittals forcing one to conclude that some sort of crude tribal realism is at work."

"Don't go fawncy on us, partner," I said. "Just come down out of the clouds and tell us in plain English what you're driving at."

"The amnesia defense seems to be rejected mainly because society and our courts apparently feel they simply cannot and dare not afford to allow a criminal defense that's so goddam easy to fake."

"But how can that same society buy all these other things you've been running on about—epilepsy and all the rest?"

"Because—and Hugh can correct me—these other things

are subject to clinical and medical confirmation and cannot easily be dissembled."

"It strikes me that if a guy's out driving," I said, "knowing he's subject to unpredictable blackout spells, the clinical proofs you mention should only afford additional reasons why the heedless bastard should be convicted."

"I was just coming to that, too," Jeremiah said. "There are indeed a few later American cases—I won't quite say it's yet a trend—holding that foreknowledge of a condition that could lead to antisocial behavior is itself reason for rejection of the defense. The English have gone even further, tending, even after acquittal in such cases, to hold such persons for further custodial treatment, much as we presently do in many insanity acquittals over here."

"Let's have the bad new American cases—possibly bad for our client, I mean."

"Well, fairly recently in Georgia the accused drank himself into a kind of snaky delirium, committed his crime—I have it down here in my notes—and tried to plead somnambulism and Fain to get himself off. The court simply wouldn't buy."

"Sounds like pretty elementary law to me," I said. "I can still hear old Professor 'Jabby' Waite telling us law school kids, 'Voluntary drunks gotta take their lumps.' At least one does not normally choose to be somnambulistic or an epileptic. Any other bad cases?"

"The most disturbing recent case of all—for our man, I mean—is that of Samuel Gooze of New Jersey, who was hospitalized following his first attack of Meniere's Syndrome."

"What in heaven's name is that?"

"A rather rare condition, I gather from the court's opinion—Hugh can correct me—caused by a malfunction of the inner ear resulting in upset equilibrium—balance to you, pard—distorted perception, violent nausea, and general drunklike behavior."

"What happened to poor brother Gooze?"

"About fifteen months later, driving alone in his brand-new Cadillac, Mr. Gooze suffered his second attack. When the fog lifted he learned he had smacked two cars in the opposing traffic lane, killing the woman driver of one."

"And?"

"At his trial for this driving homicide he predictably pleaded his sudden unconsciousness and put his doctor on the stand to back him up, which the latter did."

"What happened? Hurry, I can't wait."

"Regrettably for Mr. Gooze, the inquisitive prosecutor brought out, on cross-examination of the man's own doctor, that upon Gooze's hospital discharge he, the doctor, had specifically warned Gooze of a possible recurrence and told him never ever to drive his Cadillac alone."

"And?"

"Gooze was convicted, appealed, and lost his case with but one dissent." Jeremiah sighed and shook his head. "There must be a moral in all this for the spell-prone drivers of America."

"Simple," I said. "Drive a Cadillac."

"No, either have his doctor soft-pedal his warnings or else keep him to hell out of court."

"You seem to be touching on one of the dangerous dilemmas of ever pleading this unconsciousness thing as a criminal defense," Hugh Salter said. "If the accused fails to show previous symptoms or attacks he may be convincted for lack of adequate proof—much like the pure amnesia boys, as it were—whereas if he does dare show them, he may risk conviction under the theory of Gooze."

"Goosed either way," I said.

My partner, Jeremiah, studied me musingly over the tops of his glasses before he spoke. "You know," he said, "if only you'd said 'Goosed eider way' and ducked your head you would have cooked up a beautifully half-baked hot cross pun."

"Quack, quack," I said, dutifully ducking my head.

"Jeremiah," Hugh Salter said, "for years I've noticed that with many people, the more they concentrate the more they seem to exhibit accompanying symptoms akin to unconsciousness. Did you run across anything on that?"

"Indeed I did. Sanford Fox, in his *Columbia Law Review* article, touches precisely on that," Jeremiah said, "pointing out that unconsciousness itself is often an ambiguous state, that rarely is a person ever entirely one way or the other, that even in states of heightened consciousness—like you ecstatically beating my ass at cribbage—a person by that very fact often blots out whole areas of consciousness."

"Or like two lovers in bed," I said wistfully. "And speaking of bed, my cribbage-bent hearties, I'd better get myself there soon—I've an early fishing date in the morning."

"One more favorable thing," my partner ran on, ignoring my feeble try at adjournment, "is that the Model Penal Code itself has now come out and squarely plumped for unconsciousness as a general defense to crime."

"Is that code in force in Michigan?" Hugh Salter inquired.

"Not yet, but since the code was drafted by the American Law Institute, which includes some of the cream of the legal profession, it should be mighty persuasive."

"Speaking of cream, I'm utterly cowed," Hugh Salter said, shaking his head.

"Did I hear you say udderly?" my partner inquired.

"You men need the diversion of cribbage," I said, grabbing for my hat.

"Speaking of cribbage, I just happen to have a board and table set up over there by the fire," Hugh Salter said as he untangled himself, arose, and gestured grandly. "Will you please kindly join me there, Jeremiah?"

"I don't mind if I do," Jeremiah said, busily stuffing his papers and notes away, whereupon I left them and pointed my car homeward to dream of next day's fishing.

Chapter 15

"Gentlemen," Judge Brotherton said, our recess over, "for many hours today we've heard a lot about memory recall and hypnosis. I would now like counsel to address themselves to what they conceive to be the law applicable to their case." He smiled momentarily. "I've gone over the legal memorandums both of you have submitted to bolster your positions, and they disagree so flatly I can only assume you could not possibly have exchanged them." To this assumption Eugene Canda and I both nodded our agreement. "Now I hope we can wind up this hearing today, so I do hope you'll be brief." The judge looked at me. "Mr. Ludlow," he said, "I believe the floor is yours."

"Your Honor." I arose and began, aiming at brevity. "Perhaps, in the simplest statement I can make, the legal issues at stake here—and the consequent problems of the defense—can be boiled down to the following point: there is a growing and respectable body of law in this country, both statutory and under case law, to the effect that the impaired consciousness of the accused may be a defense to crime."

I paused and glanced at my notes. "It further appears that in every situation where such a defense has been offered and allowed, whether ultimately successful or not, the defendant has uniformly been additionally required to show the nature of his claimed impaired consciousness and what may have induced it, such as an attack of epilepsy, to give but one of many examples. In this particular case here today it further appears that the defendant, Kirk, suffers from what might be called a state of total amnesia or lack of recall, not only about what he did or why he did it but also why he cannot now recall it."

I again glanced compulsively at my notes, though I now knew by heart what I had to say. "We have also learned that amnesia alone, naked and unexplained, is never a defense to crime, whether offered as an explanation of claimed impairment of consciousness or taken alone. Indeed we have found at least one case where amnesia wasn't recognized as a valid ground even for postponing the trial until the accused might recover his lapsed memory."

I took another unneeded glance at my notes, like a ham actor pausing dramatically to let his lines sink in. "Finally," I said, "we have only within hours found eminently respectable legal authority for the proposition that where it is needed, attempted memory recall, including that stimulated by hypnosis, is now virtually everywhere considered a vital and necessary step in the constitutional right of every defendant charged with crime for a decent chance to prepare his defense."

I turned my distracting notes face down on the mahogany counsel table and faced the judge. "While I am aware that Michigan has never yet allowed the defense of impaired consciousness, by the same token it has also never yet rejected it, so the question may fairly be said to remain open, but this is not the time to argue that. To save time I shall also not now review the law upon which I base what I have said so far but leave that up to such questions as Your Honor may feel disposed to ask."

I paused a moment before launching my final pitch. "Your Honor, if our law is sound, then our whole case here today boils down to the fact that the dilemma of our client and ourselves is one that can only be solved by you," I said. "For it seems that we have been retained by a client whose only apparent defense, amnesia, turns out to be no defense at all, so that consequently his only remaining chance to build any possible defense is to recover his lost memory. Put another way, for you to deny here today what it is we seek would be tantamount to your convicting my client of murder without giving him the one lone chance of defending himself that, however remote, now seems even faintly possible. All we ask for is that one slim chance," I said, abruptly sitting down.

"Well I must say you were at least mercifully brief," the judge said, turning to my opponent. "Any response, Mr. Canda?"

"Yes indeed, Your Honor," Eugene Canda said, already launching on his rebuttal as he was getting out of his chair. "First we have here a petition to recall the memory of an accused person who has yet to offer a shred of proof that he's ever lost his memory." He went on, ticking off his points on his fingers like a prize-winning debater. "Second, we have an accused person seeking to recover that unproved lost memory by means of hypnosis, something not recognized in our law. Third, we have an offer to perform that dubious ritual by a man who's never performed the stunt before."

Eugene Canda paused and smiled amiably across at me. "And now we additionally have the candid admission just now made here by the petitioner himself, Mr. Ludlow, that the main reason he wants to recall his client's faulty memory is so that he might possibly invoke a defense—this impaired consciousness thing—that he concedes has never before been recognized in Michigan, all of which gratuitously offers me an additional reason for opposing his petition, for which I must cordially thank him."

My young opponent was in fine fettle and piling it on. He next picked up a heavy, leather-bound volume off his table and opened it. "I could probably end on this note, but, although my opponent has not seen fit to quote me a shred of law to support his views, I'd nevertheless like to quote him some law to support our own view that hypnosis and any evidence obtained by it are never admissible in the courts of our land."

"Proceed," the judge said, "though I suspect I've already read all about it in your earlier memorandum."

"Correct," Eugene Canda said, "so I shall be brief. In Volume Forty of *Lawyers Reports Annotated* beginning at page two sixty-nine there is an extended annotation on the subject of hypnotism and the law appended to the then recent California murder case of *People versus Ebanks.* In that case Ebanks sought to call as a witness an expert hypnotist to testify that the accused Ebanks, while in a state of hypnosis, had denied his guilt. In declining to admit any such testimony the trial judge said, and I quote, 'The law of the United States does not recognize hypnotism. It would be an illegal defense and I cannot admit it.' In affirming Ebanks's conviction for murder, the California Supreme Court simply said, 'We shall not stop to argue the point, and only add the trial court was right.' "

Eugene Canda expertly flipped some pages in the volume he held. "The annotation appended to Ebanks further shows on page two seventy-four that in an earlier California homicide case, *People versus Worthington,* the woman defendant there sought to exonerate herself by showing that her husband, while she was under a state of hypnosis, put her up to killing the deceased. Appended are two brief notes on the case, one of which says flatly that such a thing, if shown, still would not be a defense to murder. The other note reads in part as follows, and I quote: 'Testimony as to the effect of hypnotism . . . is not admissible in a criminal prosecution.' "

Eugene Canda clapped his book shut and returned it to his table with a thump. "I could go on reading other quotations to the same effect from that extended annotation but to save time I shall merely say that they show beyond any doubt whatever that both the law and medical professions of our land almost uniformly reject hypnotism and all its works." He sat down.

"Mr. Ludlow," the judge said, "do you have anything to say in reply?"

"Plenty," I said, rising, "beginning with reminding my opponent that he somehow forgot to tell us that the venerable annotation on hypnosis, on which he so much relies, first burst upon an unenlightened world back in 1898, while the two California cases he gleaned from it are naturally even older. Not that I can much blame my opponent for wringing so much solace from such an ancient source because, as we have learned, even to this day there is a surprising lack of mention of the realm of of hypnosis in relation to the law in most of our conventional legal sources. I know because my partner and I earlier looked high and low in our own office library and came up with nothing and, continuing our search here at the larger courthouse library, found only this musty old 1898 annotation. However, further and more recent search in our own office library has disclosed a recent case on the subject that I can only assume escaped the zealous research of my opponent, as it had indeed earlier escaped even ours. Before getting to that, however, I have this comment to make on his 1898 source."

I picked a heavy, leather-bound volume off my own table and opened it. "So sure was I that my opponent would almost necessarily have to rely heavily on that old LRA annotation that I today brought a duplicate volume along with me. Neither of the old California cases he cites go quite as far as my brother implies; namely, that hypnosis and all its works are uniformly barred from our courts. The one case, where the woman claimed her husband hypnotized her into committing a third-party homicide, simply does not apply to our present situation. As for the Ebanks case, all that case actually held was that a defense hypnotist himself could not take the stand to testify as to what the hypnotized accused might have told him. That would be as if I tried calling Dr. Salter at Kirk's approaching trial to tell the jury what it was Kirk may have told him under hypnosis rather than calling Kirk to tell it himself, once *his* memory was recovered. So I cannot quarrel with the Ebanks decision, which is really nothing more than a sound application of the rule against hearsay evidence, the best evidence rule, with possibly one or two others that momentarily elude me."

I flipped the pages of the musty volume I held before continuing. "Aside from these two old cases, then, the balance of the lengthy annotation is largely made up of foreign or domestic quotations or case histories taken from traditionally skeptical and conservative legal or medical sources, many of them antedating our own Civil War. In fact the article stands as a kind of antique and fascinating compendium of the low estate to which hypnosis had then fallen, and simply backs up the same doghouse state that Dr. Salter was at some pains to tell us about here earlier."

I reached in my briefcase and pulled out still another thick volume that was far too precious to leave lying around, and lovingly hefted it. "But whatever the state of the law regarding hypnosis back in 1898," I continued, "thanks to my ever zealous law partner, Jeremiah Dundee, I now have eloquent proof that both California's and the whole country's legal attitude toward clinical hypnosis has since vastly changed."

Once again I hefted the volume like an announcer hefting a prize country ham or mink coat on one of television's endless giveaway shows. "I hold in my hand the full text of a recent California case that not only says that an accused person is constitutionally entitled to have his faulty memory stimulated, if need be, but also that the trial court not only may but must order any reluctant jailer to admit a qualified hypnotist to attempt it. The reason I did not include the case in my earlier legal memorandum is that I did not know about it and my delving law partner only ran across it late last night."

"Tell us about your big new California gold strike," His Honor said dryly as the courtroom audience dutifully tittered.

So I launched into an exposition of our latest case, neglecting to stress that, despite his historic flight down to Ann Arbor, my partner had come up with his finest nugget in, of all places, our own modest office library.

"But how could you possibly have missed finding it down in your pet legal oasis in Ann Arbor?" I'd asked him the night before when he'd come running to me with his prize.

"Easy. Because I had an educated bug in me arse, lad," he had said, "all the while looking under such fancy topics as jails, sheriffs, mandamus, memory recall, amnesia, trials, trial preparation, and esoteric stuff like that instead of lookin' under the one simple topic any dam fool should have looked at first."

"What's that?" I said, recognizing my cue.

"Hypnotism, goddammitt!" he said, thrusting his prize at me.

"Your Honor," I began, "the newly found case I refer to is the California case of *Cornell versus Superior Court,*" and I gave him the citation. "The similarities between that case and ours are as many as they are remarkable. There, as here, the petitioner was the lawyer for a man accused of murdering a woman;

there, as here, the man's lawyer claimed his client could not recall his actions or the events during the crucial period involved; there, as here, he alleged that his client's lack of memory might have been caused by virtually the same things—except that there he added the further possibility of intoxication."

I glanced at my notes lying in the book I held. "There, as here, the lawyer for the accused sought to bring a hypnotist into the jail to stimulate recall but the sheriff turned him down. Finally, there, as here, he then asked the trial court for an order compelling the sheriff to admit them to his jail so that they might adequately prepare a defense. I repeat: The parallels between the two cases are little short of eerie. In fact the only major difference I can offhand see is that the lawyer was called Harold Cornell instead of yours truly, Frederic Ludlow."

A pained smile flickered across the judge's face at my little joke as I pushed on. "There the petitioning lawyer lost his case before the trial judge but won on his appeal to the California Supreme Court. In other words, he and his hypnotist finally won the right to enter the jail to examine the foggy-memoried accused."

"Go on," the judge murmured.

"There the defense made to the lawyer's petition was virtually the same as made here by Sheriff Wallenstein: Hypnosis and hypnotists are out as far as our law is concerned, and all the rest, which I shall not repeat." I smiled. "Another possible difference in the two cases—and one that I hope continues—is that there the lawyer had to appeal beyond the trial court in order for justice to prevail."

Again the vestige of a smile. "Anything else?" the judge said.

"To suggest the sweeping scope of the court's decision I would like to quote or paraphrase a few brief highlights from the California opinion."

"Highlight away," the judge said, leaning back in his chair.

"In answering the sheriff's no-hypnotist contention and the blanket inadmissibility of any evidence thus obtained, the California court responded that admissibility was not the issue but, and I quote, 'Cornell is now seeking to learn facts that may be of assistance in preparing for defense of the crime charged.' The court then declared that such a right is constitutional, akin to the right to have an interpreter or psychiatrist present—as we've argued all along."

"Go on."

"As for using hypnosis for this purpose, the court there quotes the 1954 edition of the *Encyclopaedia Britannica*, which flatly states, 'The use of hypnotism for the purpose desired is recognized by medical authorities.' This *Britannica* article, Dr. Salter tells me, was written by one of the country's outstanding authorities on both hypnosis and memory recall, Dr. Milton H. Erickson."

"How do you spell that last name?" the judge said, taking notes, and I told him and pushed on. "One final and I hope clinching quote from the California case is this: 'There is no substantial legal difference between the right to use a hypnotist, in an attempt to probe into the client's subconscious recollection, and the use of a psychiatrist to determine sanity.' " I closed the book and sat down, still holding it on my lap.

The judge beckoned from the bench with one finger. "If you can cease cuddling that book long enough for me to take a peek, please fetch it up here."

"Right away, sir," I said, scrambling with all the alacrity of the bailiff earlier replenishing His Honor's water jug, and returned to my table to await developments.

"I've read the California case," the judge finally looked up and said, "and regard it as conclusive on the issue before us." He smiled. "I must say I was veering that way earlier, and this about sews it up. There remains only the question of Dr. Salter's qualifications." He looked at Eugene Canda. "Does the respondent still question those?"

"Yes, Your Honor," Eugene Canda said, half-rising, "and we renew our objections on that score."

"Have you any countertestimony to offer?"

"No, Your Honor. We feel that the doctor's own testimony already reveals his lack of qualifications."

"Anything further from you, Mr. Ludlow?"

"No, Your Honor," I said.

"Very well," the judge said, glancing at the court reporter

to alert him. "While it is true that the proposed hypnotist here has never yet tried memory recall, he appears to know hypnosis well and has also done considerable reading and clinical observing in memory recall." He smiled dryly. "Moreover it seems there is no one else around these parts who can do the job if he can't, hypnotists evidently being in short supply. So I find and hold him qualified and I'll now dictate my order granting the relief prayed for, comforting myself by reflecting that no harm will be done should the good doctor fail."

Eugene Canda was quickly on his feet. "It is my understanding, Your Honor," he said, "that ineptly attempted hypnosis can do such harm."

"You failed to share your understanding with me earlier and now the proofs are closed," the judge said. "Do you want to reopen the case and offer proof on your new claim?"

"I have no exact proof on that score," Eugene Canda said after a pause, "but I thought you might wish to question Dr. Salter on the subject."

"Very well," the judge said, looking down from his bench at Hugh Salter sitting next to Jeremiah in the front row. "Stay where you are, Dr. Salter," he said, smiling and holding up a restraining hand as Hugh Salter started to uncoil himself for his trip back to the witness stand. "You've already been sworn, and our county clerk frugally administers only one oath to a customer, claiming that the hypnotic effect lasts for days. Doctor, do you see any possible harm in using hypnosis on the defendant, Kirk, if your attempted memory recall should fail?"

Hugh Salter thoughtfully recrossed his legs before answering. "Mr. Canda makes a point," he said. "In the hands of an inept, inexperienced, or mischievous operator it might indeed cause harm. It's a pretty complex subject to reduce to a mere question and answer."

"How about an attempt by an experienced operator?"

"Little chance of harm," Hugh Salter said. "The only real harm I can see in this case is if I or someone failed to try."

"Thank you, Doctor," the judge said, turning to the court reporter and dictating the formal order granting what our petition had sought. "There," he finally said, emitting a prolonged sigh. "Court is now adjourned for the day."

When the courtroom was empty except for us three—Jeremiah, Hugh Salter, and I—Doctor Hugh invited us over to his house for a celebratory supper already being prepared by his old Finnish housekeeper.

"But what if we'd lost?" I inquired.

"T'would have been a merry wake," my partner put in.

"Complete with bourbon and even champagne for the more effete mourners," Doctor Hugh said.

"Followed by umpteen games of cribbage for dessert, no doubt," I said, wearily gathering up my papers and wondering whether the cavorting trout would be dimpling in the shadowed pools and pockets come sundown.

PART TWO

Trial

Chapter 16

"Swear the jury," a hard-driving Judge Brotherton finally said just before noon on Thursday, the third day of the regular September term of court. It had all happened abruptly: After nearly a day of noisy wrangling, during which Eugene Canda and I had almost exhausted our quotas of peremptory challenges—not to mention each other's—we had finally settled upon twelve prospective jurors whose fitness to decide Randall Kirk's fate neither side further cared or dared to challenge. For both of us had early learned how dangerous it could be to risk a belated losing challenge for cause—lack of open-mindedness about guilt or innocence being one of the more common grounds—and finally find oneself stuck with a sulky and possibly vindictive juror for the rest of the trial.

Clovis the clerk popped up in his mahogany cubicle, his skinny hand already held high to administer the oath to the waiting jurors, seven men and five women, his shrill altar-boy voice quavering like an old movie Wurlitzer. "You do solemnly swear," he sang out in his rich French Canadian accent, "dat you shall well and truly try and true deliverance make, between the people of this stat' and the prisoner at the bar, 'oom you shall 'ave in char', according to the evidence and laws of dis stat', so 'elp you God."

The jury's mumbled response was all but lost in the mounting wave of excitement that rippled across the crowded courtroom grown suddenly aware the main show was about to start. Judge Brotherton frowned and fondled his gavel before restoring sufficient order to address the few remaining members of the unused jury panel still sitting in the roped-off section reserved for them in the back court.

"You are now formally excused from further attendance until one week from today," he told them. "And since the longer I sit as judge the poorer I get at predicting the length of any trial, I can only say that you will timely be notified should we need you back either sooner or not quite so soon." He smiled faintly before launching one of his more venerable shafts of judicial humor.

"This does not mean that you have been officially banished and are compelled to leave, only that you are free to go if you wish," he went on, his smile broadening. "All amateur students of criminal jurisprudence among you with time on their hands are welcome to stay." He glanced down at the sheriff, who eagerly awaited his cue. He invariably preempted the regular bailiff's mahogany cubicle during trials that were apt to attract a crowd of voters. "Adjourn till one," His Honor murmured.

I had long ago discovered that if one squinted up at the judge's mahogany bench in a certain way it gave off the illusion of being a proud mother ship from which dangled clusters of mahogany lifeboats arranged in a sort of "Charge of the Light Brigade" order: the witness box to the left of His Honor, the bailiff's box to the right of him, the clerk's cubicle to the front of him, the court reporter's station off to the side of him . . . and if one squinted hard enough, sometimes even the rigidly sprawling nearby jury box seemed to dissolve into a barge-load of exotic mahogany chairs being towed in its wake.

The sheriff, an envious student of Clovis the clerk's dramatic courtroom performances, quickly arose in his mahogany cubicle and extravagantly pantomimed the courtroom crowd to its feet, repeatedly lifting his arms, palms up, like an imploring evangelist. When the last laggard had gotten the message and arisen he dealt his own block three resounding whacks and sang out his own courtroom aria. "Hear ye, hear ye, hear ye," he bawled, "this honorable court stands adjourned until one o'-clock this afternoon." Then, before the shuffling courtroom crowd could fairly escape, he lumbered over to my counsel table and stood behind my client's chair in what my partner called his "they-shall-not-pass pose," complete with jutting jaw and resolutely folded arms. Randall Kirk glanced up at me and arose, smiling faintly, and quietly left to spend the noon recess in his cell, the Groucho-stalking sheriff following close behind him.

During this tableau the sheriff's bustling, newly appointed jury matron, who held the distinction of being the county's first deputized woman, herded her twelve new charges out the rear jury door to enjoy their first free meal on the county. I finished stashing my papers and walked out still another mahogany door to meet my partner in the defense conference room and there possibly collect my thoughts for the afternoon clash.

Several days following our successful special July courtroom hearing I had found myself trudging up the steep iron-shod stairs to Randall Kirk's third-floor cell, Hugh Salter padding along close behind me, surprisingly nimble, I thought, for a man of his years. Kirk was waiting for us, standing tall and gaunt in his open cell door, looking even more distraught and drawn than when I'd last seen him at the court hearing, probably because he'd neglected to shave.

"Hi, Randy," I said with an air of camaraderie I did not feel. "This is Dr. Hugh Salter, whom you met over at our court hearing the other day, remember?"

"Of course," Kirk replied in an expressionless monotone. "The old self-taught hypnosis buff in person."

"Hello, Kirk," Hugh Salter said, extending his hand, which my client ignored. It swept over his smarting defense attorney that our first session at memory recall was off to a dismally flying start.

Once again I fought a sudden impulse to tell Kirk to go to hell and walk out on his case. After mentally counting ten, and for Doctor Hugh's sake as much as anything, I reluctantly decided to stay and see out this strange charade.

"Do you mind too much, Kirk, if we get on with the business at hand?" I huskily said, trying to control my voice.

"Up to you," Kirk answered, standing listlessly aside and pointing at an extra wooden stool the sheriff or someone had thoughtfully added to his cell. "Be my guest."

"Suppose you take one of those stools Mr. Kirk," Hugh Salter said, pointing, "and I'll remain here." This was our prearranged signal for me to get lost, and as Kirk uneasily squatted on the stool facing Doctor Hugh who was still standing in the cell door, I faded silently down the narrow, metal-shod jail corridor to the head of the spiral stairs, where I stood under the wavering, coppery glow of a single electric bulb, still within earshot but out of sight.

"Before we get underway, Mr. Kirk," I heard Hugh Salter say, "I'd like briefly to go over with you some of the last things you do recall about that final night."

"Like what?" I heard Kirk answer in a strained voice.

"Such as that little bell you heard ringing just before your memory blanked out."

"What little bell?"

"Why, the little tinkling bell you've told your lawyer about so many times."

The next words I heard chilled me to the bone. "I never told him any such a goddamn thing," I heard Randall Kirk harshly say, "nor do I faintly recall hearing any such little bell."

There was a long silence and then I heard Hugh Salter say in measured tones, "Are you sure, Randall Kirk, that you heard no little bell ring earlier that night at your cottage shortly before Constance Farrow Spurrier met her death?"

"Absolutely not," my client loudly answered. "My lawyer's probably been talking out of turn again and peddling the wrong dope."

As I stood incredulously mulling over this latest development in my case, the jail seemed to grow hushed as a tomb. A kind of brooding silence seemed to descend upon it, broken only by the distant whine of a power lawn mower doubtless being pushed by some trusty inmate trimming the broad, sloping courthouse lawn. I took a deep breath and suddenly recalled my partner's oft-repeated claim that all jails "stink of mingled stale sweat, urine, and disinfectant."

Then above the rise and ebb of the distant, motorized whine I heard the sound of low murmuring, and I strained to hear, but all I could make out was an occasional, faintly whistled sibilant, sounding like the muffled twilight cheeping of a tiny bird. I was about to move closer when the murmur grew in volume, like the slow swell of an organ, and then I recognized Hugh Salter's voice, and cupped my ear to catch his words.

"Your eyes are closing, you are getting sleepy, your eyelids are getting heavy, you are growing drowsy, your eyes are closing," I heard the voice repeating, like the rhythmic wash and lap of quiescent waves, and I brushed my hand across my own eyes as I found myself growing unaccountably drowsy.

Again there was a spell of silence, followed by a similar low hum of words, and again I cupped my ear to hear, as though eavesdropping on some private prayer. Then again came a silence, then once again I heard a voice; this time not Hugh Salter's but another, low, petulant voice murmuring in a sort of repetitive accusatory whine, gradually mounting in volume.

"I can't stand this, I can't stand this," I heard the voice repeat until, after a sudden outburst, I knew it was Randall Kirk shouting. "Stop this, I say . . . I can't stand it . . . Please stop this dreadful nonsense . . . I've never been hypnotized, I tell you . . . I hate it, I hate it . . . I don't believe in such juvenile bullshit . . . Don't keep staring at me so . . . No, no, no . . . Please go away . . . Get the hell out of my sight . . . you *bastard!*"

Suddenly I heard the clatter of a wooden stool, then the sound of heavy breathing, almost of sobbing, then only silence. Then Hugh Salter stood before me with his finger to his lips, and we silently tiptoed down the steep iron stairway and, after negotiating several steel-shod doors that had to be unlocked and relocked by the key-dangling turnkey on duty, found ourselves standing outside blinking at each other in the bright sunlight.

"What happened?" I whispered once we were alone in my car.

"God only knows, Frederic," Hugh Salter said, himself looking almost as shaken as I felt.

"Not only has my little bell now flown up the flue," I said, heedless of my metaphors, "but it seems your first attempt at hypnotizing the guy has missed by a country mile. *What* in hell happened, Doc?"

"Rather obviously, nothing," Hugh Salter said, shaking his head. "The man simply didn't respond—I'll correct that—he responded all too beautifully but not in the way I expected." He paused and hummed to himself. "All mighty curious."

"Doc," I said, "do you think maybe the guy's suddenly gone nuts?"

"Possibly, Frederic. Surely something has happened."

"But what do we do now?" I said.

"It's rather obvious that we'll have to have a thorough clinical examination of Kirk regarding his mental state. I was going to recommend that anyway, soon as your court hearing was out of the way, but now it's imperative."

"Could such an exam be held in the jail?"

"Quite impossible, Frederic. It's got to be done at a competently staffed and well-equipped clinic—for this I recommend St. Francis here in town—so that this prickly issue of his mental state can be resolved once and for all. It's not a one-man job and could take several days."

"Hm. . . . That probably means I'll have to file another court action against the sheriff in order to get him to let Kirk go visit the clinic," I said.

Doctor Hugh shook his head. "My guess is your hypersensitive sheriff won't risk another public defeat so soon before the election. In fact I'll bet you five he won't raise a finger."

"You're on, Doc, but suppose Kirk finally clears the clinic's hurdle? What do we do then?"

He shrugged. "Then I guess I go back and give hypnosis another try."

"Doc," I said, seeking a little solace, "is this failure on your first try pretty much par for the hypnosis course?"

"That's putting it too strongly, son, though I do recall a few past cases where it took me several sessions to relax and gain the confidence of a new subject. The unusual thing here is not that I failed but the violence of Kirk's rejection." He shook his head. "Most unusual, in fact."

"How do you account for it?"

Hugh Salter turned and looked at me. "I don't, son, but I'm surely going to try to find out. Meanwhile there're several things I think ought to be done."

"Like what?" I said, grasping at straws.

"First of all I want you to stop all of Kirk's jail visitors at once—except you and me, of course. Can it be done?"

"Well, I could go ask him," I said, reaching for the car door.

"No, Frederic, not ask—*order* him. This could be crucial."

"Anything else?" I said, uneasily sitting back. "Besides getting me further into the doghouse with my client by now having me sentence him to solitary confinement?"

"Yes there is, son," Doctor Hugh said. "Since you're already so deep in the doghouse, I think you should also claim sole credit for the new visitor ban rather than blaming it on me."

"But why, Doc?" I said. "The guy barely talks to me now."

"Because, Frederic, I'm the one elected to try to recapture his memory, and to have any decent chance at that I'll have to gain his friendship and confidence. Blocking all his visitors would give me a rather poor start at that."

"All right, then," I agreed reluctantly. "Any further doghouse chores?"

"Then I want you to find out whether the jail keeps a record of all visitors—names, dates, hour, the whole bit."

"That's easy. They do."

"Fine, and I'll want a complete record of those."

"Anything else?" I said, feeling like a slow-witted office boy getting his orders for the day.

"Then find out whether they permit inmates to receive or make telephone calls," Hugh Salter said.

"Again easy. Only in strict emergencies, but I'll check on that. Do you also want his phone calls stopped?"

"Not at present," Hugh Salter said. "But do find out precisely who has visited Kirk *since* our court hearing the other day. Got it?"

"Right. I'll drive you on home now and I should have most of the dope by nightfall. But I've got one big question for you."

"Yes?"

"Why all this sudden switch?" I said. "Have you just come up with some brand-new theory about our case?"

"No, Frederic," Doctor Hugh said after a pause. "As I just told you, I've long had in mind the necessity for a thoroughgoing medical examination of Kirk to discover whether there is any clinical explanation for his original loss of memory." He shrugged. "Actually *that* should probably have been done before I ever tried to hypnotize him, but I just couldn't resist giving it a sample try, and now I'm certainly glad I did."

"What do you mean?"

"Because if I hadn't we might easily have failed to uncover Kirk's latest lapse in memory—about hearing that little bell—and have accordingly failed to take the steps to possibly unravel whatever *that* means."

"Doctor Hugh," I said, "I think you're talking in riddles."

"If I am, son, it could be because we're being pelted with so many."

"But what in hell *can* it all mean?" I said, totally at sea.

Hugh Salter reached over and briefly patted my knee and then sat erect. "Look," he said, "things are far too hazy at this moment even to guess what they might mean. The things I've just suggested doing are simply aimed at eradicating certain possible factors, however unlikely, from our case. To narrow the field, in other words."

"But *what* possible factors?" I persisted.

Hugh Salter smiled. "I've just told you it's too early to say, son." He mused a moment to himself. "Meanwhile I'll have to ask you to forsake all your probing lawyer questions for a spell and simply put your faith in this old baby doctor. In fact, I'm afraid I'll have to make that a condition to my continuing in the case." He turned and faced me inquiringly, and I could see the old boy was not fooling. "What do you say, Frederic?"

My lumps were coming in Buddy Rich drumbeats. "Of course, Doc," I said placatingly, having no other choice. "But how long—"

"You'll be the first to know when I know more and"—he paused and searched for words—"and when the time is ripe. Is it a deal, son?"

"Sure thing, Doc, but—"

"Shake on it, then, and remember—no more questions," he said extending his hand, which I glumly took. Then I started the car and maneuvered my way out of the jail parking lot, glancing up at a certain grimy, third-floor jail window, all the while trying to quell the disloyally recurring speculation that Eugene Canda just might have had something there when he'd dared question the qualifications and ability of this proud, close-mouthed old country doctor to induce memory recall in anyone by any means.

Chapter 17

"What do you think of our jury, partner?" I asked Jeremiah when I joined him and Doctor Hugh in the defense conference room during recess and found them nibbling away at a dainty luncheon prepared by Doctor Hugh's Finnish housekeeper. "No thanks," I added as the doctor gestured invitingly at all the goodies. "How about our jury, pard?" I repeated.

"Who the hell knows," Jeremiah said, gesturing with his sandwich. "Guessing what a goddam jury will do is about as chancy as chartering a world tour on the prospects of winning an undrawn lottery. Hugh here says he detects a pulse in all twelve jurors, which could help, and if my own hunch is right it ought to lean at least five-twelfths our way. Not bad odds in any league."

"You mean the presence of five women on our jury?"

"Of course. What else?"

For despite his skepticism about ever flatly predicting what any jury might do, the old boy naturally had a theory or two concerning possible mitigation of the gamble. "Every criminal trial," he had earlier explained, "presents a unique psychological problem, the correct solution to which can at least lower the chances of losing. The solution begins with the selection of the very first juror. A lawyer's job is to try to identify what that problem is, solve it, and then to use it."

"What's the magic formula on the Kirk jury?" I had finally asked Jeremiah during one of our many pretrial huddles.

"Dames," he had answered without batting an eye.

"Why?"

"Because Kirk's shy, Gary Cooper-ish good looks, augmented by that dying-poet pallor he seems to be getting lately, will arouse all of the pent-up motherhood lurking in the bosom of every dame."

"But is motherhood alone enough? After all, the victim here was herself a mother."

"I wasn't quite done," the old boy calmly went on. "Because in addition to all that, in this case we have still another strong dame-ish factor."

"What's that?"

"That no gal on this jury will be able to forget that the rich and glamorous Connie was not only two-timing her own husband but was at the same time successfully luring and winning a younger and handsomer man. For *that,* every last dame on that jury will secretly hate and envy her to a man—wups—you know what I mean."

"But how are they or anyone else on the jury ever going to know?" I said. "After all, his own lawyer had to threaten to quit his case—and accompany that with eternal vows of silence—to wring a reluctant confession from the guy."

"*They'll* know," my partner said, wagging his head and making as though to reach for his wallet. "Wanna bet a ten?"

"No I don't wanna bet a ten," I said, sensing that half the county probably already shared his belief. "But granted the whole spicy story will come out at the trial, how can any halfway responsible jury, dames or no dames, say anything but guilty to the monotonous story of a guy accused of violent murder who simply keeps repeating over and over that he can't remember a goddamn thing?"

"Maybe he'll get his memory back by the time of the trial. Don't forget, Doctor Hugh here is still in there pitching, and don't ever sell that old boy short." He sighed as his subject smiled. "Remember, pard, I dare play *cribbage* with the man."

"But what if he doesn't?" I persisted, lately more and more resigned to that very prospect. "Especially now that the unanimous report of the clinic has slammed the door on many things, including any chance of our now ever making a successful insanity plea?"

"That's both the big gamble and problem we have to face," my partner said, fighting back. "All I've been talking about is the presence of certain favorable psychological factors *if* we can get enough dames on the jury. Now we at least have the dames."

"Yes? Then what else do we need?"

"I'll concede that dames alone may still not be quite enough, for even the most pulseless juror hates, by his verdict —and here I mean by hers—to look like a goddam fool."

"I've just been trying to say that, pard."

"So our big job at the trial, partner, granted the presence of dames, is either to show enough mitigating circumstances or raise enough doubts to create a favorable climate of acquittal."

"I think maybe I'm beginning to see," I said.

And so the Kirk jury had finally been chosen, a jury containing enough "favorable factors"—as my chauvinist partner preferred calling them—to at least give us a fighting chance. But still, I glumly reflected, we remained as far away as ever from the elusive prospect of creating that magic aura of acquittal my partner had spoken of. About all that the prolonged and predictably expensive clinical examination of Kirk had accomplished, I also saw, was to narrow the field by erasing many of the legal possibilities that might otherwise have created that magic aura.

The irony of the situation was both depressing and faintly comic. With the trial itself now actually upon us, not only could my client still not remember a thing but, if my partner's theory was right, he would doubtless proudly continue to fight to the last ditch any effort to unveil one of two most powerful factors in his favor, namely, that he and Connie had long and intimately known each other "that way." All in all, I thought, it was enough to make a badgered defense lawyer flee to the woods and the simple life of fishing. . . .

Doctor Hugh had easily won our five-dollar bet. For not only had the sheriff failed to raise a finger to prevent Randall

Kirk's visit to St. Francis Clinic, he had insisted on personally accompanying him there—for a respectable per diem fee paid by the defense. He'd strutted and postured and campaigned and declaimed before all and sundry for several days, especially in the crowded main waiting room, "while," according to Doctor Hugh, "the person he was supposed to be guarding could have escaped at least a dozen times through as many exits."

Doctor Hugh explained and interpreted for us the clinic's findings; this at one of our regular weekly huddles at his old frame house located on the edge of town—thus easing the way for the inevitable cribbage clash later between him and Jeremiah. (During these I usually either played the double role of volunteer butler and bartender, mixing and serving drinks to the vying gladiators, or else ultimately wandered on home still wondering where my summer's fishing had flown.)

"I have on my desk before me," Doctor Hugh began, patting a fat file, "the final report of the earnest young doctors and technicians who have lately pawed and mauled one Randall Kirk and doubtless bled him with leeches. Since the report itself is as thick as a government report bemoaning the wastefulness of thick government reports, I will entertain a motion to summarize it."

"Please summarize ere the summer dies," I said with a languid wave of my hand. "What's the goddamn verdict?"

"They can't find a thing wrong with him."

"You mean *nothing* at all?" I said, at once surprised and relieved.

"Nothing at all," Hugh Salter repeated, "beyond a trick knee he evidently acquired on the playing fields of Princeton—along with the need for wearing a trick, removable bridge—plus a scattering of matched opals found in his gallbladder, plus a definitely high intelligence quotient."

"You mean," I said, "after all that pawing and probing they still have no notion why the man lost his memory and still later forgot that little bell?"

"Not the foggiest notion."

"Maybe their exam was only a lick and a promise," I said.

"Dead wrong, son. Their oral interviews alone took nearly half a day, and, though I hoped not to pelt you with too much trade jargon, beside the usual paces they put him through they gave him the Zondi test, the Bender-Gestalt test, a flock of Rorshach tests, an apperception test, a full-dress electroencephalogram study, and some other newer tests this shelved old country doctor hasn't yet quite learned to pronounce, much less understand."

"And still they found nothing?"

"Nothing at all—no sign of psychosis or neurosis, no delusions, no hallucinations, no conversion hysteria or dissociative reaction, no history or sign of infectious disease or chronic toxic condition, nor—and this is important—any existing or previous mental or nervous disorders, nor any sign or history of significant injury to the head—that removable bridge thing came from a playful swipe of somebody's knee to his mouth—nor any severe physical or emotional shock or fright or epilepsy nor psychasthenia"—Doctor Hugh paused and caught his breath. "There's a little more but it all adds up to the fact that Randall Kirk is so disgustingly normal that it hurts—except that all three of us know he damn well isn't."

"So what do we do now?" my partner dared to ask, not bound as I was by nonquestioning vows of silence. "What's the next step?"

"I guess I march back to jail and try to recapture his memory," Hugh Salter said with a shrug. "Let's get on with cribbage."

So after that, Doctor Hugh started revisiting the jail, but the new visitations had not been successful, or if they had, he had not shared the secret with me. The one cold comfort I found in all this was that so far at least Kirk hadn't thrown him out.

I had long since stopped accompanying Doctor Hugh on these sessions because I'd had such an unholy wrangle with my client when I'd stopped all his jail visitors that, as predicted, he had since barely talked to me. His most constant past jail visitors had been Jason Spurrier, as we already knew, and the enigmatic Viola Axholm, which came as a surprise. I also learned that on her visits she usually brought along batches of her homemade soup, the last batch having been delivered only the weekend before Doctor Hugh's abortive attempt to hypnotize Randall Kirk.

"Cut off her soup, and all outside gifts of food and drink from anyone," Doctor Hugh promptly ordered upon learning of it.

"Soup doubtless made of a memory-sapping witch's brew," was my partner's sole comment.

Both Jason Spurrier and Viola Axholm had separately visited Randall Kirk, I had learned, right after our successful summer court hearing, but neither had tried to see him since the banishment of all visitors. We also learned that Jason Spurrier had shortly left for the East.

Another reason I'd quit accompanying Doctor Hugh to the jail was my fear that I might inadvertently reveal to the old boy my growing skepticism that he was ever going to accomplish anything with my increasingly withdrawn and moody client. And now the trial itself was about to begin.

A peremptory knock on our mahogany conference room door brought me back from these doleful thoughts. The door opened and the sheriff popped his head in and announced, in the voice of a train dispatcher, "ready in five minutes" and disappeared. As I gathered up my briefcases—it now required two—I reflected that never had I found myself entering a criminal trial upon which I had lavished so much preliminary work, about which, at the same time, I felt so ill-prepared and baffled concerning the possible outcome.

Added to my woes was a growing apprehension that by so blindly following the hunches of an aging, retired baby doctor I might well also be laying myself open to the twin goblins facing every lawyer: a possible malpractice action by my client and disciplinary action by my own bar.

"Good luck, partner," Jeremiah said as I inwardly sighed and took off for court.

"Me too," Hugh Salter added, giving me a nod and a farewell wink.

"Thanks," I said, trying not to sound too cynically despondent.

Chapter 18

Eugene Canda's opening statement to the jury was brutally brief. "The People will show," he said after briskly walking up and facing the twelve intent jurors in the hushed courtroom, "that during the early hours of Saturday, June sixteenth, last, Constance Spurrier met her death by submersion and suffocation in water at the hands of the defendant, Randall Kirk; that is, she was forcibly drowned by him."

I was relieved when I heard this, as it both followed and confirmed the earlier terse autopsy report, a copy of which we already had, confining the cause of death to drowning alone, with no mention of possible strangulation as hinted at in the still earlier newspaper report. For while we were quite aware that murder by drowning was every bit as serious a crime as that by any other means we also knew that the prosecution's proof of that fact could well be considerably more difficult. Connie could scarcely have strangled herself that night, but mightn't she have drowned from a sudden heart attack or from cramps or from any other of the many misfortunes that can beset even the most experienced swimmers? And wouldn't this possibility in turn require even more powerful evidence, such as the testimony of of an eyewitness, for the People to prove beyond a reasonable doubt that Connie was drowned at the hands of Randall Kirk?

Was there finally emerging at least a dim chance of pulling this enchanted case out of the fire?

"The People will further show beyond a reasonable doubt," Eugene Canda continued, "that the killing was premeditated and the result of malice aforethought, as the judge will define those terms. In other words, ladies and gentlemen of the jury, the People will prove that the defendant Randall Kirk was guilty of the crime of murder in the first degree. Thank you," he concluded, turning away and marching briskly back to his table to call his first witness.

Judge Brotherton peered down at me. "Mr. Ludlow," he said, "do you wish to make any statement at this time?"

"Your Honor," I quickly arose and said, speaking from a half-crouch, "the defense would like to reserve its opening statement until after the People rest their case, if Your Honor please." At the same time I vaguely wondered what in hell I could possibly say to the jury about this tangled case in the unlikely event the judge would deny my request.

"Very well," the judge said, looking at Eugene Canda. "Call your first witness."

"The People will call Dr. Homer Pomper," the prosecutor announced. With a pencil he elaborately checked off the first witness's name from the long list that the People had endorsed on the formal indictment—in Michigan called an "information" —only recently filed in the case.

As the young doctor arose and came forward and was duly sworn within an inch of his life by Clovis the oath-giver, I again pondered the puzzling import of some of the many names on this list, including that of a well-known handwriting expert, for example, wondering what they could possibly testify about. Had my unpredictable client, without my knowledge, obligingly written and mailed a formal confession of guilt to the cops or to the local newspaper or indeed even to the *New York Times?*

"I do," the young doctor said, taking the witness chair and holding a sleek leather portfolio on his lap.

"Your name, please?" Eugene Canda began, and I could feel myself tense and stiffen as I realized that the actual trial was at last underway.

"Homer Pomper, sir."

"Your business or profession?"

"Doctor of medicine."

"Do you have any specialty, Doctor?"

"Pathology, sir."

"Are you associated with any professional institution?"

"Yes, St. Francis Hospital and Clinic, this city."

"How long have you practiced?"

"Five—no, six years now."

"Where did you obtain your medical education?"

"Doctor Pomper's qualifications are conceded," I arose and said, not so much out of a spirit of reciprocity but because Doctor Hugh had earlier assured me that the witness was one of the abler among the younger crop of doctors in the area.

"Thank you," the prosecutor said, making a small bow my way. He then turned and pelted questions at the witness at computer speed, adroitly bringing out that the doctor had performed an autopsy on the body of Constance Spurrier within hours of its discovery, that it was done at the official request of the county medical examiner, and that it was performed in the presence of two state police officers. . . .

"Will you please tell the jury your findings, Doctor," the prosecutor pushed on.

The witness reached in his portfolio and produced a sheaf of papers. "This is my formal autopsy report," he said, hefting it. "Because of the pressure of other work, I've only recently had a chance to assemble it. It's turned out quite long, and since the defense now has a copy I'll be glad to summarize it if that is agreeable."

Eugene Canda looked inquiringly at me and again I arose. "A summary is agreeable," I said, "though I've barely had time to finish reading the detailed report."

"You may proceed with your summary, Doctor," Eugene Canda prompted the witness.

"She met her death by drowning."

"How could you tell?"

The witness then consulted his notes and, led by the pointed questions of the prosecutor, launched into a technical discussion of his findings, including the amount of water found in her lung cavity and bronchial tubes, and the fact that her coronary arteries were normal, all adding up to the fact that Connie had indeed died of drowning. Though some of the questions were possibly leading I made no objection, by that time being quite willing to settle for the more arguably ambiguous fact of drowning rather than that of outright strangulation, which in circumstances would simply have to have been caused by another person.

Eugene Canda studied the pigeon-stained skylight before asking his next questions. "Doctor," he began slowly, choosing his words, "the People have charged that the deceased was drowned at the hands of the defendant, Randall Kirk. Now my question, Doctor, is whether you found any direct physical evidence of force having been used on her person?"

"I did not," the witness answered, and it seemed I heard a sigh of relief from my client sitting beside me, though it might have been my own.

"Did your examination disclose whether the deceased had put up any resistance?"

"It did and in my opinion she had resisted," the witness answered, and my spirits sank, making me think of the excitable old radio boxing announcer who used to shout, "He's up and circling his opponent! Wups, he's down again! Heavens, the bout's over, folks! Good night all!"

"Please explain, Doctor," the prosecutor said.

"Well, she had two broken and bloody fingernails on the third and fourth fingers of the right hand of her otherwise well-groomed hands, indicating that while she remained conscous she had fought for her life."

"Objection!" I arose and said, or rather shouted. "Deceased, in her drowning struggles, might equally have struck a rock or a raft or some other floating object. Latter part of answer draws an untenable conclusion that I move be stricken."

"Mr. Canda?" the judge inquired, peering down over his glasses.

"Then I'll ask the question," the prosecutor said. "Doctor, might not the fingernails of the deceased as likely have been broken by a rock or a raft or some other floating object?"

"Possibly," the doctor conceded, "except that both the police report and a state police officer had already told me that the defendant Kirk had two deep, fresh scratches on his upper left thigh."

"Further objection!" I arose and shouted. "Clearly hearsay and a conclusion based upon facts not yet in evidence and which in turn might ultimately prove inadmissible."

"Mr. Canda?" the judge said.

"The People can only call one witness at a time, Your Honor," he said and sat down, clearly intimating that he possessed such proof, all of which would duly be offered in the course of the trial.

"Back to you, Mr. Ludlow," the judge said.

"One moment, if Your Honor please," I said, turning to consult my client. "Is it true?" I whispered to Randall Kirk.

"Is what true?" he whispered back.

"About those bloody scratches?"

"Yes, it's true."

"But why didn't you tell *me* about them?" I almost wailed —if one can ever wail in a stifled whisper.

"Because I never knew how or where I got them, and had assumed I'd done it earlier that day, out fishing."

"You mean you never knew about Connie's broken fingernails?"

He looked at me, his eyes round and staring and suddenly welling with tears. "Good God, man, this is the first I've ever heard of it," he whispered, turning away.

"Mr. Ludlow?" the judge prompted me.

"I renew my objection," I arose and said, fighting for time, realizing that for me to withdraw my objection then would amount virtually to a public acknowledgment of guilt.

Judge Brotherton blinked up at the skylight a moment before making his ruling. "The objection is granted," he slowly said, "and the jury instructed to disregard that portion of the witness's answer pertaining to any alleged or reported scratches on the defendant's person. Proceed, Mr. Prosecutor."

"One moment, please," the beaming prosecutor said, consulting his notes. Well he might beam, I thought, recalling another recent observation by my partner that a lawyer could often disastrously lose on an objection to patently inadmissible testimony at the same time that technically he was winning on it. For surely by now it had been repeatedly and unforgettably drilled into the mind of every juror that poor Connie Spurrier had broken her fingernails while fighting off my client in a vain effort to save her own life. . . .

"Doctor," Eugene Canda pushed on, "did you find anything other than blood on the broken fingernails of the deceased?"

"Yes, there were also minute shreds of epidermal tissue still clinging to the broken nails."

"Meaning what, Doctor?"

"Bits of skin."

"Were you able to determine the source of the blood and bits of skin found on the broken fingernails of the deceased?"

"I was able to determine only that they were not her own," the witness answered, again glancing at my client.

"How were you able to reach that conclusion?"

"Primarily because I found no open lesions or scratches on her own person and no bleeding from or rupturing of the nail beds under the broken nails, as might normally have been expected had she struck some hard, inanimate object."

"Did you type the blood of the deceased?"

"I did, sir."

"And that of the defendant, Kirk?"

"No, sir, but I learned it from a sample he had given the jail physician," he said—all of which was still more surprising news to me. "It so happens that their blood types were the same—both type O."

"Were you able to type the blood you found on the broken fingernails of the deceased?"

"I tried but found it too diluted and insufficient in quantity to make a determination. You see, sir, blood cells tend to become swollen and fragmented following immersion, especially in fresh water." The witness again paused and glanced at my client. "But if it wasn't hers it would have to be his, and in either case it would have to be type O."

At least part of this answer was possibly objectionable, but my surprises were now coming in such clusters that I decided to hold both my seat and my tongue and not risk further driving home the finger of guilt already pointing toward my client by making even a winning objection.

"Doctor," Eugene Canda pushed on, still beaming and now all but purring, "could death have been caused by the things you saw during your examination and about which you have testified to here—I mean by your *admissible* testimony?"

"They could—I mean, it could, yes."

"In your opinion was death so caused?"

"Yes," the witness said, taking a long final glance down at my head-bowed client. "In my opinion death was caused by drowning at the hands of some other person."

"Your witness," Eugene Canda said, turning my way, his eyes complacently gleaming. As I reached for my notes and arose I wryly thought what an absorbing book might be written about the impact of glances and pantomime and other mute things upon the fate of all trials, not a hint of which ever shows in the official word-laden transcript. Could it be that some of the gravest courtroom decisions—indeed, those of life itself—were often powerfully influenced by such elusively eloquent rites of silence?

Chapter 19

Before the trial I had planned on asking the state's pathologist only the most perfunctory questions; this on the theory that it ill-behooved the defense to question seriously the cause or means of death, whatever the doctor's findings, in a case where the defendant had no memory of what happened and whose only defense boiled down to a claim of unconsciousness, which made him incapable of forming the necessary criminal intent of doing whatever he was accused of doing.

But now, with the very first witness, in a rush it swept over me that all that had changed, and my mind kept racing as I fussed with my papers, stalling for both time and inspiration. One new element already injected in the case, I knew, was the possibility that Connie's death might have been the result of a tragic accident. But the young doctor, by both his testimony and demeanor, had so strongly implicated Randall Kirk in an aggressive, violent act that I simply had to try to soften *that.* An equally grave companion danger was that some of the jurors might now falsely conclude that Connie's death followed an aggressive sexual attack by Kirk, during which she either drowned while resisting his advances or was drowned by him to hide his making them—either assumption pointing toward guilt—and I had also to try and soften *that.* Moreover I found myself more than a little piqued by the young doctor's lack of professional detachment in so openly betraying his settled conviction that Connie's death could only have been caused by Kirk, and I hoped to shake his general credibility while I ever so gently burned his ass on *that*. . . .

"*Mister* Ludlow," His Honor prompted me.

"Doctor," I said, arising and taking a deep breath as I advanced toward the witness, "during your autopsy did you try to determine whether the deceased had been subjected to sexual attack?"

"Of course," the witness replied, adding reprovingly, "That's routine procedure in all cases of this nature."

"So I had thought, too, Doctor, ever since law school days," I said, "which is the reason I'm now asking the question. Yet neither in your direct testimony nor in your formal report have you deigned to mention it. What did you find?"

"The results were negative," he answered, flushing over my sarcasm.

"Are you saying that she *might* have been sexually attacked, Doctor," I said, trying to pin him down, "or rather that you found no evidence of any such an attack?"

"I found no evidence of any forcible sexual attack," he said, adding, "so I did not see any point of putting it in my report any more than I would that she was free from whooping cough, say, or syphilis."

"Oh," I said in mock surprise, "so you examined the deceased for those things too?"

"Of course not," he said, glancing over at the jury and shaking his head over such a stupid question. "My only job was to determine the cause of death and I stuck to that."

"And of course, Doctor," I pushed on, "that phase of your examination included trying to determine whether the deceased had recently engaged in sexual intercourse, did it not?"

"Of course," he answered. "All part of the routine."

"Did you think, Doctor," I said, further sinking the needle, "that an affirmative finding by you of recent voluntary intercourse by the deceased might have contributed to her death?"

"Of course not," he repeated, shaking his head. "All purely routine."

"But isn't it also routine to include all significant findings in your final report?"

The witness glanced at Eugene Canda, as though for succor. "Not in my opinion," he said. "These autopsy reports have simply got to stop somewhere."

"But now that I raise the subject, Doctor, will you please reveal the results of that phase of your examination you chose not to include in your report?"

"They too were negative."

"What do you mean by negative?" I said, still wanting to pin him down.

"Well, there was no evidence of male sperm—ah—where one might expect to find it."

"Are you trying to tell us, Doctor, that a man and woman cannot collide sexually without"—I paused, groping for a more genteel way to get my message across then by using the old, familiar, idiomatic favorites that surely everyone in the room would know, just as surely as they would gasp with horror if I dared use them—"without male ejaculation?"

"Of course not," he said, smiling over my rather obvious job of courtroom editing. "But its occurrence is usually pretty conclusive evidence of that collision, as you so gallantly call it."

"So what you're really saying here, Doctor," I said, ignoring his own needle and still trying to nail him down, "is that you found no evidence of forcible sexual assault on the person of the deceased and that any evidence of possible recent voluntary cohabitation was inconclusive?"

"Well, I guess it might come down to that," he conceded, "for, short of the physical evidence I've just mentioned, there is really no way to tell whether a mature and sexually active woman has recently engaged in an act of intercourse." He shot his cuff, glanced at his watch, and gave it a few quick winds. "If she possessed the appetite and the stamina and took the proper precautions she might engage a whole regiment without leaving a trace."

"Thank you, Doctor, but a platoon will be quite enough," I said, whereupon the courtroom snickered and the judge frowned and I decided to veer to a less titillating but equally troublesome subject. "Doctor," I said, abruptly deciding to try and back him down on his harmful "broken fingernail" testimony, "you of course were not present on the fatal night when Mrs. Spurrier met her death?"

"Of course not," he said, again glancing at the jury and smiling over such a stupid question.

"And all you personally know about the cause of death from your own examination is that she died from drowning?" I said.

"Well, yes, I guess that's about it."

"And the only evidence of possible violence you found was that she had two broken fingernails and that you *heard* the defendant had two scratches on his thigh?"

"That's correct, plus the fragments of epidermal tissue I spoke of."

"Doctor," I said, taking the plunge, "aren't you both personally and professionally aware that people who are drowning sometimes, in their panic, fight off, often imperil, and sometimes even cost the lives of the very people who are trying only to save them?"

"Well, yes," he conceded.

"And couldn't precisely that have happened here?" I said.

"It *could* have," the witness answered, glancing anxiously at the judge, "except that I happen to know differently."

"What do you mean?" I said, casting all caution aside, wryly aware that anything else he might know about the case would probably ultimately come out at the trial anyway, so maybe the quicker the better. "*What* do you happen to know differently?" I pressed.

"Well," he said, glancing at my still head-bowed client, "one of the state police who attended the autopsy showed me and even let me read a photocopy of Kirk's handwritten confession that he had left behind at the scene of his crime."

This bombshell reply made me lean back against my table for support as I tried to gather my thoughts. "Your Honor," I managed to gasp, "I—I'd like a five-minute recess to confer with my client."

"It is so ordered," Judge Brotherton quickly agreed, nodding gravely at the already scrambling sheriff.

"Tell me," I said, once my client and I were alone in our conference room, and as I fought back an impulse to shout, "tell me why you ever bothered to hire a goddamn lawyer when you could have copped a plea, saved a bundle of money and maybe some time in the clink, and above all avoided associating with three toiling bastards whose every effort to help you seems only to cause you more pain?"

A frowning Randall Kirk sat staring at me from across the conference table—mahogany, of course—but made no reply.

"Or are you one of those anguished souls who once fell or was pushed off his potty and has ever since silently nursed his psychic wound along with a festering grudge against the world?" I ran on, warming to my subject. "One of those pent, brooding types I'm coming more and more to recognize the more I mess with the criminal law who, when finally they explode, hire a lawyer mainly to hide from the world, and especially from themselves, the fact that their crime was really motivated by a desire for social oblivion, by a sort of death-wish retreat to the anonymous womb of prison, in short, by nothing less than irresistible compulsion to commit civil suicide?"

I had finally stung him and he flushed and sat up so suddenly that I braced myself, thinking he might lunge across the table after me. Instead he smiled and blinked abstractedly, as though pondering a novel idea that had so far escaped him. Meanwhile I sat drumming my fingers impatiently on the mahogany table, half-wishing he would try to start something.

"Speak up, damn it," I finally said, or rather shouted, smarting under his continued silence, "or I swear I'll walk out on your goddamn case right now and leave you alone with your steamy fantasies."

"Pretty high-flown rhetoric for a backwoods lawyer," he finally said, managing a wan smile. "Why don't you come off the lay-analyst kick and tell me straight out what you're driving at?"

"Just this," I said, feeling myself flushing in turn. "Why in hell didn't you stoop to telling me a few of the goddamn things you *did* know about your case—unless it gives you some weird comfort to make a monkey out of your lawyer as he ushers you off to prison?"

"Ah, speaking of wounds, I see my sensitive lawyer's pride

is deeply hurt," he said, half to himself. "Like what things?" he added, sinking back in his chair with a look of resigned boredom.

"First," I said, holding the tip of my little finger, "why didn't you *tell* me about those telltale scratches on your thigh? Second," I ran on, moving to the next finger, "why didn't you *tell* me about giving that blood sample to the jail physician?"

"You didn't ask me," he said as I paused for breath.

"Or, despite your stubborn insistence upon waiving a preliminary examination where we might have learned some of these things, why didn't you *tell* me about you confession or whatever in hell it was?" I continued wearily, ticking off another gripe. "In fact, come to think of it, about all you've ever contributed to your case is money," I ran on, my temperature rising as I unloaded my frustrations, "and while I'm prepared to lose any case acting as a client's informed lawyer—as I've already lost my share—I'll be goddamned if I'm going to lose it being his hired patsy and playing the role of a rented clown. Speak, man! *Why* haven't you told me any of these things?"

"I know nothing about making or writing any confession," he said quietly.

My surprises were coming so fast that my orator's finger-count froze in midair and I was glad to be sitting down, finding it my turn to blink and squirm as I groped for words. "You mean," I finally said, "you mean to sit there and tell me that the doctor lied out there when he just testified he'd not only seen but read your written confession?"

"God knows," Randall Kirk said. "All I know is that I have no recollection of writing anything."

"Look, Kirk," I said, coming to a sudden decision, "this case is cracking wide open at the very start. The only possible way out I can see is for total candor. Not only between us, God knows, but with all of the People's proofs, whatever they may be."

"What do you mean?"

"Simply this. I want to go see the prosecutor right now about this confession thing. The doctor's reference to it is doubtless objectionable but winning on that or even gaining a mistrial because of it won't make the thing itself go away. We've got to face up to it, and fast."

"What do you propose?"

"That if you did write and leave something behind at the scene, we at once admit it—not only as a fact but also into evidence."

"But, God man, I have no recollection of writing *anything.*"

"That's precisely what I'm driving at," I said. "If you wrote the thing and can't remember doing it, however incriminating, this could be still further compelling proof of your total unconsciousness of whatever it was you did do that night. Will you go along?"

He shut his eyes and swayed a little in his chair before he spoke. "About now I don't give a damn what happens to me or my case." He shrugged and tried to smile. "Do whatever you want—as I have an intuition you're determined to do anyway, or walk out on me. Am I right?"

"You're not far off target," I said grimly, rising and grabbing up my battery of briefcases nimbly as a bellhop. "You wait here while I go call your guardian bailiff, square this further delay with the judge, and then go see the prosecutor for a showdown on this whole confession thing." I started for the door.

"One moment," I heard him saying, and I wheeled around inquiringly.

"Yes?" I said.

"While we're playing at our new game of candor and truth," he said, "I'd like to unveil a little gripe of my own."

"Yes?" I repeated.

"Tell me," Randall Kirk began in an imitation of the way his lawyer had earlier launched his own gripe-unveiling, "tell me, if you can, why you went back on your word to me with your very first question to the very first witness in the case?"

"What do you mean?" I said, puzzled.

"Injecting all that crude sex stuff about Connie and me."

I stood staring at the man, torn between breaking out in raucous laughter and hurling my swollen briefcases at the poor, confused bastard, one by one.

"Look, Randy," I said, a feeling of pity mingling with my

impatience, "far from injecting sex into your case I was simply trying my damndest to eradicate it from the jury's mind. Can't you *see* that, man?"

He sat frowning at me as I pondered the man's helpless compulsion to mangle and twist around everything I tried to do for him. Was this part of the swarm of psychological goblins that were pursuing him? Was I being too hard on a poor, tormented soul wrestling with his private devils?

"Hang in there, Randy," I said, feeling a wave of compassion for the man. "Try to look upon me as one must a dentist, who sometimes hurts his patient even as he tries to help him." I turned to leave. "Be back real soon."

"With your line of bullshit, sir," I heard him saying, "you ought to be composing greeting cards."

"Thanks," I said over my shoulder, my wave of compassion shattering abruptly on the rocks of reality. "Thank you very much."

Chapter 20

When court reconvened following the extended recess, I found a fidgety Dr. Pomper already back on the witness stand, glancing anxiously at his wristwatch, giving it a few more unneeded winds, peering out at the courtroom clock as though to confirm the incredible delay, then thumbing through what I guessed to be an appointment book, the routine of which we thoughtless legal beagles had so callously upset.

"You may proceed with your cross-examination, Mr. Ludlow," Judge Brotherton said, having already been clued by counsel on what was in the wind.

"No further questions, Your Honor," I popped up and said. It was all aprt of the understanding I'd just reached with him and Eugene Canda on how best to handle the ticklish question of the doctor's unfortunate, but obviously innocent, reference to an alleged confession not yet even produced by the prosecution, much less received in evidence.

"Any redirect, Mr. Canda?" the judge said, playing out the charade.

"None, Your Honor," the prosecutor predictably arose and said.

"The witness is excused," the judge said, nodding benignly

at the puzzled doctor, who fairly leaped off the witness stand and sped from the room, shaking his head over the baffling ways of a rival profession that had so needlessly kept him from his appointed rounds.

"Call your next witness, Mr. Prosecutor," the judge crisply said, resuming his role as the relentless courtroom driver, who must, in a previous incarnation, have, as my law partner had recently declared in his best barroom idiom, "cussed and whupped the poor enslaved bastards who built them there here now pyramids."

"The People will call Sergeant Roland Oliver," the prosecutor arose and said, and the uniformed state police officer who had found the handwritten note that Randall Kirk had left at the scene—something I had only learned during the recent recess—arose and marched briskly toward the witness stand, there to be met and challenged to tell the eternal truth by Clovis the oath-giver.

His testimony was brief and to the point—and, I soon learned, utterly devastating to my client. Yes, he and a fellow officer were the first to arrive at the scene; yes, the housekeeper of the deceased, Viola Axholm, had led them to the spot on the moonlit beach where she had found the body of her dead mistress; yes, they had immediately traced and also measured the distance she had dragged the body from the beach to the nearby screened-in summer house and there covered it with a beach towel.

The courtroom re-creation of this macabre scene was followed by a small avalanche of testimony about the various distances and measurements involved, which were given both in conventional and metric scale. I, who had barely wriggled my way through high school math, found myself nodding to their usual sedative effect on me and my "negative attention span"—as chronic classroom boredom later came to be called by those resourceful modern-day word merchants whom my law partner had recently called "those goddam rhetorical wizards of ooze."

At this juncture the prosecutor produced a small piece of note paper and requested that the court reporter mark it People's Exhibit A for identification. This done, he walked up to the witness and handed him the paper, at the same time saying, "I show you the People's proposed exhibit and ask if you've ever seen it before?"

"Yes, sir," the witness said, after carefully scanning the paper. "The same green ink written on four-by-six-inch note paper which was part of a gummed pad."

"Where did you find it?"

"I found the exhibit lying on a small wicker coffee table in the screened summer house, not far from the victim's shrouded body—about five feet, in fact—held from blowing away by a teaspoon," the witness answered, after first consulting a notebook evidently bulging with measurements.

"Any evidence that the note was written before or after the paper was folded?"

"In my opinion, sir, the folding clearly followed the writing."

At this point the prosecutor produced and held up a small spoon with the flourish of a stage magician and asked to have it tagged and marked as People's Exhibit B for identification. This done, he handed the spoon to the witness and pushed on with his questions.

"Did you retrieve both the paper and the spoon?"

"Yes, sir, but only after my brother officer had first checked them for fingerprints."

"Did he find any?"

"He did, sir, on both objects."

"Were they made by the same person?"

"They were."

"Do you know whose fingerprints they were?"

"I now do, sir."

"Whose?"

"They were those of the defendant, Randall Kirk," the witness answered, glancing down at my head-bowed client sitting next to me.

Both the question and answer were probably objectionable, I felt, as the witness had just testified that the prints were taken by a fellow officer. But I also saw that for me to object and win would simply delay the inevitable, besides probably only irritating the jury to boot, all members of which were absorbedly hanging on every word.

So instead I inwardly shrugged and arose and addressed the judge as follows: "Your Honor, during the recent recess my client had the opportunity to examine both proposed exhibits in the prosecutor's and my presence. My client then and now concedes that the note is indeed in his handwriting but has no recollection of writing or leaving it or any spoon."

"Yes?" the judge said, pressing me to come to the point.

"Accordingly, to save time and expense, the defense formally waives any further proof of the authenticity of the written exhibit and consents that it forthwith be received in evidence as People's Exhibit A," I said. "And while the note alone should create quite enough stir without the added agitation of the spoon," I ran on, noting the judge's grimace of pain, "for good measure we throw in the spoon and consent that it be received as People's Exhibit B."

"Does your offer also include a waiver of any further proof that the defendant's fingerprints appeared on both exhibits?" the judge inquired, rallying gamely from my rash of puns.

"Yes, Your Honor," I agreed, swiftly concluding that the absence or presence of my man's fingerprints became quite academic once he'd admitted to writing and leaving the note.

"Mr. Prosecutor?" the judge said.

"The People accept the defense offer," Eugene Canda said, "and now offer both exhibits in evidence as People's Exhibits A and B respectively."

"They may be so received and marked," His Honor said. "Anything else?"

"People also move that the name of its handwriting expert, Anselm Joachim, be stricken from the information and the witness be so notified."

"Agreed," I arose and said.

"So ordered," the judge said, getting into the rhythm of the thing. "Anything else?"

"People also move that its Exhibit A now be copied into the record and also forthwith shown to the jury so that all further testimony may be received with its contents in mind."

"Agreed," I arose and said, inwardly envying and applauding the dispatch with which my clever opponent was tightening the noose of guilt around my client.

"So ordered," the judge said, squinting out at the thronged and buzzing chamber. "This courtroom will meanwhile remain at ease while the reporter copies the written exhibit into the record and also while the members of the jury examine it." He smiled frostily. "That done, as a final therapeutic measure I suggest that the prosecutor read aloud the exhibit so that those avid students of crime sitting out yonder won't either swoon or explode out of sheer frustrated curiosity."

While the assemblage dutifully giggled and the court reporter did his stuff, the nearest juryman was duly handed the damning note. As he read intently with a growing expression of mingled wonderment and horror and gingerly passed it along, I sat glumly reviewing the hectic events of the preceding half-hour.

After leaving my client sulking in the conference room, I had raced to find my law partner and Doctor Hugh to tell them about my ultimatum to Kirk and my plan to go level with the prosecutor.

"Go to it, lad," my partner quickly agreed, nodding approvingly. "Fact is I wouldn't blame you if you *had* walked out on the ungrateful bastard."

"Are you sure Kirk said he couldn't remember writing or leaving behind any note?" Hugh Salter asked me.

"Absolutely, Doc."

"Do you believe him, son?"

It was a good question, and I reflected a spell before answering. "Well, Doc," I finally said, "let's say I believe him about as much as I believe anything he tells me lately."

"It'll be interesting to learn precisely what he did write," Doctor Hugh said reflectively, pursing his lips and nodding.

"Understatements, understatements," Jeremiah said, or rather snorted, as I hurried away to see the prosecutor, whom I luckily found alone in his office.

"Gene," I said, coming abruptly to the point, "if you've got that note handy and can show it to me, maybe all of us could be spared a lot of unnecessary tugging and hauling."

"What's the pitch, Fritz?" my opponent said, reaching for one of his own battery of pregnant briefcases.

"I'd also like Kirk to look at it," I said. "If he agrees that he wrote it I'll agree to admit it in evidence without further proof, pronto, first chance you get back in court."

"The note was found by a state cop, weighted under a spoon," he said. "Would you admit that too?"

"Yes, even along with a set of matched china."

"Hm," the prosecutor hummed to himself as he pondered what I was up to. "What's in it for me?"

"No losing objection for the DA because of the goof of his own witness, however innocent. No prolonged wrangle over whether the damned note is or is not a full confession about which the defense should have earlier been clued. No need to import a busy and expensive handwriting expert to show in ten thousand words who the hell wrote and signed it. No risk of the People possibly losing a defense motion in asking the judge to declare a mistrial because of its untimely mention, or failure earlier to clue us about it. Chance for frugal prosecutor publicly to save taxpayers wads of dough. Ah—let's see—prosecutor gets hot document fast before the jury plus possibly even wins a switch to a defense guilty plea, who knows, if the note's bad enough."

"Quite a handsome basket of goodies, Fritz, but bad as the note is for your side I don't think it's a full confession," the prosecutor said. "Moreover, remember, whatever it is, it was left at the scene by your man himself and was not made to the cops or me."

"That's one reason I'm here making my pitch," I said.

"What's in it for you?"

"Facing up fast to what's ultimately going to come out anyway. Avoiding the inevitable trial delay if you force me to move successfully for a mistrial, during which my unbailable client simply further cools his patrician ass in jail."

"But doesn't he need the extra time to recover his strayed memory?" my opponent countered.

"How do you know he hasn't?" I sparred. "In any case I'll take a chance on that."

"How come the sudden switch?"

"Simply to face up to what's coming out anyway, as I said,

and maybe get this goddamn case over with in time to get a little fishing in before winter moves in."

"Still chasing after those speckled mermaids are you, Fritzy? Could it be you'd also like to get rid of your sulky client?"

"You said that, Gene, I didn't," I quickly put in, not wanting to arm my opponent with *that* shrewd guess.

"Just kidding, Fritz," he said, producing and smoothing out a wrinkled paper on his table. "Anyway, whatever your reasons, it sounds like a good deal to me, so go get your man —along with his armed bailiff, mind—and we'll see how the ball bounces."

In a matter of minutes Randall Kirk sat reading the original note, now held under a small pane of protective glass—"just in case," the prosecutor shrugged and explained. My client's face drained of all color as he read.

"Well?" I said.

"It's in my handwriting, without a doubt," he looked up and said in awed, husky voice. "Even to the green ink I usually use."

"Any recollection of writing it?" I pressed.

"None," he answered, slowly shaking his head.

"Or of leaving it in the summer house weighted under a spoon?"

"None," he repeated

"Read the note aloud," I said, slipping on my Freudian wig. "Maybe it will stimulate your memory."

Randall Kirk cleared his throat and read in a low monotone. " 'I'm sorry I did it but I had to. Can explain all. Will be waiting at my cottage. Randall Kirk.' "

"Still no recollection of writing it and leaving it under any spoon?" I said.

He slowly shook his head no.

"Or why?"

"Christ, no!" he said, or rather wailed, burying his face in his hands.

"Gene," I said quietly, fighting off any threatening waves

of compassion, "we'd better quick go and clue the judge before he throws a tantrum over all the delay."

"Right-o," the prosecutor said, retrieving the damning note and spoon, along with his briefcases, while the bailiff kept coaxing and prodding my benumbed client up from his chair.

Chapter 21

With the People's first two exhibits safely in the case, the prosecutor deftly drew from the same police witness the remaining measurements lurking in his trusty notebook, all of which again nearly put me to sleep as his droning testimony wove tighter the web of guilt around my client.

Yes, it was so many feet from the anchored diving raft to the island shore where the body was found, so many more feet from the same raft to the mainland shoreline close to the defendant's cottage, all of which came to a total of X feet from the place where the body was found, making, let's see, a grand total of Y feet from the mainland to the screened summer house, where the defendant's handwritten note was found. . . .

Some of these distances and measurements seemed quite irrelevant, based upon any proofs so far in the case, I noted, but I'd been around long enough to know that if I dared object on that score, almost surely I would be met by a pained assertion from the prosecutor, gravely agreed to by the judge, that their relevance would soon enough become apparent by the testimony of other witnesses who knew certain things this one couldn't possibly have known. Plus receive a possible lecture on the virtues of patience . . . moreover, et cetera, whereas, notwithstanding, ad infinitum, God bless America.

So I held my tongue and thus avoided losing on a frivolous objection before a watchful, score-keeping jury which, like others I had faced, instead of weighing the merits of many cases, kept score on the relative number of judicial slapdowns suffered by the opposing lawyers. I sat listening in silence while waves of ennui gently washed over me, all due of course to the flaring of a recurring ailment, that incurable old negative attention span.

"Your witness," I heard the prosecutor saying, making me sit up with a start.

"One moment, please, Your Honor," I said, shuffling my notes as I debated what to do.

There were lots of questions I could have asked this witness, I saw, some of them rather probing. Why hadn't he or someone mentioned the damning note to Kirk at the police huddle right after they'd picked him up? Oh, so you wanted first to check out for possible fingerprints? Very well, but whose note did you *think* it was, man, signed with his own name and promising to explain all? Oh, I see, you decided it was better to cool it on all your evidence once he'd claimed forgetfulness. . . .

"No questions, Your Honor," I arose and said, figuring I could get to these and other questions later with other witnesses and yet avoid appearing at the outset to be challenging the integrity and fairness of a careful police witness who'd just unveiled what simply had to be some of the most damning of the People's proofs.

"One moment, please," the prosecutor said, evidently surprised by my failure to cross-examine. "I'll have to check whether my next witness is here."

As I sat awaiting the People's next witness, a recent comment by my law partner on the same subject came back to me. "Modern jurors, possessing as they do the high cultural advantage of having been raised watching the rantings and finger-waggings of most TV courtroom dramas, are apt to equate all cross-examination with accusatory disputation; that is, with calling the witness a goddam liar," he had declaimed. "So if your opponent throws an obviously honest and neutral witness at you who badly hurts your case, 'tis often better to ask him nothing at all, lad, rather than drive his story home twice while at the same time making the jury madder and madder at you."

"Sorry, Your Honor," the prosecutor said. "We can't seem to locate our next witness."

"It's about time for the noon recess anyway," the judge said, turning to the jury. "Let's all be back sharp at one."

"The People will call Viola Axholm," the prosecutor arose and said after the noon recess, while I sat wondering what new bombshells my law partner's favorite witch might explode.

I knew that the old girl had been haunting the courtroom for days, sitting disdainfully erect with folded, sinewy arms, even during the tedious jury selection; either that or frowningly striding up and down the adjoining marble halls and mahogany-lined corridors in her swishing long black dress.

As she arose and made her way up from the rear of the crowded chamber to be challenged by Clovis I had to agree that she *did* look rather witchlike, moving along with her skinny erectness and faintly rickety stride, with her jutting jaw and perpetual frown, all topped by a wedge of rather obviously dyed jet-black hair tightly skinned back into a gleaming knot that looked more like a coiled serpent about to strike.

"Your name, please," Eugene Canda asked after Clovis's shouted oath had further deepened her frown.

"Viola Axholm," she answered in a high, querulous voice that sounded not unlike a feminine version of Clovis's own unmodulated shout.

"Married or single?" the prosecutor continued.

"None of your business, young man," she snapped, drawing back offended, hugging even more tightly the large black cloth bag she was clinging to—and which my dependable partner had already guessed, "probably contained booties she was knitting for some imminent son of a witch."

"Just a routine question," the prosecutor said softly, trying to soothe her, "so the jurors may have your correct civil status before them as we proceed."

"They why didn't you ask that young state cop if *he* was married?" she shot back. "Why make *me* publicly confess I'm just another one of those dried-prune old maids?"

"I guess you've pretty well answered my question," the prosecutor said placatingly, glancing at the judge. "So with the court's permission I'll push on to other things."

"By all means," His Honor hastily agreed, "before the courthouse gets surrounded by marching feminist picket lines."

Viola Axholm shot a look of triumph at the prosecutor and further smoothed down the same long black dress she had worn all week and which had earlier moved my partner to declare that she "looks and dresses like a surrealist version of the painting of Whistler's mother coming off a three-week drunk."

As the prosecutor concluded his preliminary questions to the scowling witness, treading carefully as a doctor treating a crusty patient, I reflected that the world's grudge-bearers came in many shapes and sizes, and the skinny Viola Axholm bade fair to be a prize exhibit.

Yes, the scowling witness testified—grudgingly conceded might be a better term—she was employed as a housekeeper by Constance Spurrier at her island home at the time of her death. Yes, she had worked for both her and her parents, and indeed even for her grandparents, ever since she herself was a young woman, in her teens.

"How many years would that add up to?" the prosecutor gamely asked, all but wincing over her anticipated reaction.

"None of your business," the witness dependably snapped, again going through her purse-clutching dress-smoothing routine. "What has telling you precisely how old an old maid I am possibly got to do with poor Randall's guilt or innocence?"

"Poor Randall," I repeated to myself, resolving to explore *that* interesting phrase when it came my turn to examine.

"The witness just may have a point there," the judge gently put in, pouring oil upon the troubled waters. "Maybe we'd better get down to cases before those pickets start marching."

"Very well, Your Honor," the prosecutor said, flushing as he consulted his notes. I knew from long experience that it was not Eugene Canda's way to back down before a hostile or touchy witness, and felt she must indeed be an important People's witness for him to surrender so meekly.

"Were you so employed by Constance Spurrier at the time of her death?" the prosecutor said, getting abruptly down to cases.

"I was," the witness replied tartly.

"At her island home in this county, known as Treasure Island on Treasure Island Lake?"

"Of course," she answered, shooting a scornful look at the prosecutor that all but shouted, *"you dummy."*

"Where there did Constance Spurrier live?"

"In the big main house, of course."

"And you?"

"In one of the nearby cottages."

"Alone?"

"Of course."

"Were there any other persons then living in the main house?"

"Not after Spurrier cleared out," she answered, all but hissing the name as I made a mental note that he too must be high on her voluminous hit list, give or take a sibilant.

"Any other employees?"

"Of course."

"How many?"

"Well, there was Fred the gardener and general handyman, Aune the cleaning lady, André the cook," she answered, searching her memory, "besides several full- and part-time maids and other help, depending."

"Did all of these people live on the island, too?"

"No, Fred either motorboated or snowmobiled them across to the island in the morning and back after work. Also the number and hours varied with the seasons and on whether Commo was home."

"Who is Commo?"

For an instant a look almost of tenderness appeared on her face. "It's the way Miss Constance pronounced her name as a child and which later became her lifelong nickname with her friends and among the help."

"And who is Miss Constance?" the prosecutor inquired patiently, with the restrained air of a jumpy dentist drilling the molar of a jumpy patient.

"My own private name for the lady I worked for," she answered almost civilly, adding with pursed lips, "I never did like to use either of her married names or even think of them."

"Why?"

There was a pause and again the almost tender look.

"Why?" the prosecutor repeated.

"Because poor, impulsive, headstrong Commo made not only one but two bad choices in husbands and never did live to marry the man I know she really loved," she answered softly, turning and casting an almost motherly look down at my still head-bowed client.

The courtroom had grown as hushed as the high noon of a soap opera, a silence broken only by discreet coughing and assorted low-tar throat-clearings. Watching, I observed one of the lady jurors evidently dabbing a mote from her eye, which seemed to cast one possible vote for my partner's jury theory. Meanwhile the witness sat with folded hands and downcast eyes, grieving for her lost Commo. What an actress the old girl might have made, indeed was, I thought, and in what a gilded fairy world of romantic fantasy she must dwell.

The prosecutor understandably didn't like the drift of the testimony and so, equally understandably, didn't inquire who the lucky man might be that poor Commo should have wed. I longed to look around and see how one of the rejected husbands on the witness's list was taking it, but the prosecutor's next question abruptly stopped all that.

"Who besides you and Miss Constance were on the island the night she met her death?" the prosecutor asked, evidently determined to get the crucial facts out before the witness once again exploded or else the jury dissolved into tears.

"Only Randall, there," she answered, pointing. "That is, not counting all those prowling policemen with flashlights who came along later."

"By Randall you mean the defendant, Randall Kirk, sitting there at counsel table next to his lawyer?" he inquired patiently, in turn pointing.

"Who else?" she snapped, back once again in her favorite role as the aggrieved lady who'd take no guff from any stupid, posturing male.

The prosecutor looked up at the judge with a slight hand-raised shrug, which, to this old shrug interpreter, shouted loud as a bull horn this eloquent plea: Look, Judge, I know I could and probably should ask you to warn or even discipline this old biddy, but that might only make her carry on worse, if possible, and maybe even make her change her earlier story she told the police and blow my case right out of court.

"Proceed," the judge said quietly, getting the message, and I sat back, shrugging inwardly, recalling one of my law partner's latest edicts on the chanciness of all trials. "Most jury trials, especially criminal, are a sort of legalized state lottery," he had said, "being little more than ceremonial games of chance where the dignified gamblers carry shiny simulated-leather briefcases stuffed with invisible darts, which they keep hurling —along with reams of rhetoric—at whirling psychological dartboards."

"Did you see Randall and Miss Constance together that night?" the prosecutor asked, doggedly boring in.

"I did."

"When and where?"

"Around midnight together out in the lake."

"What, if anything, were they doing?"

"They seemed to be playing together in the water just off the diving raft."

"How do you mean, playing?"

"Well, they seemed to be splashing each other and playing a game of ducking each other under water."

"Where were you?"

"Standing near the summer house not far from shore."

"How could you see them from so far away?"

"There was a full moon and I had my field glasses."

"You mean binoculars?"

"I mean my field glasses," she repeated severely.

"How come they couldn't see you?" the prosecutor pushed on, not risking another courtroom crisis over *that*.

"I was standing in the shadows of the summer house."

"What happened then?"

"Well, I heard the phone ringing in the main house—there's an outside buzzer—so I hurried back to answer it."

"Then what?"

"There was nobody on the line, just a buzz."

"And?" the prosecutor said.

"So I waited awhile for it to ring again and then went back outside."

"Then what?"

"I found poor Commo lying face down on the beach," she said, "and I shook her but she didn't stir."

"Why?"

"Because—because I'm afraid she was already dead," she said, closing her eyes and biting her lips to keep from breaking down.

"Where was Randy?"

"It was too far to see just who it was, but I saw someone moving away in a canoe, which occasionally gleamed and glistened in the moonlight."

The prosecutor paused to consult his notes for his final thrust while I idly wondered how many bushels of unpublished verse this obscure Emily Dickinson had squirreled away in her island cottage.

"Did Randy often use a canoe?"

"Yes, when he didn't swim across."

"Had he used a canoe that night?"

"Yes, I saw it earlier floating near the raft."

"What next did you do?" the prosecutor pushed on.

"First I tried to bring her to, but when I saw that was no use I dragged her to the summer house and ran to phone the police."

"Do you now know how she met her death?"

"For hours I lay awake that night refusing to believe what I had really seen."

"And precisely *what* did you conclude you had seen?"

"Poor Randall, for some awful reason, in the act of taking the life of the woman he loved," she said, closing her eyes and bowing her head.

"Your witness," the prosecutor abruptly turned to me and said.

Chapter 22

"Did you actually see Randall kill Miss Constance?" I began, deciding to plunge at once to the heart of the case.

"I've just told here what it was I saw," she said, shaking her head reprovingly.

"That's what I'm driving at," I said. "You just testified, did you not, that you saw the two 'playing,' to use your own word, out in the lake near a tethered raft; that you left to answer the phone; and that when you returned you found her lying alone on the beach?"

"You were here and heard me," she said severely.

"I'm also representing a man charged with first degree murder," I said. "Did you or did you not just say these things?"

She still remained silent, glancing over at the jury with pursed lips, and so, thus stymied, I looked inquiringly up at the judge.

"Please answer the question," the judge said curtly.

"And what if I don't?" she said coolly, turning and giving him a withering look.

"Then I could send you to jail for contempt," the judge said quietly, "which, I might also inform you, I'm not too far from doing anyway."

"What's the question?" she said, after a prolonged pause, as though weighing the pros and cons of going to jail for her principles.

"The court reporter will please read the last question," the judge said.

" 'That's what I'm driving at,' " the reporter read in a bored monotone when he'd flipped back some pages and found the place. " 'You just testified, did you not, that you saw the two "playing," to use your own word, out in the lake near a tethered raft; that you left to answer the phone; and that when you returned you found her lying alone on the beach?' "

"Answer the question," the judge ordered bluntly, plainly itching to show this crotchety old girl just who was running his court.

"Yes," she answered, almost biting the word, and so another courtroom crisis was narrowly averted.

"Miss Axholm," I began—

"Don't you dare call me Miss!" she loudly interrupted, glaring at me. "My name is Viola Axholm."

"Your Honor," I said, "in the interest of possibly concluding this trial by Christmas, may opposing counsel and I please confer with you privately up at the bench?"

"By all means," the judge said, plainly as eager as my opponent and I were not to imperil the course of a well-advanced trial by having to bundle a key witness off to jail for an open contempt of court.

The judge arose and leaned forward over the bench, resting on his palms, as Eugene Canda and I craned forward on tiptoe to confer with him, forming quite a conspiratorial tableau, all of which the witness sat beadily watching with a scornful smile.

"The old girl seems on the verge of cracking up," I whispered.

"I'd say one leg was over the ledge," the judge whispered back as the prosecutor nodded.

"What did you call her, Gene, during your pretrial huddles?" I whispered to my opponent.

"Nothing," the prosecutor whispered back. "I avoided calling her anything after one initial blast and after that I cravenly sent my assistant to her island lair to beard the lioness in her den."

"Why not ask her what she *wants* to be called," the judge whispered, "though I have a few suggestions in case she needs any help."

"Good idea," I whispered back, and the three of us sagely nodded and resumed our respective places.

"What would you prefer that I call you?" I bluntly asked, once back on the barricades.

"Axholm," she snapped, shooting another look of triumph at the jury.

"Axholm," I said, accepting her gracious invitation, "when did you first conclude that Randall had intentionally killed Miss Constance?"

"After that nice policeman who just sat here asked me if I knew Randall and his handwriting and I told him yes."

"Go on."

"So he let me read but not handle the paper they'd found signed and left by Randall, and I told him yes, it was Randall's writing all right, made on the same kind of pads he used and in his usual green ink." She sadly shook her head. "What else could I think than he'd done it on purpose?"

It was an excellent question for defense counsel to ignore, which I did. Instead I asked, "How come you hadn't spotted the note lying there under a spoon long before the police ever showed up?"

"Who said I didn't?" she snapped back.

"Are you now saying you *did* see and read the note before the police arrived?"

"Yes," she finally answered after taking an appraising glance over at the frowning judge.

"But why didn't you tell *them* about it the moment they arrived?"

"They didn't ask me," she answered, further twisting the wad of handkerchief she held. "And anyway I—I guess I was far too upset."

"But still not upset enough to leave *your* fingerprints behind," I said. "How did you ever manage that?"

"I used this to remove the spoon and read the note," she answered, dangling her limp handkerchief and giving the jury a sly glance.

"But why, in your state of shock and grief," I said, truly marveling, "would you have ever thought of doing that?"

"So as not to blot out any other fingerprints," she answered, "or maybe make the cops think I was involved." Another sly glance at the jury. "Something I picked up watching television" —she smiled craftily—"where they show you in pictures even how to rob a bank."

"Up to the time you read Randall's note," I doggedly pushed on after this testimonial to the cultural enlightenment shed by television, "did you still think that the two had been 'playing,' to use your own word?"

She moistened her lips several times as she pondered her reply. "Well," she finally said, for the first time showing signs of uncertainty, "I couldn't help but feel something dreadful had happened when I left to go answer the phone and then came back and found poor Miss Constance lying there alone and unconscious on the deserted beach."

"And poor Randall far out there in the lake sneaking away in his gleaming metal canoe?" I inquired, lowering my voice to a purr.

"Yes, yes. It all seemed and still seems so weirdly incredible."

"Why incredible?" I said even more softly.

"Because," she began and then paused for a moment, seeming on the verge of breaking down.

"Because what?" I all but whispered, feeling like old Doctor Hugh himself invoking a state of hypnotic trance in one of his expectant mothers.

"Because I knew they were so much in love," she answered softly, almost tenderly, along with a certain air of defiance.

At this point the crowded courtroom seemed to gasp and emit a prolonged communal sigh, so I pretended to fuss with my notes and let the message sink in. For I now saw that for the first time, however obliquely, we were veering to the very heart of our defense. How could poor Randall have ever *consciously* killed and so callously abandoned the woman he loved? So I determined to pursue this tack however much it might pain my touchy client.

"Have we ever talked about this case?" I inquired, wanting first to get that possibility out of the way.

"Never."

"Have we ever met or talked about anything anywhere before today?"

"Never."

"Tell me," I doggedly pushed on, "how did you know they were so much in love?"

"I don't quite see the relevance of all this," Eugene Canda quickly arose and said.

"Counsel means he does see the relevance and doesn't like what he sees," I countered. "Moreover the subject first came up during his own examination of his witness," I added, as much for my client as anyone; at least I couldn't be accused of being the first to ghoulishly pry open the forbidden door.

"I didn't ask her," my opponent said hotly. "She just blurted it out."

"But—" I began, and then the judge took over.

"Gentlemen, gentlemen," he said, turning to the still bristling prosecutor. "I think we'll take the answer while the witness is available and on the stand as possibly bearing on some pertinent issues in the case. The prosecutor may renew his objection later should he wish. The witness may answer."

Viola Axholm still sat arm-folded and haughtily disdainful and I was afraid my opponent's interruption had broken the romantic spell, which he'd probably intended.

"It's all right," I said to the waiting witness. "All we seek is the truth. How could you have known they were so much in love?"

While waiting for her reply I glanced sideways at my client, who sat glaring stonily across at me, so I arose and grabbed up my notes and moved away to a warmer climate, feeling I had quite enough to do without weighing his views on preserving the sanctity of bygone adulteries. The witness still remained silent and for a moment I thought she had been permanently clammed up.

"The truth could help Randall," I prodded her, risking another objection, but none came. Then gradually her expression softened and she finally unfolded her arms. "I've known they were in love for many years," she said simply.

"But how could you have known?" I gently persisted. "Did either or both of them ever tell you?"

"Of course not," she said, bridling. "A woman has her intuitions, hasn't she?"

"I'm sure she has," I said, not wanting to get into *that* hornet's nest, and suddenly feeling just as sure that there was something she was trying to hide. "Did you run across some old love letters?"

"Of course not," the witness answered with a frown.

"I still object to all this," the prosecutor said.

"Overruled," the judge said, leaning sideways to listen.

"Intuition is fine, but a fair-minded and intelligent woman also likes to have her intuitions confirmed," I went on, this time risking not only a further objection from my opponent but a volunteered slapdown from the judge for such a crude buttering-up of this touchy old girl. But nothing from either, so I concluded both were more concerned with or resigned to my getting the cross-examination over with and the hell off the stand. "Wasn't there at least some occasion or little sign or *something* that confirmed your intuition?"

"There were plenty," she answered quietly, sitting even more erect, and I sensed a sudden resolve on her part to speak out and let the chips fall where they might.

"Such as?" I prompted her.

"I've often seen them making love," she said simply.

Again the gasping sigh from the attending students of crime as I groped to phrase a question that might disclose just how much ground her delicate euphemism covered.

"Such as playing together in the water?" I said, plumping for the gradual approach.

"Yes," she answered, squirming a little in the witness chair. "Many times, though not quite the way they were *that* night."

"Maybe holding hands and occasionally even kissing?"

"Yes," she answered, nervously moistening her lips. "Many times."

"Maybe even *more* than that?" I inquired softly as if I were wooing the old girl.

"Yes," she answered, flushing deeply and looking down at her cupped hands lying on her lap. "Many, many times."

"Where would these—ah—encounters usually take place?" I asked, deliberately hitting the euphemistic trail on my own because I wanted *her* to tell it, thus possibly somewhat appeasing my sensitive client and also robbing my opponent of any later argument that it was I who'd led her down the rosy paths of sin.

"Many places."

"Such as?"

"On the raft, on the beach, often in the summer house, sometimes in the main house."

"Ever in the main bed?" I softly inquired.

"Yes," she said, and I half looked around to make sure my client wasn't stalking me.

"But how could you possibly *know* about such things?" I asked, genuinely wondering.

"Because I sometimes peeked," she answered after a pause, her face now aflame.

"More than once?"

"Many times."

"But *why?*" I said, feeling Krafft-Ebing himself breathing down my neck.

"Because I've loved those two ever since they were children and always hoped one day the would get married," she said, holding her head up proudly.

"But how would—ah—watching them make love, as you call it, ever help *that?*" I gently pushed on.

"Because I could stand guard over them and keep them from being disturbed or getting caught—which I'm sure I prevented several times, though they never knew I had. Then, too, I—"

"Yes?" I prompted her.

"I liked to watch because it made me feel so good," she blurted, turning and glaring defiantly at the enrapt jury.

"Axholm," I said softly, feeling a bit voyeuristic myself, "since you knew Miss Constance's husband was far away in New York and that all the help was gone for the day wasn't *that* the real reason you happened to be out so late that final night, standing there alone in the shadows with your field glasses?"

"Yes," she said quietly, moistening her lips and glancing guiltily over at the judge and then busily smoothing out her dress as I again consulted my notes.

"One final question before we leave this absorbing subject," I said. "What about the times you couldn't watch them, such as those occasions when they might have been in the main bedroom, say, behind closed doors?"

"Then I'd listen," she answered softly, her eyes suddenly alight and gleaming over the recollection. "Sometimes that was almost even more"—she paused.

"Yes?"

"Exciting," she said with a downcast look, at the same time watching me like a naughty child from under upraised brows.

I glanced halfway around to see how my client was weathering the storm and found him sitting hunched forward with bowed head and closed eyes, his elbows resting on the table and his hands clapped over his ears. My diagnosis: incipient nausea complicated by massive lawyer gripe.

"At this juncture I think we'll adjourn until nine tomorrow morning," I heard the judge saying in a small voice. "Mr. Sheriff."

Chapter 23

The next morning my client remained silent, disdainfully looking away when I greeted him at the defense table. Progress, I thought, making a mental shrug as I dug out the notes for further cross-examination I'd made the night before.

"You may proceed, Mr. Ludlow," the judge prodded me once the jury was in place and the frowning Axholm and her long black dress were back on the stand, basking in the curious stares of the jurors so recently enlightened on some of the quirkier byways of sex.

"Thank you, Your Honor," I said, rising and leaving my silent client and moving up toward the witness box, feeling rather like a highly resented family doctor struggling to keep alive a suffering patient who no longer gave a damn. Even Viola Axholm seemed to stiffen and recoil the closer I got, I noticed, so I stopped about midway between her and my client to sort of distribute the wind-chill factor, as our modern weather prophets delight in calling it when it's mighty damn cold outside.

"Yesterday you testified, did you not, that after you dragged the body back to the beach house you ran to phone the police?" I began, kicking off still another day of fun and frolic.

"No, I didn't," she calmly replied as I almost did a backward flip out of surprise over her answer.

"What *did* you say, then?" I finally managed to gasp.

"I said that I hurried to the phone from the summer house, *not* from the beach house," she frowningly corrected me, making me think of my old grade-school teacher, sweet Miss Fisher, who first opened my eyes to the often surprising utility of trying to say the first time what one should have said.

"Thank you," I said. "And did you complete the call?"

"I did."

"To what police?"

"The state police, of course," she said, darting a withering glance over at the arm-folded sheriff. "I wouldn't call *that* character even to manure a lawn—though he'd sure never lack the stuff to do it."

All this and a sense of humor, too, I thought, as I waited for the snickers to die down under the frowning glare of the judge, studying my notes to hide my own giggles.

"Did you also phone the surviving husband, Jason Spurrier?" I went on.

"I certainly did *not* phone that—that two-timing old—"

"Stop!" the judge broke in, glaring at the witness as he addressed her. "Do you have any proof of what you've just now implied?"

"That's my business," she snapped her reply, glaring back. "If I wanted I could—"

"Stop!" the judge repeated, louder this time, holding up his hand as he turned and spoke to the jury. "Please ignore and utterly disregard what you've just heard. It has no bearing whatever on this case and I order it expunged from the record." He then turned to me. "Please proceed with your examination, Mr. Ludlow."

"Who informed the bereaved husband of what happened?" I asked, wryly aware that far from erasing anything from the jury's mind, His Honor had just figuratively carved it in granite.

"The state cops, of course. They phoned him at a New York City number he'd left behind."

"I see," I said, taking a new tack, sensing that even an oblique mention of Connie's husband seemed to agitate her so.

"Tell me, have you seen and talked with my client, Randall, since that fatal night?"

"Of course," she said testily, still upset. "Why shouldn't I?"

"Where?" I said, ignoring the challenge.

"In the smelly visiting room of the county jail across the way," she said, hooking a thumb, ever the critical housekeeper. "Where else?"

"Did you and he ever discuss the case?"

"Of course not," she said. "Any more than I'd pry into what happened with the grieving kin of a suicide." She glanced down at my expressionless client and her eyes softened. "I only tried to comfort the poor boy and bring him clean laundry and his mail and his favorite homemade cookies and soup and other things."

"So then you were not and still are not angry at Randall?" I said, wanting, if possible, to make that clear while at the same time quelling an impulse to exchange recipes.

My question touched her to the quick and again I was afraid she might break down. "No, just heartbroken and terribly sorry for him and poor Commo," she finally said, "and awfully puzzled over how it all could ever have happened."

"Then you never asked him to 'explain all' as he'd promised in the note he left in the beach—I mean—summer house?"

"I did not."

"Or ever mention the note?"

"I did not."

"But why not?"

"I've just *told* you why," she said, shaking her head over my stupidity. "Also because the state cops made me promise not to discuss the case, or they'd cut off my jail visits."

"What would you have particularly wanted to ask Randall if you hadn't promised the police otherwise?" I pushed on, risking an objection that did not come.

"How he could possibly have written that awful note even before he crossed over to the island that night," she answered swiftly. "Made everything look so plotted and planned ahead."

"You mean the note Randall finally did leave behind weighted under a spoon?" I said, knowing full well she did and smarting over how efficiently the defendant's own lawyer was bringing out such crucial proof of premeditation.

"Of course," she snapped.

"But how could you possibly have known where or when Randall wrote any note?" I pushed on.

"Because I know his handwriting so well, always in his favorite green ink and usually written on those same little note pads," she continued in a rush of words. "You see, I regularly tidy up his cottage on my Thursday afternoon off—as I once used to do for his dear parents," she ran on as though reading my mind. "Anyway, Commo never used green ink or note pads and never kept stationery in the summer house, which I ought to know because after all I looked after the place."

"Anything else?" I asked weakly, trying to draw comfort from the thought that all this already had or would have eventually come out at any rate and might somehow bolster our defense of impaired consciousness.

"Further, the poor boy could barely have had time to write anything on the island, even if he'd fetched along a pen and dry paper, after all that ducking and splashing."

"Then how do you think he ever got his already-written note across from the mainland, still dry and readable?" I finally asked, mainly because I had to.

"Damned if I know," she shot back, triumphantly folding her skinny arms. "That's for you nosy and overpaid lawyers to find out."

I glanced down at my notes and then across at my opponent's table, groping for a graceful way to get this unpredictable witness out of my hair and off the stand. Eugene Canda turned and quickly winked at me, and from the sly smirk on his face I wryly realized that two could play at this little courtroom trapping game; that he'd obviously known all along where the cryptic note was written but preferred that defense counsel confirm it and further let that mewling cat out of the bag.

"Axholm," I lamely pushed on, "do I correctly gather, then, that you have never really discussed the case with Randall?"

"Yes," she fairly hissed.

"And that accordingly the state police never did cut off your visits to him in jail?"

"No, but *you* did," she suddenly shrieked, leaning far forward in her chair, dangling her handkerchief, and aiming an accusing, skinny finger out at me. "*You* are the cruel, insensitive schemer who weeks ago cut off all poor, lonely Randall's visitors," she shouted. "*You,* the same wretched man who only yesterday wrenched from me all those awful, sexy stories about their private affairs."

"Are you now saying under oath," I shot back, raising my own voice and pointing back at her, readying her for a charge of perjury if she now dared to recant, "that you lied yesterday when you testified here for nearly an hour about all the sexual bouts and engagements between those two you'd either watched or listened to?"

"I didn't quite get the question?" she asked, leaning forward and cupping her ear.

"You heard me," I shouted. "Yes or no?"

"Yes, but that's not the point," she wailed, again tossing her head. "It's the devilish, sneaky way you lured me on to the subject and got me in the mood so that I ran *on* and *on* and *on,* you—you nasty *sadist* you!" Suddenly she broke down into a piteous spell of sobbing, at the same time tightly clasping her hands and joining her skinny, sinewy arms together, reminding me of wrenching pictures in old *National Geographics* of grief-stricken old women in far-off places.

"No further questions," I said, turning away and moving back beside my stony-faced client. Meanwhile the courtroom had grown deathly still except for occasional low, hiccuping sobs from the witness.

"Any redirect?" the judge asked the prosecutor, or rather challenged him.

"No, Your Honor," Eugene Canda popped up and said, evidently as anxious as His Honor and I to get this explosive creature off the stand before she blew the skylight off the courthouse.

"The court matron will please assist the witness from the stand," the judge said, whereupon the lady bustled forward to help the still-sobbing Viola Axholm.

"*You bastard!*" I heard my client whispering to me, or rather hissing from the side of his mouth.

"That makes two of us," I hissed back, without turning, debating lobbing a roundhouse swing to the jaw of my first sitting target ever, in court or out.

"Call your next witness," the judge said to the prosecutor, delivering me from temptation.

"The People will call Jason Spurrier," the prosecutor said.

"We'll take a five-minute recess here," the judge said thoughtfully.

"Your name, please?" the prosecutor began after recess.

"Jason Spurrier, sir," the witness leaned forward and answered graciously in his cultured Eastern accent, while casually fingering and adjusting the knot on his tie.

"Are you the surviving husband of the late Constance Spurrier?"

"I am, sir."

"Were you in this area when she met her death?"

"Regrettably, I was not, sir."

"Where were you?"

"Visiting friends in New York City," he said, "where the thoughtful state police finally telephoned and notified me of the tragic event."

The testimony ran on in this vein: brief, urbanely restrained, and quite innocuous as far as the basic issue of guilt or innocence was concerned. Eugene Canda had doubtless bothered to call Jason Spurrier to the stand at all not because his testimony was important or even necessary—after all he'd been almost half a continent away on the fatal evening—but simply to gratify the natural curiosity of the jury and let its members get a good look at the bereaved *and* cuckolded husband. The prosecutor probably also hoped to quell any small-town rumors (which not calling him might only feed) that his marriage to Connie had gone irreparably on the rocks, which might possibly ease the burden of guilt on the homicidal adulterer.

"Your witness," Eugene Canda abruptly said, turning to me.

"How long have you known the defendant, Randall Kirk?"

I arose and said, leading up to the interesting fact that the witness had kept visiting my client in jail after Connie's death and so apparently bore him no malice.

"I've known Randall, Mr. Ludlow, ever since I moved out here from the East."

"How long ago was that?"

"It must be several—heavens, how time flies—it's nearly four years now," he said, shaking his head over that singular phenomenon. "My late wife introduced us, probably because she knew we shared a common passion for fishing for trout with the artificial fly."

Not to mention one for their introducer, I wryly thought. "Then you and he were on friendly terms?" I asked.

"Indeed yes, Mr. Ludlow. You see, we were summer neighbors on the same lake and when I discovered he too was a fellow angler we often went on fishing trips together, frequently spending the night out at my little country place. Sometimes we went sailing out on the big lake."

"In other words you two became and remained good friends?" I pushed on, wanting to nail that down.

"One might call it that, though men who fish together tend to form a sort of indefinable rapport, a special bond of camaraderie, going quite beyond the realm of mere friendship." He paused and gave the jury an amused smile as I listened for the muted strains of his rhetorical obbligato. "If you'd ever fished yourself, Mr. Ludlow, you'd perhaps more readily grasp the feel of what I'm so inadequately groping to express."

"I have fished once or twice," I confessed, knowing he already knew. At the same time I reflected that with *his* magnificent line of bullshit Jason Spurrier should not only be composing greeting cards but own the goddamn factory. "But whatever your mystic bond was, Mr. Spurrier, I now ask you whether or not it survived the death of your wife?"

He seemed to ponder my question carefully, blinking thoughtfully up at the courtroom skylight before he spoke. "Well, naturally Randy and I haven't fished together since he's been in jail," he finally said, "but all along I've tried to remain open-minded on the question of his guilt or innocence and give him the benefit of any doubt."

"Let me put it this way, Mr. Spurrier," I said, still trying to pin down this elusive witness. "Whatever the present state of your friendship with Randall may be, do you or do you not harbor any feeling of rancor against him?"

"Rancor?" he said, repeating the word, as though tasting a new vintage of wine and wanting to be meticulously fair. "Naturally I am both distressed and depressed over the tragic events that appear to have taken place at my home during my absence." He sighed and shrugged, again making me think of a certain suave old movie actor. "But rancor, no, Mr. Ludlow, only sadness for all concerned—that and a certain puzzlement."

"Then you're not mad at Randall?" I said bluntly, reverting to barroom idiom in my efforts to get some straight talk out of this character.

"I assume you're using the word in its popular sense, Mr. Ludlow," he said, like a reproving lecturer in semantics. "If poor Randall ever fell in love with my wife, about which I personally have no knowledge or proof, I can only admire his vast good taste, however I may regret its tragic consequences. But mad at him, in the vulgar sense, I must say no, never."

"And as evidence of your fair-minded detachment you have frequently visited him in jail after his arrest, have you not?" I pushed on.

"Oh, yes," he answered brightly, again giving the jury his disarming smile. "As you doubtless rapidly learned yourself during your law school days, Mr. Ludlow, I concluded it was not for me to prejudge Randall's guilt or innocence, however bleak the evidence might be against him, and that my only proper concern was that justice might prevail"—here he paused and cast a paternal look down at my client—"a concern which I'm sure Randall shares with me." He blinked up at the skylight for a reflective moment. "Although I do hope the poor man can explain away the insinuation we've just heard here that any note he left, he may have written before he ever arrived at the island."

"Why?" I asked, marveling over the adroit way he'd just injected *that* while at the same time protesting his lofty detachment from deciding guilt or innocence.

"Because of the implication of deliberate premeditation,

that could only add to his woes—that and what I think you lawyers used to call 'malice aforethought.' "

"And still do," I said. "And how many times a week did you visit poor Randall in jail?" I pushed on, again attempting to pin down this evident master at using words either to persuade or baffle his listeners rather than to enlighten them. "How many visits a week?" I repeated.

"Who knows?" he answered, smiling indulgently. "I suppose only the calculating souls in our society—of which we appear to have no shortage, alas—ever keep count of their errands of mercy."

"At least once a week?" I pushed on doggedly, admiring the way this smooth calculator had just evaded my question. He was a man who seemed able, without effort, to cloud his most casual utterances with a fine film of ambiguity. "Or maybe more than once?"

"I've just tried to give you a civil answer to that, sir," he said, smiling faintly as he hurled still another dart my way. "All I do know is that I've been unable to see poor Randall for many weeks now, ever since his own attorney, the very man I'm talking to"—here he unfolded one limp hand down at me like a ballet dancer—"so cruelly cut him off from having any visitors."

Again I consulted my notes, feeling my face reddening as I sensed vaguely that it was I who was now being worked over rather than he, so almost defensively I veered to a different subject. "Mr. Spurrier, wasn't your wife suing you for divorce at the time of her death?" I bluntly asked, wanting, if possible, to take at least some of the adulterous sting out of her and my client's torrid romance.

"She was, sir," he answered lightly with an amiable smile, as though I had alluded to some minor bridge-table spat. "We had our occasional little domestic differences—who hasn't?—but I was confident of patching them up."

"I see," I said, consulting my notes. "Earlier in your testimony, Mr. Spurrier, you also said something about the possibility of Randall's having fallen in love with your wife, did you not?"

"In passing, I believe I may have, sir."

"And that you had no personal knowledge or proof of its existence?"

"That is correct, sir."

"Now were you present here in court yesterday and earlier this morning when the previous witness, Viola Axholm, gave her testimony?"

"I was, sir," he said, his eyes flickering warily as he divined what I was driving at.

"And I assume you heard all of her testimony here, did you not?"

"Yes, I certainly did," he said, the look of wariness now replaced with one of tolerant amusement. "All and all, quite a remarkable performance."

"Then you must have heard her testify, did you not, that for years she'd known your wife and my client Randall Kirk were deeply in love?"

"I certainly did."

"And so now I must ask you: Do you question the soundness of her observations and conclusions on that score?"

"Let me put it this way," Jason Spurrier answered, after a prolonged, chin-stroking pause. "The state of being in love is a most subtle and subjective one, even to those deeply enmeshed in it, as I'm sure you've long been aware, sir. Consequently I, for one, prefer not to judge its presence or absence based on the romantic fantasizings of one's own domestic help, especially of one whose leisure hours seemed to have been filled with the avid consumption of books and periodicals devoted solely to sex or authentic romance—either that or voyeuristically watching on television an endless round of all the sudsier soap operas."

It was quite a speech for the spur of the moment, as one gasping onlooker in the back of the courtroom quickly confirmed. I, wheeling around, confirmed the gasp as emanating from none other than a head-tossing and scowling Viola Axholm herself.

"Quiet back there!" the judge ordered, squinting and glaring, and again I faced the witness as peace slowly descended.

"You may have a point there," I conceded as I strove to make a larger point of my own. "But surely there is no subjective speculation or uncertainty involved, would you say, in the testimony of a witness who swears she has many times seen or listened to these two people making ardent sexual love on all manner of occasions in all manner of places? Do you think she made *that* up?"

Again there was the profound air of judicious contemplation before the witness answered. "Mr. Ludlow," he began, "I wasn't there so I can't say what the witness *thought* she saw or didn't see. But it does seem to me not too excessive to question the veracity of *anything* a witness might say who so coolly also testifies here that she watched a man in the act of drowning her mistress and thought they were engaged in mere play."

What a superb job of avoidance, I thought, of befuddling the jury while at the same time subtly pointing the finger of guilt at one's old fishing pal, "poor Randall"—not to mention also adroitly uncuckolding himself.

"Tell me, Mr. Spurrier," I said softly, "do you think Viola Axholm was also fantasizing that final night when, as she has testified here, she phoned the police that something awful had happened to the woman you'd married?"

"It is barely possible," he quickly replied with equal softness, "that the grim specter of death itself may have momentarily reprieved her from the lubricious world of ravening sexuality in which she usually dwelt."

Again I heard an angry mumbling from the rear of the chamber as I decided to quickly get this chameleon character off the stand before he convicted *me.* "Would you also please enlighten us, Mr. Spurrier," I said, still trying to pierce his armor of aplomb, "concerning your theory about why your wife and Randall happened to be alone together after midnight in a secluded woods area while you were away in a distant city?"

"I prefer not to speculate about that," he answered easily, seeming to sense his imminent reprieve. "Perhaps poor Randall could shed some light on that interesting subject if and when he should ever take the stand," he concluded, casting a final benevolent look down at my client. "That's if by any chance he has recovered his poor faltering memory," he added as a parting shot.

I could not resist hurling one final question for the witness to try to wriggle out of. "In summary, then, is it fair to say, Mr.

Spurrier," I said, "that you are quite willing to believe anything Viola Axholm may have said here that might embarrass her or others but unwilling to believe anything that might possibly offend one Jason Spurrier or wound his modest pride?"

"Objection, *objection!*" the prosecutor arose and shouted. "Leading, prejudicial, not warranted by previous—"

"I withdraw the question," I interrupted, moving quickly back to my table.

"I insist upon answering this snide insinuation," I heard Jason Spurrier saying as I quickly wheeled around, "one totally unwarranted both by the facts and by my testimony, and a shabby discredit by the asker on the ethics of an ancient and honorable profession." He glanced at the judge and then over at the jury. "He ought to be ashamed of himself and publicly apologize to this august assemblage. That's all I have to say."

"I'm still waiting for your answer," I said.

"The answer is no," he said firmly, folding his arms.

"Thank you very much for the first straightforward answer I've heard from you today," I said. "No further questions."

"Any redirect, Mr. Prosecutor?" the judge said crisply.

"None, Your Honor."

"The witness is excused," the judge said, and I stood speculatively watching Jason Spurrier as he moved almost jauntily off the stand, smiling and nodding at the jury like an actor leaving the stage, the tip of his beret protruding casually from the pocket of his elegant woolen jacket. "Natty" and "dapper," my mother would doubtless have called him, I reflected nostalgically, as I groped for the one elusive word that might even begin to hint at the labyrinthine complexities of this enigmatic man. "Call your next witness," His Honor ordered.

Chapter 24

"The People will call Detective Sergeant Clement Barnett," the prosecutor said, and another alert, crew-cut young state police officer—this one in civilian garb—survived the ordeal of his swearing in by Clovis and sat convalescing in the witness chair.

Much of his testimony was repetitious of what his brother officer had earlier testified to, including yards and yards of old measurements and distances, plus a few new ones thrown in for good measure, and I envied my law partner as I saw him arise and make his tiptoed escape out the nearest mahogany door while his poor law partner had to sit there numbly taking it on the chin.

Yes, the detective was saying, he had been one of the first state police officers to arrive at the scene; yes, quite a number of his fellow officers had arrived shortly, including the fingerprint man, a first-aid man "just in case," the official photographer—among quite a few others. Yes, he had been present when Sergeant Oliver had found the note, now admitted to have been written by the defendant, lying under a spoon. Yes, he had also been present later in the county jail during the subsequent police conference with the defendant following his arrest. Yes, the defendant had been duly warned of his legal rights, including the right to have an attorney present if he so wished, which right he'd expressly declined to exercise.

"Officer, were you present when the defendant was taken into custody for the murder of Constance Spurrier?" the prosecutor next asked.

"Yes, sir, I was one of the two arresting officers."

"When and where did the arrest take place?"

"Shortly before daylight at the defendant's cottage on the mainland—where his note said he'd be waiting to explain everything."

"Was he waiting at the cottage?"

"He was there and evidently sound asleep, as it took quite a while for him to answer the door."

"What was his reaction when he was told the reason for his arrest?"

"I'd say one of shocked unbelief."

"So you arrested him and took him to jail?"

"Yes, but first he asked permission to pack a few personal belongings, so while my fellow officer accompanied him for that purpose, I looked around the cottage a bit."

"Find anything of interest?"

"Yes, sir, I think I did."

"What?"

"On a small telephone table near the front door I found a blank pad of four-by-six-inch pinkish note paper gummed on one end. Resting open on it was a ball-point pen containing green ink."

"Was there any writing on the pad?"

"No, but there was the clear, indented impression of a message earlier written on a piece of note paper that had evidently been removed."

"Were you able to read it?"

"Not all of it then. Later we discovered that the full impression duplicated word for word the original message left under the spoon in the summer house."

"You mean the note pad and ball-point pen are still in the People's possession?" the prosecutor asked—as if the wily fox didn't know, I wryly thought.

"They are."

"With the defendant's knowledge and consent?"

"Yes, sir. When we left his cottage for the jail I pointed at the pad and pen and asked if we might take them along for use as possible evidence."

"And what did he say?"

"He agreed, sir."

"Do you recall his precise words?"

"Yes, sir. He said, 'Help yourself to any damned thing you see or want or find in this whole crummy place.' He seemed quite depressed."

Eugene Canda reached into a folder and withdrew—big surprise—a blank note pad and a ball-point pen and had them marked and offered as additional People's exhibits.

"Any objections?" the judge asked me.

"One moment, Your Honor," I said, and leaned over to whisper to my client: "Did it happen?"

"Yes," he whispered back.

"May I ask a few clarifying questions?" I asked the judge, who nodded. I then addressed the witness: "You were actually looking for this pad and the pen when you came to the cottage to make the arrest, were you not?"

"Yes, sir."

"On a suggestion given you by the housekeeper, Axholm, right?"

"Yes, sir."

"Did Axholm ever tell or hint to you men about any note before you found it?"

"She did not."

"And you've since learned that the entire writing on the note left on the island fits exactly the impression left on the blank pad found by you at the defendant's cottage?"

"That is correct, sir."

"No objection," I said to the judge.

"The People's exhibits are admitted," the judge said. "Any further questions of this witness, Mr. Prosecutor?"

"No, Your Honor. The defense may proceed to cross-examine."

"Sergeant," I continued, this time remaining seated, as His Honor had earlier thoughtfully suggested that we lawyers might do when fatigue or whatever so moved us. "You were present, then, when the defendant told the assembled officers that he had no recollection of being with the deceased earlier that night?"

"I was, sir."

"So you personally heard him make that claim?"

"I did, sir."

"And that he had no recollection whatever of harming her?"

"I heard him say that several times, yes sir."

"Or of writing and leaving behind any sort of confessional note?" I pushed on.

"That subject was never brought up, sir."

"Why not, Officer?"

The young officer glanced quickly at the prosecutor and then over at the sheriff and cleared his throat.

"Why not, Officer?" I repeated.

"Well—ah—when we heard the defendant's claim of total loss of memory the questioning officer apparently decided it was better not to mention the note lest it and its contents prematurely get out," he said. "At times we sort of have to play it by ear."

"And perhaps you also wanted to await the fingerprint report?" I suggested, feeling rather sorry for the young man, as I sensed from his glancing pantomime that probably the main reason the note wasn't mentioned was indeed to keep its existence and contents from prematurely getting out, as he'd just said—a reason possibly augmented by the presence of the garrulous sheriff.

"That's right sir," he answered relievedly, giving me a grateful smile. "Had first to compare fingerprints."

"Officer, was the county sheriff present at the earlier police investigation on the island?"

"No, sir."

"Why not?"

"I'm not quite sure," he said, again glancing at the prosecutor. "Possibly someone forgot to notify him."

"But he was present at the later jail conference?" I ran on.

"He was, sir. After all, it was held in his own jail."

"And was he there during all of it?"

"Yes, I'm sure he was, sir."

"Including when the defendant claimed to have no recollection of the events of that evening?"

"Correct, sir."

"May I ask what part the sheriff took in this jail phase of the investigation?" I pushed on.

I'd struck a sensitive chord, I saw, as I waited for his reply. "Well, mostly he ran the coffee machine," he said, quickly adding as the wave of snickers mounted, "In fact, most of us were there merely as observers. If we had a suggestion we'd pass a note to the questioning officer."

"Perhaps to avoid a sort of 'third degree' atmosphere, Officer?"

"Perhaps, sir."

"Getting back to the defendant's note," I said, "is it accurate to say that there was no public disclosure of its contents until this present trial?"

"That's right, sir."

"Except for the officer who inadvertently revealed its contents to the People's pathologist, Dr. Pomper?"

"Well, it still did not get out *publicly* until this trial," the witness answered, gamely fighting back.

"Were you by any chance the officer who tipped off the doctor?" I said, feeling pretty certain he wasn't.

"No, *sir,*" he said, shaking his head over such a ghastly thought, "and the young, newly commissioned officer who did so has already been—ah—spoken to."

"Officer," I continued, "if you happen to know, could you tell us whether anybody's fingerprints were found on the body of the deceased?"

"There were, sir."

"Whose?" I inquired.

"Those of the housekeeper, Viola Axholm, found on a metal bracelet worn on the left arm of the deceased."

"Do you know how or when these prints got there?"

"Well, I assume they did when the housekeeper dragged the body from the beach to the summer house, sir."

"An assumption, is it not, Officer, based solely upon what she told you and the others?"

"That is correct, sir. There were no eyewitnesses of which I am aware."

I decided to leave this interesting new development until I could gather my thoughts—and more notes—so I quickly got back to the police huddle. "Aside from the defendant's claim of total forgetfulness," I said, "did he otherwise cooperate with the police at the jail investigation following his arrest?"

"He did, sir."

"Can you be more specific?"

Well, the witness went on, the defendant had, among other things, been routinely fingerprinted; had given the police several samples of his handwriting, including his signature; had allowed the jail physician to take a blood sample; and had finally stripped nude, upon request, and allowed the photographer to take a number of pictures of the bloody scratches on his thigh."

"In other words, Officer, the defendant did everything you asked of him, including making and signing a final police statement?"

"That is correct, sir."

"And in that statement he reiterated, did he not, his claimed total lack of memory regarding the events of that fatal evening?"

"He did, sir."

"Was he then or later given a lie-detector test on his lack-of-memory claim?" I asked, peripherally observing the prosecutor arise and start padding restlessly back and forth.

"Not to my knowledge, sir."

"Why not, Officer?"

"I'm not quite sure I know why, sir."

"Has the defendant since been given any such polygraph test?" I said.

"Not to my knowledge, sir."

"Would you have known if he had?"

"Yes, sir," he said. "Just as you too would surely have known."

"No further questions," I said.

"No redirect," the frowning prosecutor jumped up and said, beating His Honor to the punch.

"We'll take our noon recess here," the judge said. "Please be back sharp at one."

After scrawling down some further thoughts before they soared away, I headed for the defense conference room, where I found Doctor Hugh and Jeremiah munching Amanda's—Doctor Hugh's housekeeper—sandwiches and awaiting me.

"Congratulations," Doctor Hugh gravely greeted me, "on so deftly bringing out from that candid young officer that bit about Randall's claimed loss of memory. In fact I've just been telling Jeremiah here about it. He seems quite unimpressed."

"Why, pard?" I turned to him and said. "I thought that was pretty nifty going."

"Nifty, yes," my partner conceded, "but it still leaves us precisely where we were when we first got hooked by this goddam case."

"What do you mean?"

"That we still have a client whose only defense is he can't remember something which, in case you too can't remember, simply spells AMNESIA, which ain't no defense to crime. Fact is, I'm far more impressed with your bringing out that marvelous stuff about Axholm knowing about the note before the cops arrived, and that only her fingerprints were found on the body, as Hugh just told me."

"How come? It was only a shot in the dark."

"Because it may open up whole new vistas," Jeremiah said mysteriously, moving his open hand, palm down, in a half-moon over our table.

"Spill it, pard," I said. "I've just had my weekly tolerance for double-talk exhausted by brother Jason."

"Because I've been stalking the probate court records for weeks for possible leads," he said, still with an air of mystery. "And today I just may have run across a big one."

"Please let's have it, pard," I begged, sinking wearily into the nearest mahogany chair, "before I throw up."

"Connie's last will and testament—as we reticent lawyers

so love to call these earthly farewells—has just been filed in probate court in connection with guardianship proceedings being instituted on behalf of her young son by her first husband."

"That'd be Marius Blair the Third," I said, still not following what he was getting at.

"In it she leaves most of her property in trust to young Marius and—here's the interesting part—also a handsome cash bequest plus a monthly life income and an island cottage to live in, all for our favorite witch."

"Axholm?"

"Of course."

"How about our friend Jason?"

"He gets the back of Miss Connie's hand; in fact, worse than that—one measly, solitary buck, to avert any possible later legal claim by him that maybe she had forgotten the bastard."

"So where's the big clue?" I pressed, still at sea.

"Yes, where?" Doctor Hugh put in, glancing at me. "I'm hearing all this for the first time, too, and I'd certainly like to hear Jeremiah's latest clue—that's if he can ever bring himself to divulge it."

"It could open up the interesting question of possible motivation, which this crazy case so far sadly lacks."

"Such as?" I said.

"Well," Jeremiah said, "if I were writing a soap opera about this case I'd wind up today's episode with a string of questions —pregnant questions, I think they're called in the trade."

"Such as?" I repeated.

"Did the prying Axholm already know the contents of Miss Connie's will, treating her so handsomely?" my partner demanded in the ringing voice of a carnival barker. "And had Connie caught Axholm spying on her and Randy that final night, whereupon the two violently quarreled *after* Randy had left? And had Axholm simply done her mistress in so she wouldn't be able to cut her out of her will? Or instead had the quirkily jealous Axholm herself been madly in love with Randy all along and could no longer endure watching him repeatedly making love to her young and beautiful and boundlessly horny rival? Tune in tomorrow, folks, and learn all about it!"

"Are you by any chance inferring, partner—?" I began, aghast at the thought.

"No, son, in a few isolated crannies of our society, still only the listener may *infer,*" he broke in, "and still only the speaker *imply.*"

"Are you implying, partner?" I doggedly corrected myself.

"Only that all these things I spoke of are possibilities, son," he said, shrugging. "And now that you've just brought out the things you did—as Clovis might put it—zee plot she zicken."

"But what about Randall Kirk's presence at the scene and his leaving that dreadful note behind?" I said, fighting back.

"We have only her word for that, remember, and maybe the ambiguous note is only a clever forgery or even an old, undated note he'd once left for Axholm with his soiled laundry."

"But how did she ever make him forget he wasn't even there or else had already left before whatever happened happened? And what about the blank pad and pen found at his cottage by the cops? And how about his fingerprints on the note and spoon and those bloody scratches on his thigh?"

"I'll be goddammed if I know," my partner said, wagging his head. "But you just asked me to open some new vistas."

"Incredible," I said, shaking my head.

"The only incredible thing about it is that an old criminal law hand like you should regard *anything* as incredible," he shot back. "If you can dream it, son, people will do it—or bust a gut trying."

"Amen," Hugh Salter said.

"That reminds me," I said, turning to Doctor Hugh. "Vistas or no vistas, we've still got a client who can't remember where he was or what he did that night. And the way His Honor is pounding Gene Canda and me on the back, the People's proofs could well be in before the day is out and it'll be *our* turn to bleep or get off the pot. What are the prospects?"

"I plan to have a final session before the weekend is out, son," Doctor Hugh quietly said. "More than that I cannot say —remember?"

I ruefully recalled my earlier vows of silence just as a warning buzzer sounded and I glumly gathered up my battery of swollen briefcases and lugged them off to court.

That Friday afternoon the jury listened to a constant parade of clean-up witnesses, mostly state police officers, who—after being sworn by the increasingly hoarse and strident Clovis—reeled off still more depressing measurements and statistics—how far from this to that to the other thing.

It soon became evident that Eugene Canda was indeed striving to finish his proofs before the day's adjournment, while I, seeing little point in prolonging the agony, helped speed things as much as I could, already having taken a private vow that, come hell or high water, one Frederic Ludlow was going *fishing* that weekend. To this end I quickly stipulated that my client's police statement be received in evidence without the usual time-killing proofs—and was charmed to see in my photocopy that my client had in several places indeed claimed a total lack of memory.

I did the same with a small flood of assorted graphs and charts and various blowups, including several of my client's fingerprints, not to mention a virtual billboard-size enlargement of his damning note. Then, following the usual mid-afternoon pee recess, the official photographer resumed the stand and routinely identified still another sheaf of glossy enlargements of photos he had earlier taken: photos of Connie's seminude body still lying in the summer house, both shrouded and unshrouded; flashlight photos of the scuffed and sandy beach trail where Axholm had dragged her body; another one of Connie, lying on a slab in the county morgue—still oddly beautiful in a rigidly macabre way, I was soon to learn, leaving me in turn wondering whether this qualified me as a paid-up member of the "don't-he-look-nat'ral" school of funeral parlor condolers; enlarged close-ups of Connie's broken fingernails; more photos of my virtually nude client showing the telltale scratches on his thigh; enlarged close-ups of these same scratches.

"If I may first have a look at these proposed photo exhibits," I arose and said, "we could possibly save time by my stiuplating the admission of these and all other photos without further ado."

"Very well," the prosecutor said—after observing the vigorous nods of assent by our hard-driving judge—and promptly marched over to my table, reached in front of my client, and thrust across at me a whole stack of glossy photographs.

"Christ!" I heard escaping the lips of my client in a kind of low, moaning shriek that sounded less like any word I'd ever heard than an elemental bleat of anguish.

I grabbed at the sheaf of photos, knowing in my guts what I would find, and there, lying on top, was a photo of poor Connie lying seminude on a slab in the morgue. After absently shuffling the photos to get her decently buried I arose and spoke—"The defense consents to the admission of these and all similar photos"—then walked over and plopped the lot down on the prosecutor's table, wondering if the wily bastard had *planned* it that way.

"Your witness," Eugene Canda turned to me and said.

"No cross-examination," I said.

Eugene Canda then stood and faced the judge, the latter still visibly shaken by my client's outburst, and spoke. "Your Honor," he said, "the People rest their case."

"Your Honor," I arose and said, "I apologize for my client's —ah—untimely interruption, but I must also inform you that I believe it was precipitated by the shock of his inadvertently seeing a photograph of the deceased."

"Some people are allergic to freshly developed photographs, I have heard," the judge said after a pause, having evidently decided to overlook an incident that could well have stalled our trial in its tracks. "Makes some of 'em sneeze and carry on something awful."

"Thank you, Your Honor," I said as he calmly turned to the jury and addressed that body. "You will be excused until Monday morning sharp at nine," he told its members. "Meanwhile, as I've said earlier, please do not discuss the case among yourselves or with anyone. Should any person try to talk to you about it please report the incident and his identity to me at once." He turned toward the sheriff. "If you please, Mr. Sheriff."

After the sheriff had arisen and floridly delivered his adjournment speech and the crowd had started to disperse, I sat at my table scribbling notes for next week's assault while the thoughts were still fresh in my mind.

"There," I said aloud, stashing my notebook and lining up my briefcases for a hasty exit. I then glanced around to see if my partner and Doctor Hugh were still there so that I might possibly persuade them to join me in a stop at the Midway Bar for a midway-in-the-trial drink. There they sat, I saw, still waiting in the front row. At the same time I also saw—among the usual know of curious courtroom loiterers—a stone-faced Axholm sitting alone in the back of the court and an imperturbable, armfolded Jason Spurrier also sitting alone about halfway up—the first time *they* had lingered after adjournment, I recalled, during the entire trial.

"See you Monday," I arose and said to my client, mostly for the sake of showing some of those present that we two were still communicating, after a fashion.

"Not if I can help it, you bastard," my client shot back in a low voice, all the while staring stoically straight ahead.

I seemed to be getting used to my new nickname, I reflected, smiling and nodding amiably as I gathered up my briefcases. Giving a cheery farewell salute to my client—like any good member of Jason's fishing fraternity—I moved back to consult my associates about that upcoming drink. Both were agreeable to joining me, I was relieved to learn. "But not till I personally help the officer accompany our boy Randall safely back to his cell," Doctor Hugh added in a low voice, half glancing around.

"You mean you're going to try to do your memory thing over there right now?" I said petulantly, seeing my drink going down the drain.

"No, not that, son—only that I don't want anyone else trying to have at him."

"What in hell do you mean, Doc?" I said, both parched and puzzled.

"Just look around the courtroom again and venture a guess," Doctor Hugh whispered.

I looked around and guessed I vaguely got the message, all right, but also guessed that I needed a drink far more. "See you two at the Midway," I said, quickly turning away and heading out for my car through a forest of marble and mahogany, like a thirsting pilgrim crossing a broad and saloonless desert, my fatigued mind a whirl of conjecture and foreboding and more dangling thoughts I'd forgotten to scrawl.

Chapter 25

The big trout rose again near the edge of the pool in the slow, tranquil back-eddy just below the steep rock ledge, and again the fisherman braced himself and made another cast, and, lo, once again nothing happened. So the fisherman reeled in and, after much contemplation, selected and tied on another fly, at the same time dreamily conjecturing that the storm-ravaged giant pine still clinging there so precariously to the rocky ledge above him could well have been teetering thus since Paul Revere's last ride.

The trout rose again; the fisherman gingerly waded a few steps closer and braced himself and again cast his fly; the trout struck and leapt high over the pool, creating a miniature waterfall crowned by a tiny rainbow. The fisherman retrieved line furiously and took another step and slipped, losing, in swift succession, his balance, his fish, and his temper, whereupon, splashing clumsily ashore and swearing ever so softly, he squished his way back out to his car, dripping like a miniature waterfall—this one lacking only one tiny rainbow.

It was approaching dusk that Sunday evening when, dog-tired and still damp, I plodded up the wooden steps to Doctor Hugh's vine-covered verandah and reached for the ancient metal door-pull, already rehearsing my excuses for being tardy for one of the old-fashioned Sunday night suppers prepared by Amanda.

Just as I heard the dissonant clang of the bell Doctor Hugh himself opened the stained-glass door, holding a tall, clinking highball which he thrust out at me, saying, "Better take this, son. You may need it more than I when I break the news—though heaven knows you appear to need it badly enough, the way you're shivering."

"Thanks, Doc," I said, gratefully downing a swig. "Sorry I'm late. I not only had an epic blowout driving home but also got mixed up with a sassy mermaid out on the big river, who gaily swished her tail at me as she broke our date, my leader, and finally my heart." I took another swig. "What's up?"

"Things seem to be hitting the fan down at the county jail," he said, leading the way to his den to join Jeremiah, whom we found crouched impatiently over a card-strewn cribbage table. "There've been three phone calls for you in the last hour."

"Maybe it's Kirk calling to tell me he's recovered his memory," I said, generously refreshing my drink.

"No, Frederic, it's some young jailer called Kallio, who says he knows and has gone fishing with you—evidently a local distinction shared by throngs. Wants you to phone him soon as you get here. You can use the hallway phone while Jeremiah and I finish our cribbage game."

"Wonder how he ever tracked me down here," I said.

"Tried me earlier at my bachelor digs," Jeremiah said from his table, "and I told him you were expected here at Hugh's for supper. Glad you finally decided to drop by, however tardily." He gestured disgustedly at the card table. "Might have saved millions had you only shown up on time."

"My, my—that makes four calls," I said. "Excuse me while I go see what's cooking."

Five minutes later I thoughtfully returned to the cribbage game and, miracle of miracles, found both players not only *not* playing cribbage but anxiously awaiting the word.

"Let's have it, pard," my partner said as I further refreshed my drink.

"The young jailer tells me our man Kirk is on some kind

of a rampage and wants to see me down there right away," I reported.

"What kind of a rampage?" my partner demanded. "From the shock of recovered memory, I hope?"

"No way, pard," I said. "Seems he's been in an awful sweat to see me ever since he talked with Jason Spurrier a coupla-three hours ago."

"But that cannot *be!*" Jeremiah said, pounding the cribbage table till the cards and pegs jumped around like popping corn. "Weeks ago we left strict orders that nobody, but *nobody,* was to visit our boy Kirk. Why, even Axholm and Jason both needled you about that earlier out in court, remember?"

"Talked on the phone, I mean, Kallio reminding me that our no-visitor orders never covered emergency phone calls—the only kind they'll ever allow," I said, turning to Doctor Hugh. "I guess maybe we goofed on that one, Doc, or didn't we?"

"We just may have, son," he replied thoughtfully. "But, tell me, has your client quieted down yet?"

"I clean forgot to ask, Doc," I said. "But he did tell me that Axholm had tried to visit our boy personally yesterday but that the jailer then on duty turned her away and she'd made quite a scene."

"Poor jailer," Jeremiah said, at which point Amanda appeared in the doorway.

"Yentlemen," she announced, making a little curtsy, "com' quvick. Supper he's now be serfed an' time for eats."

By the time Amanda's banquet was over, washed down with what seemed to be flagons of wine, I felt far more like curling up on the neearest sofa than driving down to the county jail to face a rampaging client. During supper it was decided that Doctor Hugh would accompany me to the jail while Jeremiah would return to the office for a final go at our requested jury instructions which, under the court rules, had to be in the hands of the judge not later than the close of the evidence—now probably only hours away—and a copy of them served on the prosecutor.

"I've got our impaired-consciousness theory laid out cold, Hugh," he said, "and now it's up to you guys to find out and clue me on the one *big* thing—how and why our boy's ever *got* impaired."

"It's tonight or never," Doctor Hugh replied grimly, and shortly he and I found ourselves rolling along together toward the county seat in my mud-bespattered car, Doctor Hugh hugging on his lap a rounded little old-fashioned doctor's valise of a kind I hadn't seen in years outside a museum.

"That your overnight bag, Doc?" I quipped, since as usual he didn't seem to want to talk about our case.

"Precisely, son," he agreed. "Who knows how long I may have to hang around?"

Once I had rolled into the semidarkened and sparsely occupied jail parking lot Doctor Hugh persuaded me that I should go first to see my client. "After all, son, it's you he's panting to see," he pointed out. "I'll just wait out here and listen to the decay of popular music on your car radio."

"Doc," I said about a half-hour later, opening the car door and shaking a dozing Doctor Hugh awake, "how would you like to buy a secondhand trial brief and a virgin set of requested jury instructions real cheap?"

"Who? What?" the old boy mumbled, sitting up. "Oh, so you're back already? My, my. . . . What's up?"

"Not much, Doc," I said. "We've been reprieved—Kirk's just fired me."

"Ah, at last it's happened," Doctor Hugh said, now thoroughly awake. "Tell me about it, son. Did you and he have a quarrel?"

"No, Doc, more like a glacial encounter. Right off the bat he told me he thought he needed a new lawyer."

"Yes?"

"At first I didn't get the drift, reminding him he already had two, plus the services of a free memory-restorer thrown in. So he quick told me he didn't mean an additional lawyer but a brand-new one to take over the case and handle everything."

"Go on," Doctor Hugh said, leaning forward.

"My first reaction was one of immense relief mingled with utter fatigue, like an adrenalin-drained boxer after a tough fight."

"Nice figure of speech. Did you try to talk him out of it?"

"Not so much that, Doc, as to point out to the poor deluded bastard that no lawyer worth his salt would either care or dare to take over such a complex case on such short notice at such a crucial stage."

"How did he respond to that, son?" Doctor Hugh pressed.

"He merely said that in that event he'd handle his own case but that the one thing he was sure of was that he no longer wanted me or my wisecracking Irish pal on his case."

"You mean he omitted me, son?" Doctor Hugh said. "I'm not sure whether I should feel neglected or flattered."

"He didn't mention you, Doc, which I suppose *is* a kind of bass-ackward compliment."

"Did he give any reason for his action?" Doctor Hugh pressed, and for the first time in my professional life I sensed how helpless a witness on the stand must feel under the probing scrutiny of a searching cross-examiner.

"He didn't volunteer any reason," I said, "so finally I asked him straight out why in God's name he was taking such a crazy step."

"And?" Doctor Hugh prodded softly.

"For two reasons, he said: first, that he was fed up with my continued messing around with this childish hypnotism stuff."

"Ah," Doc murmured, nodding. "And second?"

"And that he highly resented my shabby courtroom tactics and my repeated references to and insinuations about his having illicit relations with Mrs. Spurrier."

"He used those words and called her *that?*"

"He sure did, Doc," I said glumly, "winding up by calling me, quote, 'a cheap, posturing shyster,' unquote, who was only selfishly using his plight to advance my own legal career."

"Did you try to fight back, son?"

"No, Doc. I overcame a sudden urge to haul off and sock the ungrateful bastard—lately almost a chronic impulse, I may add. Instead I simply repeated what I'd already told him, namely, that no lawyer in the land, however brilliant, could possibly step into his case on such short notice and do much good; also that what he was doing was little short of suicidal." I shook my head. "The guy must be mad."

"Anything else?"

"I also reminded him—not in order to change his mind but simply to keep the record straight, as we lawyers so love to say —that it was the prosecution and not I who first injected romance into his case."

"Yes?"

"Then I repeated that old line about there coming a time in the affairs of men when only the naked truth might prevail."

"Then what?"

"Then I got the hell out of there," I said, yawning. "Boy, will I ever sleep tonight."

"How did he take it all, son?"

"Cool as a cucumber, Doc. Even forgot to call me a bastard. In fact he finally yawned in my face and flopped down on his cot and, I swear, in nothing flat was fast asleep as a breast-fed babe." I shrugged in the semidarkness. "So there you have it, Doc. We're fired and now I'm free to fish and you to write up a scientific paper or whatever on the case. Let's go celebrate our emancipation at the Midway."

"Not a bad idea, son," Doctor Hugh said, clicking open the car door on his side and thrusting out his long, water-bird legs. "But first I got to go see my patient, remember?"

"But Doc," I protested, "we've just been fired—remember? The goddamn show is over."

"Maybe you and Jeremiah have been fired," he replied, nimbly stepping out of the car, clutching his doctor satchel, "but I haven't—remember? The only man who can fire me is the judge who appointed me."

The old boy had a point there, I saw, so I shrugged and took my lumps for the second time that night. "Want me to wait out here?" I inquired.

"That'll be fine," the old boy said, after a pause. "Please stick it out until I either show up or you get some word." With that he shifted his satchel and walked away toward the jail, looking, in the looming shadows, like some kind of ambulant scarecrow lurching along on rickety stilts.

"Good luck, Doc," I called after him and then curled up and promptly fell asleep almost as fast as my former client had.

It seemed hours later when I felt someone shaking me. "Wake up, Mr. Ludlow. . . . It's me, your jailer pal, Gary Kallio. . . . Wake up, Fritz. . . ."

"Oh it's you, Gary," I said, coming to and sitting up. "What's up? Kirk off on another rampage?"

"Not that, but I'm just going off shift and stopped to tell you that your old doc friend says for you to get the hell on home."

"You mean without him?"

"That's what the old guy just tottered down out of Kirk's cell block and told me to tell you."

"But how will he ever get home, Gary?"

"Says he ain't goin' home, Fritz, and that no bourbon-soaked trout-crazed fisherman is gonna make him leave. Oh yes, also says he wants to see you down there in the courtroom first thing in the morning, at least a half-hour earlier 'n usual, no questions, no excuses."

"Sounds like the old boy means it," I said. "Anything else, Gary?"

"That's all the man said."

"Thanks, Gary," I said, groping for the ignition key. "What the hell time is it?"

"Just past midnight. Late man just relieved me."

"Thanks again, Gary," I said, starting up the car. "Could I give you a lift somewhere?"

"No thanks, Mr. Fritz, I'm driving a gas-eating chattel mortgage of my own. Take it easy on the curves."

"Good night, Gary," I said, groggily driving off to join the vast army of the unemployed.

Chapter 26

Following Doctor Hugh's stern injunction of the night before that I show up early in court, almost predictably I obediently overslept. It wasn't that my alarm clock failed to ring, for it futilely rang and rang, but the temperamental thing clean forgot to shake me, further proof of the flight of pride in craftsmanship in our mass-production society. Consequently the jury was already filing into the courtroom when, half-shaven and still panting from all the mad rush, I tardily joined my client—or whatever in hell he was—at the defense table.

"Terribly sorry for everything," he leaned over and whispered to me. "All a ghastly mistake."

"Thanks," I said, trying to keep the sarcasm out of my voice.

"Doctor Salter just left this note for you," he further whispered, handing me a folded slip of paper.

"Thanks," I again said, relieved to have something else to occupy me than trying to carry on a stilted conversation with my solemnly contrite client.

"Frederic," the note ran. "Please arrange to have me sit at your table. Absolutely essential. Hugh."

By this time, court had formally been convened and the

judge fixed me with his magnified stare and spoke. "Mr. Ludlow," he said, "the defense may proceed."

"Your Honor," I arose and said, "before making my opening statement I should first like to ask leave of court for Dr. Hugh Salter to join me at the defense table during the upcoming examination of defense witnesses."

"Any objection, Mr. Prosecutor?" the judge inquired.

"None, Your Honor," Eugene Canda half-rose and said.

"Leave is granted," the judge ruled. "Dr. Salter will please come forward."

As Doctor Hugh slowly picked his storklike way forward to join me, I addressed still another request to the judge. "I should also like the court's permission to remain seated during my examination of witnesses so that I may more readily confer with Dr. Salter on technical and other matters."

"Permission for counsel to remain seated has already been granted at my own suggestion," the judge said, frowning, "but I'll cheerfully renew the grant if you prefer double coverage."

"Thank you, Your Honor," I said, quickly crouching beside Doctor Hugh at my table for our first judicially blessed conference. "Doc," I whispered, "no time for palaver, I know, but is unconsciousness still our main pitch?"

Doctor Hugh gravely nodded yes and the judge prodded me with a brusque "Proceed!" I arose and walked up before the jury and delivered what may some day rate a footnote as being possibly the shortest opening defense statement in the annals of Michigan criminal jurisprudence, an exercise in legal utterance scarcely notable for its brevity.

"Ladies and gentlemen of the jury," I said, "the defense will undertake to show and prove that the defendant is not guilty of the crime charged, or of any crime, because of his impaired consciousness at the time of the alleged offense. Thank you."

Returning to my table I saw an arm-folded Jason Spurrier sitting in the front row of benches directly behind our table, a picture of sartorial elegance and faintly disdainful calm. In the row behind him sat a smiling and nodding Gary Kallio, next to a state cop, and I felt reassured to have one possible fan in the house.

"Call your first witness," the judge prodded me.

"One minute, please, Your Honor," I said, leaning over for my second whispered conference with Doctor Hugh. "I suppose we call Kirk first, don't we, Doc?" I inquired.

"No," he whispered, wagging his head. "Call the sheriff."

"The defense will call Sheriff Matthew Wallenstein," I said, feeling almost as surprised over this development as the sheriff himself looked as he arose from his mahogany cubicle beside the judge's bench. He lumbered over to be sworn by his archrival in courtroom dramatics, Clovis the oath-giver, and then sat facing me with a look of perplexed and wounded wonderment.

"Your name is Matthew P. Wallenstein and you are the duly elected sheriff of this county?" I began without further consultation, feeling moderately sure of that one.

"I am that," he answered proudly, nodding and glancing over at the jury. Already he was rather obviously enjoying this unexpected thrust into the spotlight—not to mention onto the front page of the *Gazette.*

"And as such do you have the care and custody of the county jail as well as of such prisoners who may be confined there either serving sentence or awaiting trial?"

"I am—wups—I mean I have."

"Including the custody of the defendant in this case, Randall Kirk?"

"Right."

I looked inquiringly at Doctor Hugh, who tersely whispered, "Cover background," as I again faced the witness, suddenly recalling that the People had *not* called the sheriff on its main case; the prosecutor was evidently trying to soft-pedal the courtroom clash we'd earlier had that summer.

"Sheriff, do you recall that during the past summer I appeared at your jail with a medical doctor from this county and asked that we might visit Randall Kirk in an effort to stimulate his memory?"

"I sure do, Fritz—I mean, Mr. Ludlow."

"And that you refused that request?"

The sheriff was gaining confidence and now thoroughly enjoying his new role. "Yass," he answered, "on account of you wanted to do it with that there phony hypnotism stuff."

"Correct, Sheriff, and do you further recall that I then took you into this very circuit court, where, after a hearing before our present judge, an order was entered permitting Dr. Hugh Salter access to my client for the purpose of attempting to stimulate memory recall by the means you just mentioned?"

The sheriff was getting a little bored with my belaboring of the obvious. "Yaas, all that there's ancient history and was in all the newspapers."

"But not yet in the official record of this trial, Sheriff," I said. "And do you further recall that following that court order, Dr. Salter visited the defendant in your jail a number of times?"

"Yass, I seen him prowling in and out of the place quite a few times," he answered, adding, as he scented a chance to figuratively pass out some campaign matches, "that's when I wasn't out on highway patrol."

"And are you aware that Dr. Salter's latest visit to your jail for that purpose occurred only last night?"

"Yass, my night man already told me that the old gent spent the whole night there."

"Objection," Eugene Canda arose and said. "To save time I've gone along with this series of obviously leading questions of his own witness, and I suggest it has gone far enough."

"Yes?" the judge demanded sharply. "What is the point of all this?"

"I too have been trying to save time, Your Honor," I said with a confidence I scarcely felt, "and shortly expect to tie this in with later testimony. Moreover, all this is necessary background to the very nature of our defense and includes questions which only this witness can answer."

"Proceed," the judge said, raising his brows and shaking his head over this delaying exchange between counsel.

"Sheriff," I went on, "I assume you were present when Randall Kirk was questioned in your jail following his arrest?"

"I sure was—right in the thick of it."

"And were you also at the island home of the deceased prior to Kirk's arrest?"

"No, I couldn't make it out there that night."

"How come, Sheriff?"

"Must a been out on highway patrol where they couldn't get hold of me. Yass, I now recall I was."

"And by 'they' do you mean the state police?"

"Yass, me and them work real close together."

I decided not to explore this modest self-tribute to interpolice harmony, and pushed on. "At the later jail session with Kirk did you hear him state that he could not recall the events of the evening prior to his arrest?"

"That's all in that police statement over there," he said, pointing at the mound of various People's exhibits stacked on a second table near that of the busy court stenographer.

"But I just asked you, Sheriff, did *you* hear him say he could not recall what had happened?"

"Oh that? Yass, I heard him spring that forgetful line several times."

"Do I correctly gather from your answer, Sheriff, that you were not overly impressed by his 'forgetful line'?"

"Correct, I sure wasn't."

"Why not?"

"Well, it seemed too handy for a guy to go and drown a lady and leave a note confessing it all and just a few hours later up and claim he clean forgot the whole thing."

"But at that time, Sheriff, you didn't know of the existence of any note, did you?"

"Let's see," he said, going into an eye-blinking pantomime of deep recall, with the rosy tip of his tongue protruding. "I guess that's so, which maybe only goes to show how dead right I was all along."

"By 'right,' Sheriff, do you mean in your conclusion that he was lying all along?"

"Right," he repeated, reminding me of the scathing backhanded compliment my partner had recently paid that loquacious man. "Our sheriff is a man of few words," he had solemnly assured me, "except that, regrettably, he keeps using them over and over."

"And have you since changed your mind on that score?" I said.

"I sure haven't."

"In other words, Sheriff, up to this very hour and moment you still think Randall Kirk was lying with his forgetful line?"

"I sure do," he said, glancing over at the jury and bestowing upon it a Socratic nod.

"Sheriff," I went on, "do you recall the previous requests made to you on behalf of Kirk that he be given a test to possibly determine whether he was telling the truth about his claimed lack of memory?"

"I do."

"Did you ever grant those requests?"

"Nope."

"Why not?"

"Because I don't believe in them lie-detector gadgets—"

"Objection, objection!" shouted Eugene Canda, already on his feet and waving the witness silent. "Highly prejudicial question before jury. . . . Results of a polygraph test in any event inadmissible . . . .Leading his own witness. . . . Move question and answer be stricken and jury instructed to disregard."

"Mr. Ludlow?" the judge patiently inquired.

"The defense is not trying to show the results of any such test but simply that one was asked for," I said, rising out of habit. "No question of admissibility is involved because, as the witness has just said, no such test was ever given. Moreover, since the People saw fit not to call the sheriff as a witness here, it is rather obvious that I had to do so myself in order to ask him anything. Finally, I suggest that any police officer who publicly declares under oath that; one, he believes a criminal defendant is lying on a crucial issue in a case and still fails to use the one available means that might enlighten him or; two, fails to freely permit a defense doctor access to his jail for the purpose of possibly refreshing the defendant's lost memory, just might qualify as a hostile and prejudiced witness, which I am entitled to cross-examine."

It was quite an impromptu speech to have been made without notes and I gratefully sat down and gulped a glass of water.

"Anything further, Mr. Prosecutor?" the judge said to my opponent.

"I've said my say, Your Honor."

The judge leaned forward and glanced sideways down at the poised court reporter as though to make sure he missed nothing, and spoke in a low voice. "The objection is overruled," he said. "The witness may complete his answer to the question."

"What do you say, Sheriff?" I prompted the witness.

"What's the question?" the sheriff answered, flushing. "During all this here lawyer palaver and snipping I guess I clean forgot."

"I was asking you, Sheriff," I further prompted him, "why you didn't ever permit Kirk to take the lie-detector test both he and I earlier requested?"

"Oh, that. Like I say, I don't trust them gadgets."

"Preferring instead, Sheriff, to be guided by your own infallible intuitions?"

"You said it, Counselor, I didn't."

"Your unambiguous answer, please, Sheriff," I persisted.

"Right. I'll buy my own hunches before I'll believe in them gadgets."

"Any more than you believe, say, in using hypnosis for memory recall?"

"Right," he said. "In my book that's also for the birds."

I felt Doctor Hugh plucking at my sleeve and, after excusing myself to the judge, we conferred at some length, during which he suggested a new line of questions I found so bizarre and disturbing that I pondered asking for a recess so that I might either debate the issue with him or at least seek further enlightenment.

"Please proceed," the judge said, jolting me out of my dilemma.

"Sheriff," I began, shrugging mentally as I resignedly groped for an opening for my strange new line of questions. "As the chief elected law-enforcement officer of this county, you, I assume keep yourself well-posted on all rumors and reports of dangerous persons who may be at large around the county, do you not?"

"Of course yes," he said, proudly jutting out both his chest and chin and all but buffing his sheriff badge. "As your sheriff I'm always amongst the first to get the word."

"Then may I ask you, Sheriff, whether during recent months this past summer you have known or heard of any person or persons believed or suspected of haunting the wooded areas of this county, particularly the area of our resort lakes, threatening harm to others living or staying in such areas?"

"If you mean all them cottage break-ins by thieves and booze-an-pot-partying kids, yes, they're a dime a dozen an' me and my staff's busy night and day workin' on 'em."

"Not quite that, Sheriff," I said, gingerly feeling my way. "I mean have you during the past summer known or heard of any person who has threatened by word or act the lives and safety of others in such rural areas, more particularly those of boaters or swimmers on or in any of our outlying resort lakes?"

"Nope," the sheriff said positively, wagging his head. "Never heard tell of any such kooky characters."

"And if there were any such dangerous persons abroad would you have known about it?"

"Not only known but been out there and nabbed the sons of"—he paused and glanced guiltily over at the judge—"the goldarn rascals."

I glanced questioningly at Doctor Hugh, who whispered, "That's enough," so I arose and looked across at Eugene Canda and said, "Your witness."

"No questions," he arose and said, "though I fail to see any remote connection between this last series of questions and any possible issues in this trial"—a prosecution sentiment which I, for once, was inclined to share with him.

"Call your next witness," the hard-driving judge brusquely said, dashing my hopes for at least a brief respite so that Doctor Hugh might better fill me in.

"Call the defendant," I heard Doctor Hugh whispering. "Cover the memory thing first."

"The defense will call the defendant, Randall Kirk," I arose and said, feeling much like a ventriloquist's dummy, quickly sinking back for a hurried huddle with Doctor Hugh, as my client, looking unusually pale even for him, made his way up to the witness stand in the tense and hushed courtroom.

Chapter 27

"Your name, please?" I began.

"Randall Kirk," he replied.

"Your age?"

"Twenty-eight—no, twenty-nine." He smiled faintly. "Since I've been in jail across the way it seems I've enjoyed a birthday celebration—if that's quite the phrase."

"You are the defendant in this case?"

"I am."

"Did you know Constance Farrow Spurrier during her lifetime?"

"I did," he answered steadily.

"For how long?"

"Since we were children."

"You were summer neighbors, then, and remained so until her death?"

"That is correct."

Doctor Hugh had suggested covering the memory thing first, so I turned to that. "Mr. Kirk," I said, "are you aware that you are now on trial here for her deliberate and premeditated murder?"

"I am," he answered, for the first time showing signs of

emotion, his hands whitening as he kept gripping the arms of the witness chair. "All too dreadfully aware."

"Do you recall when you were put under arrest for that crime?"

"I do."

"When and where did that occur?"

"At my summer cottage during the early hours of the morning after I was supposed to have"—he paused, searching for a less wrenching phrase than the one that had evidently occurred to him—"committed my crime."

"Mr. Kirk, at the time of your arrest did you or did you not recall being with Mrs. Spurrier the night before?"

"I did not," he answered steadily.

"Or recall harming her in any way?"

"I did not," he repeated.

"Or of writing and leaving behind a certain incriminating note?"

"No," he said, shaking his head. "I remembered nothing."

"And did you so tell the investigating officers?"

"I did, except that I never knew about my leaving any note until this trial."

"You told them this more than once?"

"Many times."

"And you so told your own lawyer?" I asked, risking a successful objection by my opponent but figuring he might let it pass, not only to spare me the time-consuming chore of so testifying, but also to spare himself the pain of having to listen to me.

"Yes, sir, I've always told you and everyone the same story," he said.

"Right down to the time of this trial?" I pressed, wanting to nail that down.

"Yes," he answered simply, "because it was and had remained the truth."

His use of the past tense was not lost on me. As I leaned toward Doctor Hugh he whispered, "Push it," and I turned back to the witness and began pushing away.

"Mr. Kirk," I began, "I now ask you whether there has been any change in your loss-of-memory situation?"

"There has," he answered quietly.

Again I paused, sensing we were at a crucial stage in our defense and again feeling Doctor Hugh plucking at my sleeve. "Keep pushing, but avoid any hint or mention of hypnosis until I give you the signal," he whispered cryptically. "Kirk's already been warned."

"Mr. Kirk," I pushed away, feeling more and more like a dangling puppet possessing a correspondence-course law degree. "When did you first recover any memory of that fatal night?"

"Late last night in my jail cell," he answered quietly, and the crowded courtroom grew as hushed and still as a deserted church.

"Randall Kirk," I said. "Will you now please face the jury and tell what it is you now recall about that fatal night?"

"Yes," he answered, almost in a whisper, briefly bowing his head and then turning and resolutely facing the jury. "It must have been after eleven o'clock that night when I took off alone in my canoe in the moonlight to paddle across to Treasure Island."

"To visit any particular person?" I said.

"Yes," he answered, speaking in a kind of expressionless monotone. "Mrs. Constance Spurrier."

"Did you—ah—have a prior understanding to see her?" I asked, treading gingerly on sensitive territory.

"Yes, we had talked on the phone just before I left."

"So she was expecting to see you?" I all but blurted, all this being news to me since he had earlier been quite vague on that point.

"Yes, she was," he said, momentarily closing his eyes.

My next question was inevitable and I mentally ducked as I asked it. "And did you and she shortly see each other?" I inquired.

"We did not," he answered in the same listless monotone. My own gasp of surprise was lost in that of the jury's and crowded courtroom's.

"Whom," I cautiously began, feeling like a man canoeing

down a rocky rapids in the dark, "whom if anyone *did* you see?"

"When I reached the anchored diving raft," he went on, much like an awakened sleepwalker recounting a vivid dream, "I tethered my canoe to it and got out and lay on the raft, waiting for Connie to join me."

"How were you clad?" I asked with some trepidation.

"In swimming trunks," he answered steadily.

"Anything else?" I could not resist asking.

"I also wore a waterproof pouch hanging around my neck."

As I paused to ponder how best to explore *that* intriguing subject Doctor Hugh, who seemed to read my mind, leaned over and whispered, "Lay off that for now."

"What happened after that?" I next inquired.

"Presently I saw someone swimming out toward the raft in the moonlight, coming from the island shore, coming closer and closer . . ." he went on, speaking faster, his eyes widening at the memory.

"Yes?"

"So I slid off the raft and clung to it, waiting to greet Connie, and then—and then—"

"Yes?"

"Then suddenly she was upon me and threw her arms around me and for the first time I saw—"

The witness paused and in his agitation suddenly stood up in the witness box. As I was about to rise and motion him to sit down Doctor Hugh reached over and restrained me.

"What did you see?"

"And for the first time I saw," he repeated, speaking faster, his voice grown even more shrill, "that it was not Connie but another woman, an almost-naked woman who was a total stranger to me."

Once again he paused until the electronic click of the clock in the hushed courtroom seemed to urge him on.

"As her arms drew tighter and tighter around me, I tried to fight her off," he quickly went on, almost in a chatter. "Finally I broke her grip and managed to hold her under water. Still she clung to me and repeatedly shouted my name—'Randy, *Randy*'—but I managed to hold her under until gradually she went limp." He paused and breathed deeply, as though he had himself just emerged from deep water. "By then I concluded I'd not only saved myself from danger but Connie as well, so I swam this strange intruder in to shore and left her lying on the sand and went to find Connie. She wasn't in the summer house so after waiting for an interval I left her a note and canoed on back to my cottage."

The courtroom by now was in a kind of muted uproar, and above the din I heard Doctor Hugh hoarsely whispering, "Tell him to sit down—and still lay off the note."

"You may now please be seated, Mr. Kirk," I arose and said, motioning him down with my hand like a teacher guiding a confused child.

"Thank you," he said, almost absently, obediently resuming the witness chair while I once again conferred with Doctor Hugh.

"Mr. Kirk," I went on, again facing him, "I now ask you whether or not you saw Constance Spurrier at any time during that final evening."

"I did not," he answered in a small voice, momentarily closing his eyes. "Not that night or ever again."

"When you finally left the island did you know whether the stranger you had encountered was living or dead?"

"I did not."

"Do you now know?"

"Yes, yes—the person I saw that night was dead."

"When did you first become aware of that?"

"Only last night in my jail cell."

"Were you alone when this awareness struck you?" I said, slowly feeling my way.

"Mercifully I was not."

"Mr. Kirk," I pushed on, veering even closer to the expected explosion, "do you now know the true identity of the person you encountered that night off the diving raft?" He nodded and lowered his head at my question and then looked up at the skylight, his face contorted with anguish. "Can you tell us who?" I pressed.

"Oh God help me, God forgive me, God help me," he suddenly blurted in a kind of despairing wail, "I now know it was my Connie—*that I killed the woman I loved!*"

After the first horrified gasps subsided the courtroom grew as hushed as if laid under a spell. Kirk was now sitting with his head bowed, one hand shading his eyes.

"Randall," I finally said, "can you now tell us the identity of the person who last night helped you recall the things you've just told us here today?"

"Dr. Hugh Salter," he said in a low voice, glancing briefly at my table mate.

I turned to Doctor Hugh for confirmation of my next question, which by now seemed inevitable, and he again nodded gravely. "If you know, Mr. Kirk, would you please tell us what means Dr. Salter used to help you recall your lost memories?"

"Hypnosis," the witness answered.

"Objection!" Eugene Canda thundered, and for the first time during the trial the red-faced judge had actually to pound rather than brandish his gavel to restore sufficient order to be heard above the clatter.

"One more such outbreak," the judge said sternly, pointing out at the back court with his gavel, "and I'll be forced to clear the court of all spectators, and I mean *all.* You have now been warned." He turned to the jury matron. "Please take the jurors out to their room so that I may hear the pending objection."

Chapter 28

"Proceed with your objection, Mr. Prosecutor," the judge said after the jury had retired.

"Your Honor," Eugene Canda quickly arose and began, "the People urge that this whole line of testimony by the defendant, Kirk, is objectionable and should be stricken and the jury instructed to disregard it. We do this for two reasons: one, that it was elicited under a state of hypnotic trance, which in itself makes it inadmissible—as I've argued here on an earlier occasion—and two, because it further appears that the defendant now seeks to defend his murder charge on the grounds of insane delusion."

He stepped back and raised one hand and deftly ticked off his points. "Insane delusion is out for two reasons," he ran on. "One, he has failed timely to file the advance notice of the defense of insanity, as required by law; and two, even if he had he would still have no right to kill the unarmed woman he now claims he deludedly mistook for a total stranger."

Eugene Canda kept banging away at his points like a bemicrophoned rock guitarist in full twang, citing still another venerable *L.R.A.* source, which Jeremiah and I already knew about from our own research, concerning the still prevailing but often criticized majority rule that such a deluded defendant must, at his peril, pick out a delusion that, if true, would have constituted a recognized legal defense to his crime if he were sane.

He paused and took a sip of water and pushed on, rehashing much of the same argument he had made at our summer hearing. Meanwhile I sat there nagged by the worrisome fear that, however exciting Kirk's apparent memory recall may have been, it could raise as many questions as it answered. Chief among these was the one big, gnawing question, insistent as a drumbeat: *Why* had he mistaken the lovely and loving Connie for a total stranger bent upon harming him?

"Further, Your Honor," my opponent ran on, rattling off still more points, "neither the recent California Cornell case nor your own even more recent order permitting attempted hypnotic memory recall passes on the *admissibility* of the evidence thus obtained. In fact the opinion in the Cornell case expressly disavowed it was deciding that question, and hinted that any results might be limited to the establishment of the kind of defense not requiring the defendant himself to give any such recalled testimony, such as an alibi—as though Kirk, say, had last night recalled he'd been playing pool in a neighborhood tavern all that fatal evening and was thus able to recall and then produce his fellow players to prove it."

Again he paused to consult his notes and once again bored in. "Finally, taking his story in its most favorable light—to him, I mean—it seems to boil down to the dubious defense of unconsciousness, a rare and offbeat defense that has never been recognized in Michigan. For all these reasons we renew our objection and move that all the testimony of the defendant induced by hypnosis be stricken from the record and the jury instructed to disregard it." With that he snapped shut his briefcase and abruptly sat down, patting his forehead with a neatly folded handkerchief, then returning it to his breast pocket with a practiced, overhand flip.

"Up to you, Mr. Ludlow," the judge said.

"Your Honor," I began, well aware that the fate of the whole trial could now be hanging in the balance, "my opponent seems to be laboring under a singular delusion of his own, I am afraid. I speak of his groundless assumption that our defense has suddenly become one of insane delusion rather than impaired consciousness; this despite my opening statement stressing the latter defense delivered here scarcely an hour ago. But at least the latest annotation he cites on the subject has crept all of seventeen years into the present century, for which I compliment him at the same time that I must decline walking into his trap."

I glanced at my notes and pushed on. "For what he is in effect saying is that we have no defense, and for that proposition, both ironically and illogically enough, he depends upon the very testimony that at the same time he seeks to expunge. In other words, Kirk's testimony isn't good enough for the jury to hear, but is quite good enough, thank you, to support his objection and so neatly help him win his case. Let me give a crude example of what I'm driving at, if I may, in case Your Honor has not lately had occasion to review the law of insane delusion," I said, again glancing at my notes.

"I'm all ears," the judge prodded me.

"After a hard day at the office a suburban toiler arrives home and is greeted by his wife with open arms," I began. "Instead of embracing her he deludedly mistakes her for a waiter rushing at him with a double martini and fatally smites her with his loaded attaché case—surely a deadly weapon everywhere these days. At his trial his lawyer pleads insane delusion, but it's no dice and his man is promptly found guilty. Why? Because in our society the prevailing rule is that giving a tip rather than taking a life is the going price for such a delightful intrusion. On the other hand, should our deluded suburbanite mistake his wife for the same waiter rushing at him with a drawn sword, he may fatally smite her, but this time with at least a fighting chance of success. Why? Simply because the prevailing law says that any sane man may do the same in such circumstances and at least make the claim of self-defense."

"I have a vague recollection of the rule," the judge said, glancing anxiously out at the clock.

"In other words, it seems the muddled defendant must pass a course in criminal law and show method in his madness," I said. "You may also recall that this is the prevailing, if often criticized, rule throughout the country," I ran on. "It likewise still seems to be the rule in Michigan. And so, to be quite candid, this is one of the biggest reasons we dared not plead insane delusion in this case. A companion reason is that we have scarcely been in a position to plead much of anything because, as we are just now discovering, only last night did my client recover his lost memory of the tragic events. Still another reason is that we early became convinced that, whatever illusions or delusions our client might be suffering from, they did not spring from insanity."

"If you'll pardon my intrusion I think you've slain insane delusion," the judge said in a burst of poetic rhetoric. "Please move on to something else."

"Thank you, Your Honor," I said, wondering how many bushels of unpublished verse *he* had squirreled away behind his rows of dusty law books. "My opponent next argues that the Cornell case did not decide the issue of the *admissibility* of testimony resulting from a lost memory successfully recovered by hypnosis. For once I heartily agree for the simple reason that *that* issue was never before it—any more than that issue was before Your Honor at our earlier session, held in this very chamber this summer. It must follow, then, that the issue remains open and that any contrary hints the Cornell opinion may have thrown out must be regarded as gratuitous surplusage."

"Please proceed," the judge said, nodding gravely.

"From this premise my opponent moves to the unsupported claim that any such recalled testimony must be limited to *other* witnesses, as in a plea of alibi, citing the example of the defense calling on the poolroom pals of the accused to prove the accused was there with them," I said. "But suppose the poor defendant had played pool alone that night in a deserted bar presided over by a tippling and snoozing bartender? Is he thereby barred from telling the jury where he'd been? If his hypnotically recovered memory is good enough to recall and let his pals come here to testify for him then why can't he do so himself? What is the fatal flaw in such recalled testimony that so contaminates *his* testimony but not *theirs?* One final question that my opponent might for once seriously ask himself: Would we be wasting all this time here wrangling over this whole subject had my client's memory been jogged by conventional psychiatry rather than by hypnosis?"

I was heartened to observe the judge jotting down a note at this point, so I quickly consulted my own notes and pushed on. "Perhaps I can best reveal the basic flaw in my opponent's argument by posing one final question. Why would the California court in the Cornell case or this court in the Kirk case have ever bothered to go through the futile and time-wasting motions of allowing *any* attempted memory recall by hypnosis if at the same time they were already determined to seal the lips of the accused if the attempt worked?"

I glanced around at the courtroom clock and at the same time glimpsed an intent Jason Spurrier still sitting in the front row, now wearing a large pair of dark glasses, and my jailer pal Gary Kallio and the young state cop still sitting there in the row behind him.

"Passing now to my opponent's final argument, namely, that the defense of unconsciousness has never been allowed in Michigan. I freely concede this is so, but by the same token I must point out it has never yet been rejected. In other words the question is, and remains, wide open in this state. Moreover the prestigious American Law Institute's Model Penal Code accepts the defense; more and more of our sister states are accepting it, both by statute and court decision; and I cannot believe that this court would, at least in midtrial and before the accused has had a decent chance to tell his story, flatly reject the defense out of hand. Finally, Your Honor, Michigan has long recognized the classic and ancient defense of insanity, which is really nothing more than one form of impaired consciousness and one which asks the same old question the larger defense itself invariably asks: whether the act done was the conscious, voluntary act of an aware and sapient human being."

I took a few steps toward the bench to make my final plea. "The issue before us is not whether a violent act of homicide has been committed. That such an act *was* committed is now all too brutally evident to all of us. Rather the issue to be resolved here is whether that admitted act of violence was a voluntary and conscious one—and therefore murder—or an involuntary and unconscious one—and therefore possibly excusable under the law. We have only barely begun to explore that latter question."

I returned to my table and lowered my voice. "I'm afraid

that my earnest young opponent, in his zeal, has confused the admissibility of evidence with the right of the accused to tell his story. That the latter's story may sound bizarre and incredible —and ultimately be rejected by all who hear it—does not lessen his right to tell it. That right is all we seek to exercise here and I hope we can now get on with that interrupted chore." I abruptly sat down and reached for my empty water glass.

The judge peered out at the courtroom clock as though to mark the moment of his decision. Then he poured and took a sip of water and cleared his throat. "The People's objection is overruled and the defendant's testimony will stand," he said. "The matron will bring back the jury and the examination of the defendant will continue." Hugh Salter reached over and squeezed my knee and I moistened my parched lips and wigwagged the sheriff to bring me another batch of his apparently inexhaustible supply of two-day-old water.

Chapter 29

"Randall," I began, the jury back, and swiftly boring in, "when did you write the note you now recall you left under a spoon in the island summer house?"

"I wrote and brought it with me from my cottage," he replied.

"You mean you knew what you were about to do even before you canoed across to the island?"

"I did," he replied simply. "And that's why I wore the waterproof pouch—to keep the note dry."

Showers of questions now came tumbling at me, and I plucked one out of thin air. "But what on earth ever made you write and leave behind such a damning note?"

"I was told to do so," he replied quietly.

This opened up still new vistas which I at once began to explore. "For whom was the note intended?"

"Connie."

"But why would you ever write such a stilted, formal note, Randall, to the woman you say you loved?"

"Because I was told to write it that way."

"By some other person, you mean?" I managed to say when I'd rallied enough to go on.

"By the same person who also told me to leave it in the summer house when my mission was over."

"Then the words in this note weren't your words but those of this other person?" I helplessly repeated.

"Yes."

To relieve my own mounting tension I arose and paced back and forth behind my table, finally pausing beside the seated Doctor Hugh. "And did this same person also tell you to do the things you did when you arrived at Connie's island?"

"Yes," he answered, bowing his head. "In great detail."

"But Mr. Kirk," I said, feeling more like a prying inquisitor than the man's own lawyer, "what could possibly have made you do the things you did simply because some other person suggested them?"

"Because not only were they suggested to me but I was also commanded to do them," he answered steadily, almost doggedly.

I felt a nudge and, leaning, heard Doctor Hugh whisper, "Push hard and fast."

"Randall," I went on, "how could another person possibly *make* you do the tragic, dreadful things you did that night?"

"I was commanded to do these things," he repeated slowly, "just as, by the same means, I was commanded to forget having done them."

"By what means?" I said, suddenly chilled to the spine.

"By hypnosis," Randall Kirk answered.

"Objection!" the prosecutor shouted.

"Overruled," the judge shouted back in order to be heard above the sudden din, once again grimly raising his gavel to remind the spectators that their Roman circus would end abruptly if they didn't cease. "Proceed," the judge tersely said and I left my table and moved closer to the witness.

"Mr. Kirk," I said, "when did you first become aware that someone had hypnotized you and made you do the things you did?"

"Last night in my jail cell."

"Who, if anyone, helped you in gaining that revelation?"

"Dr. Hugh Salter."

"By what means?"

"Also by hypnosis."

"But how?" I persisted, genuinely puzzled.

"By its use, he made me recall what had happened under my previous states of hypnosis, except that when he had finished he did not erase those memories, as this other person invariably had."

This was pretty heavy going and I wondered how the jury was weathering it. There was another bug that also bothered me, and I decided to confront it, come what may, before my busily note-scratching opponent did. "Randall," I pushed on, "how long have you known Dr. Salter?"

"Since back in July when, for the first time, he tried to hypnotize me in my jail cell," he said. "In fact I recall you accompanied him."

"And how many times have you seen him since?"

"So many times I can't recall," he said. "At least once and often twice a week, sometimes oftener."

"And always up in your own cell?" I said, surprised at the large number of visits I had known nothing about.

"That is correct."

I decided to take a more direct tack. "Randall, what I'm driving at is this: Why, after all the times he has tried to hypnotize you during his many visits, did Dr. Salter succeed only last night?"

"Mr. Ludlow," the witness answered, smiling faintly, "I'm afraid communication between you and Dr. Salter has not always been perfect."

"What do you mean?" I asked, both startled and puzzled.

"Because the only other time Dr. Salter ever tried to hypnotize me since that first time was last night."

I wheeled around and looked at Doctor Hugh, who gave me the barest of confessional shrugs, then once again I faced the witness. "But what did you and he do and talk about all those other times?" I demanded, seeking enlightenment as much for myself as for the absorbed jury.

"Many things."

"Such as?" I prompted.

"Things like gardening and growing flowers and the amazing variety of songbirds in this vast Upper Peninsula of Michigan. Also the wide variety of wild mushrooms, a fascinating subject in itself. He also brought me books and pamphlets on these and other subjects, including some on mushrooms by Alex Smith and by Dr. Salter's talented friend, Ingrid Bartelli."

"Any books on hypnosis?"

"He did, and they helped soften my whole previously hostile attitude toward the phenomenon, though we rarely if ever discussed it. In fact we never did, come to think of it."

"But only the other day you—ah—chewed me out about the whole idea of hypnosis, did you not?"

"The repeatedly planted hostility to it sometimes tended to return when Dr. Salter wasn't around."

"Mr. Kirk," I doggedly pushed on, wondering whether I had lately been groping around in a state of trance myself, "please tell me, if you can, why Dr. Salter failed to hypnotize you the first time and yet succeeded last night?"

"He could doubtless explain that far better than I," he answered, "but I do have a few ideas."

"Please share them."

"One, I'm not sure he really ever tried to hypnotize me that first time, something I felt even at the time. Two, because last night he used a different approach. A third possible reason is that this other person, as I just said, repeatedly forbade me to recall what had happened on that fatal night, and above all, ever to allow myself to be hypnotized by another. From my reading I now gather this is technically known as posthypnotic amnesia, I believe, accompanied by a planted aversion and resistance to any rival hypnosis. But, I repeat, Dr. Salter can probably explain this far better than I." There was the faint hint of a smile. "I seem to be a far better guinea pig for hypnosis than a student."

"Then why didn't this planted aversion you speak of also work last night?"

"Perhaps because I've grown to know and like and trust Hugh Salter," he said, glancing at our table, "and been so long out of touch with this other person, since all my other visitors were cut off, that both my planted amnesia and aversion to rival hypnosis must have weakened." He paused for a moment, speaking slowly. "I also suspect I have lately begun to see this other person in a new and more revealing light."

This was touchy going, I saw, as well as possibly objectionable, so I veered to another approach. "Randall," I said, "when did this other person first ever hypnotize you, do you know?"

"Many months ago, possibly even a year, I'd guess, while we were sitting before an open fireplace playing a little game this person had one evening suggested, picking out faces and shapes in the flames."

"Was it during these little games, Randall," I asked, "that you first heard of a strange woman who periodically appeared and vanished on your and Connie's lake?"

"Yes, first heard and saw her."

"What do you mean, *saw* her?" I said, once again jolted.

"This person frequently described to me this enigmatic woman, described her in such detail that I too began to see her in the dancing flames."

"While you were in a state of hypnosis?"

"Invariably, I'd guess. It was all so terribly real—*she* became so real, as in a vivid dream."

"What was the purpose of this little game?"

He shut his eyes for a moment before he spoke. "To build me up to do what I finally did."

"You mean, to *kill* her?"

"Yes, though that word was never used."

"But how can you say that? How could that possibly be done?"

"I didn't realize it then, but I was being put through a subtle course of learning to grow both to hate and fear this woman, as well as to want to try to save her."

"Please explain?" I said, miles at sea.

"Much time was spent explaining to me that this woman was some sort of distracted, half-human siren who haunted rural lake areas, particularly resort lakes, and more particularly the lake where her archrival dwelt."

"And who was she?" I asked, a light beginning to dawn.

"Constance Spurrier," he replied simply. "And only last night, for the first time, did I learn that this strange creature was purely an hallucination created and carefully planted in me by this other person."

The courtroom had grown hushed with an almost ticking silence as I returned to my table and took a hurried gulp of the sheriff's tepid water. "Randall," I said, standing close beside Doctor Hugh, "what else were you told about this strange woman?"

"As time passed this game-playing person also planted in me a growing fear that this woman might one day try to molest and harm both Mrs. Spurrier and me. I was repeatedly warned to remain alert to protect ourselves, and especially her, when the time came."

"But why?"

"Because I was told this woman was falling madly in love with me and also growing insanely jealous of her beautiful rival."

"Again meaning Connie Spurrier?"

"Yes."

"And you actually believed it?"

"Intensely crazy and egoistic as it all sounds, I did, yes."

"How were you supposed to know when danger impended?"

"This person said I would be adequately warned, either in person or by telephone, when danger was imminent, and that I must move decisively and at once to subdue her."

"You mean you were told to kill her?"

"Never quite that. Always I was told I must act to quiet and subdue her."

"How were you supposed to do that?"

"I was repeatedly told she was essentially a strayed and bored water creature, rebelling against the dullness of her realm, and that the only way to calm and subdue her—always *that* word—was to submerge her in her natural environment until calm returned and all resistance stopped." He took a deep, sighing breath. "In effect I was told that I would not only be helping Connie and myself but society and this troubled creature as well."

"Go on," I said.

"It became to me almost a form of civic duty in which I would flatteringly emerge as a kind of folk hero. At no time was I led to believe that I might do lasting harm to her much less take her life, however incredible all this may sound. She—she was so real she still haunts me as I speak these words."

I stared at the man and suddenly resolved, at whatever risk, to bear down and ask some of the many troublesome questions that kept nagging me. For if the man's own retained lawyer couldn't quite swallow his story, I asked myself, how could he ever expect a neutral jury to do so?

"Look, Randall," I blurted in a rush of words, "during these sessions weren't you ever aware that something mighty strange was going on? During your normal waking hours weren't you ever suspicious or uneasy about the odd hours you must have kept? Weren't there puzzling and unexplained time gaps that made you wonder and should have warned you that surely *something* was terribly amiss? Or are you now trying to tell us you were kept in a constant state of hypnotic trance?"

"None of these things," he answered steadily enough, "incredible as this too must sound." He paused and stared out at the tensely hushed courtroom. "Much still remains hazy, but as nearly as I can now reconstruct it, these sessions were as comparatively short and intense as they were infrequent and somehow always seemed to take place after I'd been aroused from my normal sleep."

"Aroused by this other person, you mean?"

"Invariably," he said, nodding, "so that any occasional questionings and qualms I may have felt, and there were a few, I tended to ascribe to my own bad dreams." He managed a wan smile. "Either that or to possibly having had one or two too many before retiring."

"But qualms or no qualms, how could you," I persisted boring in before the prosecutor did, "an intelligent, mature, educated man, presumably possessing all his marbles, have possibly swallowed this lake siren thing?" I shook my head. "How could this other person have possibly sold you such a bill of goods?" As I awaited his answer I heard a whispering in my ear saying, "Good boy. Keep it up."

"I've just tried to tell you," he said resignedly, and again there was the faint smile. "Perhaps it shows some of the strange power of this hypnosis thing. Perhaps Dr. Salter can better explain it. Maybe I read too many fairy tales as a boy. Perhaps the course in Greek mythology I took back in college made me more susceptible. I can't say."

"Did this other person know of your interest in these things?"

"Yes, and also that while in college I spent most of one summer on Loch Ness vainly looking for the so-called monster."

"Do you believe that such a Loch Ness creature exists?" I asked after a quick swallow, for I knew my opponent surely would if I didn't. My question seemed to perturb him but there was now no holding back. "Do you?" I persisted. "Yes or no?"

"It's a long story, almost as complicated and controversial as hypnosis itself." Again the faint smile. "Let's say I'm open-mindedly agnostic on the subject." He glanced over at the jury and then turned back to me, his face suddenly clouding. "But I *did* see this siren I've just told about on that moonlit night last summer, far more plainly, I swear, than I'm now seeing you."

The courtroom by now was seething with excitement as I pondered the inevitable question. "Since your arrest, Randall have you seen this other person you keep referring to?"

"Many times."

"Where?" I asked, knowing there could only have been one place.

"In the county jail."

The field of candidates was now sharply narrowed, and I tried to keep the throb of excitement out of my voice as I quickly pushed on. "Why did this person keep visiting you?"

"Out of friendship and concern for me, I then thought, but I now know differently."

"For what reason, then?"

"To keep rehypnotizing me and renewing my amnesia and again warning me against ever allowing anyone else—particularly Dr. Salter—to hypnotize me or even to try." He paused briefly. "Also to find out about our latest defense plans."

"You mean," I went on with an involuntary shiver, "this person could make you tell anything he or she wanted to know?"

"Not only could but consistently did."

"Even about past events in your life, however personal and private?" I said, thinking of Axholm's testimony about our client's and Connie's sexual gymnastics.

"Everything," he answered grimly.

"But how could this person keep rehypnotizing you with all the distractions in a noisy, crowded jail?"

"Simply by uttering a code phrase I'd previously been taught by this person, over and over. By using it I could instantly be put back into deep hypnosis and become virtual putty in this person's hands."

"What was this code phrase?"

For a moment he had a hunted look, glancing to the right and left. "I—I'm almost afraid to say."

"Try," I said. "Your trusted friend Hugh Salter sits right here."

"Marcel Proust," he said, almost in a whisper, then repeating it almost in a shout—"*Marcel Proust!*"

"You mean the dandified Frenchman who later took to wearing ladies' shawls as he crouched in his cork-lined rooms writing the world's longest novel about a cookie dipped in tea he had once eaten?"

"I think they were called madeleines, after the lady who created them," he answered, smiling faintly. "But the very same man."

"You mean that all this person had to say was this name and, presto, you would again be hypnotized?"

"Instantly."

I found all this disturbing even to listen to and I studied the skylight for a moment to steady myself before the impending storm. "Randall," I went on, "did this person employ this signal on the day of Connie's death?"

"Yes," he answered, again convulsively gripping the arms of his chair.

"When and where did you and this person meet so that you could be give your signal?"

"There was no personal meeting—it took place over the telephone."

I stood frozen by my table as a revealing bell rang in my

mind. "You mean," I managed to say, "this person rehypnotized you over the phone?"

"Yes."

"But how could that be?"

"We had practiced it many times," he answered, "except that on this day, or rather night, something more was added."

"Go on," I barely whispered.

"I was told to go at once to Connie's island to protect her from this evil woman."

"And so you did?"

"And so I did," he echoed, bowing his head.

"When, if ever, were these code words used again?"

"After I was in jail."

"To what end?"

"When, after using them on me, this person first learned that I'd told you something about remembering the ringing of a little bell. The purpose was to erase even this blurred and vestigial memory, which was then successfully done."

"You mean, then, that this person later additionally erased your faint recollection of the earlier phone call made to you?"

"I do."

"But how," I pressed on, fighting the chill in my spine, "how could this person have known you'd ever told me that in the first place?"

"Simply by making me review everything you and I ever talked about—something which occurred regularly."

"Including anything you may ever have told me about your relations with Connie?"

"Yes."

I glanced down at Hugh Salter, almost hating to ask what was now inevitable, and his lips silently formed a single word: "Push."

Again I faced the witness. "Randall, when was this code last used on you?"

"Yesterday, about midafternoon."

"In person or by phone?"

"When I received an emergency telephone call at the jail."

This time a large bell rang, a wild, reverberant gong, and

I fought an impulse to wheel and see if anyone was leaving the courtroom.

"Phoned for what purpose?" I asked.

"To hear me confirm the state of my continuing amnesia, which I did, and also to command me to immediately discharge you as my lawyer, which I also did."

"When you fired me last night, Randall, were you aware you had been ordered to do so?"

"I was not," he said, looking almost grateful for my question, "because at the same time I was ordered to forget it—as well as again strongly urged to resist attempted hypnosis by anyone."

"Then the reasons you gave me last night for firing me were not your own sentiments but those of this other person?" I could not resist asking.

"They were this other person's," he answered, "and were also but the latest in many previous efforts to turn me against you."

"But why me?"

"Mainly, through you, to reach this person's real target, Dr. Salter."

"I don't quite follow."

"With you out of the way this person evidently thought any further attempt at memory recall would finally be stopped—memory recall being this person's greatest fear."

"But why?"

"Because if my memory were ever restored this person knew the whole devious plan would lay exposed."

"And so last night Dr. Salter succeeded in restoring your memory?"

"He did," came the grim answer. "I now recall everything."

"Randall," I said, "when you say you recall everything, do you mean you now remember doing what you did to Connie that night or only to that—that other woman?"

He closed his eyes for a moment, breathing deeply. "Only to that other woman, thank God," he answered. "Mercifully she is the only memory I have or ever will have of that dreadful night, my sole reality."

The moment of truth had arrived and I pretended to consult my notes while I tried to order my racing thoughts. "Randall," I said, feeling as though I were igniting a short-fused bomb, "is the person who earlier hypnotized you and made you do the things you did that fatal night still in this Lake Superior area?"

"Yes," he answered.

"Where?"

"In this very room."

This is it, I thought, blurting my next words. "Will you now please rise and identify that person for us?"

Randall Kirk was suddenly on his feet, pointing in my direction, but beyond me, as though sighting a rifle, which slowly began moving as he spoke, as though he were making a running shot. "He's sitting there now in the front row. . . . No, he's getting up and leaving. . . . He's now opening the courtroom door and standing there. . . . Look! Can't you see? *It's Jason Spurrier!*"

"It's a damned lie!" Jason Spurrier shouted from the open courtroom door, whipping off his dark glasses and brandishing them as he spoke, his pale eyes ablaze. "It's a lie! It's a lie!" he kept repeating, like a stuck phonograph record, then turned and suddenly disappeared. The door sighed shut behind him, but the chanted words still echoed back to the stunned courtroom, gradually growing fainter and finally dying away into a plaintive murmur.

Chapter 30

The courtroom throbbed with an insistent dynamo hum while the judge, visibly shaken, for once forgot even to brandish his gavel. When a measure of calm had descended without benefit of gavel he turned and spoke to the jury. "We will now take our noon recess till one o'clock—no, better make it one-thirty today," he said. "Meanwhile I'd like both counsels to join me at once in chambers, along with the county sheriff."

Randall Kirk rejoined us at our table, still highly agitated, and as Doctor Hugh sought to calm him I rounded up my gear to go see the judge. That done I glanced about the courtroom and quickly saw that many of the spectators were staying over through the noon recess, evidently worried about being able to find a seat later if they dared leave now. I also spotted a still smiling Gary Kallio, who gave me a little wave, still sitting next to the young state cop. Some of the crowd already discreetly nibbled away at the verboten lunches they had smuggled in.

My, my, I thought, at last we're playing to a full house, with champing lines probably already waiting out there in those marble halls. As I arose and tugged at my array of pregnant briefcases I wondered vaguely when the S.R.O. signs would start appearing and the friendly scalpers would move in.

"Hi," the sheriff greeted us as he came tromping up. "I've just fixed it for my deputy Kallio to fetch your man Kirk back over to jail this noon on account of the judge wants to see me in private real bad."

"Mind if I tag along, Sheriff?" I said, proud to be a witness to such an historic confrontation.

"Be my guest," the sheriff said, so together we headed for the judge's chambers for what turned out to be a session that consumed most of the noon recess.

Promptly at one-thirty, court reconvened with most of the cast once again assembled: the judge back on his bench going over some papers, the jury waiting expectantly in its box, my opponent busily shuffling papers at his table, I dependably jotting a few more notes at mine, my client back on the witness stand tensely awaiting further questioning.

My law partner and Doctor Hugh were nowhere to be seen and while I suspected cribbage I hoped the old boy had instead found an empty chair somewhere and was catching one of his "country doctor" naps—"First thing they used to teach us lads in medical school was how to nap sitting up," I'd often heard him say—as I planned calling him as my next witness and felt he'd really have to be on the ball to deal with the fusillade of questions I expected from my opponent.

Still missing was the dramatic star of the morning session, Jason Spurrier, and few in the crowded courtroom knew that, on the judge's orders, several crews of officers were already out looking for him to bring him in for contempt of court—largely for his "bold attempt to sway the course of a pending trial," as the judge had phrased it, by his shouted denial of the charges my client had made against him that was *not* made under oath from the witness stand. This circumstance seemed to bother the judge almost as much as the grave charges themselves.

Both my opponent and I shared the judge's wish not to do anything that might imperil the course of such a well-advanced trial, and we further agreed that probably the safest course was simply to have Jason quietly brought in, as the judge planned, until we learned whether or not he meant to be sworn and take the stand and face up to the charges my client had made against him.

The sheriff had begged off from guiding the state police helicopter up to Jason's fishing lodge in search of him, claiming not to be sure of the way, though I suspected the real reason was a reluctance to miss his coveted matinee performance at the afternoon session. So the judge had instead directed the sheriff's jailer, Gary Kallio, to take his place, and I wondered if they'd yet flown up there and retrieved the missing Jason.

"Mr. Ludlow," the judge said, finally looking up from his papers, "you may now continue with your direct examination of the defendant, Randall Kirk."

There were many questions I still could have asked my client, I knew, but his continued state of agitation and my own feeling that a crucial peak of the trial had now been reached held me back.

"No further questions at this time, Your Honor," I arose and said.

"Your witness, Mr. Prosecutor," the judge said.

"Your Honor," Eugene Canda arose and said, "if possible, the People would like to defer cross-examination of the defendant until later."

"How much later?"

"Until certain of the—ah—steps and contingencies we discussed this noon in chambers might be resolved, Your Honor."

"Any objection, Mr. Ludlow?"

"None, sir," I quickly arose and said, sensing that the prosecutor was waiting and wondering like the rest of us just what might happen if and when Jason Spurrier was brought in. Might he not also be holding out at least a tacit prospect that he might not cross-examine my client at all? Or was all this merely a clever shift in strategy, such as possibly trying to refute and discredit the defendant's story by maybe confusing and breaking down one tired old country doctor?

"Call your next witness," the judge said to me.

I glanced anxiously around the crowded chamber for the missing Doctor Hugh, and was about to ask leave of court to go look for him when I saw the old boy slowly making his way into court through the main mahogany door, carrying before him in one hand a large brown paper bag, of all things.

"The defense will call Dr. Hugh Salter," I quickly arose and said. I watched with mixed emotions as the weary and unshaven old boy continued to approach me instead of heading for the witness stand, at which I stood gesturing and pointing.

"Ask me about these," he whispered hoarsely as he drew close, hefting his heavy paper bag.

"Tell me more," I whispered back.

"No time. . . . Young jailer Gary just flew back from Jason's lodge. . . . Found no Jason but maybe something even better."

"Tell me more," I ruefully repeated as Doctor Hugh turned and headed for the witness stand, there to be sworn by another weary old man, Clovis the oath-giver, whose shout was now reduced to a raspy whisper.

"Proceed," the judge said, once Doctor Hugh was sworn and seated.

I longed to solve the mystery of the paper bag at the outset, but decided it was better to start at the beginning. So instead I had the witness trace his background in and long experience with hypnosis, his extensive library and reading on the subject, and the various huddles and seminars he'd attended around the country, pretty much as he'd unfolded it during our summer session. All during this prolonged recital Doctor Hugh held the paper bag carefully poised on his lap, as though it held a treasure of precious eggs, possibly even golden ones.

"Doctor, I'll gladly relieve you of that bag until you're ready for it," I finally suggested. "Or you might even rest it on the floor."

"No, thank you, Frederic," the witness quickly answered, clutching his cumbrous prize even more tightly. "I'm quite comfortable where it is."

"Doctor," I pushed on, plunging into the heart of our defense, "was last night the first inkling you had that hypnosis by another might be involved in this case?'

"No," was his surprising answer. "I have suspected it for a long time."

"For how long?"

"Almost from the beginning, when I first learned that Randall's amnesia so untypically preceded the events that might normally have precipitated it. I refer to the sound of a little bell he vaguely remembered having heard at his cottage before he canoed over to the island that night. When, shortly following last summer's courtroom hearing, that bell suddenly stopped ringing, there was added to my suspicion the possible presence of some form of hypnotically induced amnesia."

"Go on."

"This feeling was further buttressed the time I failed to hypnotize Randall in his jail cell, the violence of his rejection making me also suspect a planted aversion to any attempted hypnosis by any other person." He shrugged and spread his hands. "After that it was largely a question of finding out who that person was—one reason I suggested cutting off Randall's jail visitors."

"But would *that* help?"

"I figured this would not only stop many things but, as the trial progressed and the tension grew, that *someone* might feel compelled to risk making an emergency telephone call."

"You mean the emergency phone call to the jail that Jason Spurrier is supposed to have made only yesterday, according to the defendant."

"Precisely, and a call that can be backed up by your young jailer friend. Then your abrupt firing last night confirmed a growing companion suspicion that at least one of the signals for reinducing deep hypnosis simply had to be by word of mouth."

"Yes, but wouldn't that same phone call have also told the caller that you had so far failed to recover Randall's memory?"

"Yes, it could have encouraged the caller to believe that his planted aversion to any rival hypnosis was still working."

"Doctor," I said, posing a further searching question I knew my opponent would surely ask if I failed, "how could this rival hypnotist have so successfully gotten me fired but failed to stop you from rehypnotizing Randall?"

"The answer to that one, Frederic, goes to the very heart of hypnosis itself. All I can say, and perhaps lamely, is that our two situations were vastly different."

"In what way, Doctor?"

"After all it was *you* who cut off Randall's jail visitors last summer—though at my suggestion, you may recall."

"I have a faint recollection. Go on."

"It was also *you* who earlier had to keep probing away at him privately about the intimate facets of his personal life."

"Go on."

"Finally it was *you* who ultimately brought out in a public courtroom certain—ah—lurid revelations about his most private, personal life." Doctor Hugh shrugged. "Meanwhile all I had to do was to keep visiting him and bringing him books and newspapers to help him pass the time of day. Our situations were completely different."

"Doctor," I said, deciding to switch to another ticklish subject I simply dared not ignore and thus let my gleeful opponent be the first to pounce upon it, "aren't there quite a few respected psychologists and other students of hypnosis who flatly deny that any person can, by its means, ever make another do what the defendant has testified Jason Spurrier made him do?"

"There are, and while I haven't taken any head count, perhaps even a majority who say and honestly believe that such a thing can never be done. Indeed, had you asked me the same question only a few months ago I might probably have agreed with them."

"Would you please name some of these nonbelievers?"

"I can, at least some of the older ones, as I've lately been reviewing the subject for this trial and found it to be one of the most fascinating and controversial in the entire field of experimental psychology." He consulted his notebook and cleared his throat and continued. "Among those either outrightly committed or leaning to the view that hypnosis may never successfully be used to make another person commit a crime—'antisocial act' is the favorite professional euphemism for what we're talking about—are the prestigious Milton Erickson and men like him—Orne, Hollander, Lowenfeld, Mears and—oh, yes—the team of Schilder and Kauders, among others whose names temporarily escape me."

Sounds more like the defensive line of the Green Bay Packers, I thought but did not say. Instead I asked, "Are there any books on the subject, Doctor?"

"Mostly these views, both pro and con, are confined to brief sections in books or articles in professional journals. But there is one fairly recent book by Bryan on hypnosis and the law—there aren't too many of these, oddly enough—which almost derisively scorns the idea that one person may, by hypnosis, ever persuade another to commit a crime."

"How did you come to switch your own views, Doctor?"

"Simply that the more one studies the subject the more one hesitates ever to flatly assert that a crafty, patient, and ruthless hypnotist, over the course of many months, may never by its means persuade one person to harm another. Look at the leader of that religious cult who some time back almost overnight persuaded hundreds of his followers to kill themselves and even their own children. Incredible, one is apt to say in horror, except that we know it happened. And all apparently without any prolonged buildup by hypnosis, as we have here. More recently I've read that as far back as 1951 the CIA, while experimenting with hypnosis, successfully persuaded a female employee to aim and fire a pistol point-blank at a reclining colleague."

"You mean it commanded her to kill a co-worker?"

"No, for the gun was empty, but she didn't know it and later vehemently denied ever doing such a thing, which further suggests the presence of hypnotically induced amnesia, as we rather clearly have here in my opinion. The report hasn't yet gotten into the literature and is too sparse to appraise how elaborate was the buildup, but there it is. Unless the CIA was lying about an experiment it was reluctantly compelled to divulge under recent so-called freedom-of-information legislation, here is still another dramatic instance where it actually happened."

"Who are some of the procrime supporters of your view?"

"Among some of the older and better-known believers or leaners are Wells, Rowland, Estabrooks, Wolberg, Weitzenhoffer, Kline, Watkins, Margaret Brennan, among others, and last but not least, to my mind perhaps the most persuasive of the lot, Paul C. Young."

"Who is he?" I asked, as all this was just as new to me as it was to the jurors.

"Paul C. Young is one of American's pioneer psychologists, now retired and living not far from the university where he once taught in Baton Rouge. In my view he is also probably the most eloquent and persuasive proponent of the view that a subject under hypnosis can be persuaded by the hypnotist to do just about anything, provided only that his technique is adequate. His proviso tells all. Only yesterday I reread his brilliant article in LeCron's book, *Experimental Hypnosis,* and rediscovered that he is also a member of that small band of academic heretics who refuse to write with their feet."

"What's Young's theory, Doctor?"

"His article is much too long to read here but I've jotted down some of the highlights," Doctor Hugh said, again reaching for his notebook and flipping the pages until he found his place. "Young takes the position that if you assume both a talented and knavish operator, which you must, you've also got to assume that he'll shoot the works to gain his end. In other words the wily hypnotist doesn't hand his subject a loaded thirty-eight on Mother's Day and order him to go home and drill the old girl, despite the apparent bold crudity of the successful CIA experiment I just mentioned."

"What would *he* do?"

"Let me read a brief passage," Doctor Hugh said, adjusting his spectacles and holding his notebook up at another angle to better catch the courtroom light. " 'If one were seriously attempting to induce antisocial conduct he would seek to falsify the whole external and subjective situations,' Young writes, so that finally the hypnotized subject has—and once again I quote —'an altered conception of reality.' " Doctor Hugh closed his notebook and faced me. "And Randall's moving story here this forenoon beautifully shows that this apparently is precisely what Jason Spurrier so brilliantly did."

"What does Young say about those who fail to share his view?"

"Plenty, though he expresses it with characteristic restraint and respect for his peers, pointing out that this is what so many modern skeptics of his position so often fail to do, namely, ever so patiently to implant an altered conception of reality. He also ever so gently implies that many of his dissenting colleagues probably nurse an unconscious desire to fail at any such experiments."

"But why?"

"Motivated largely by a natural reluctance to see something they've studied and revered for years ever able to be used for evil." He paused and reflected a moment. "Something akin to another modern dilemma: the growing split among scientists over the splitting of the atom."

"Let's get back to brother Young, Doctor," I said.

"Ah yes . . . Young further stresses that many of his colleagues perform their experiments in a routine, laboratory atmosphere, often fatally insisting that the subject himself always know that he is being asked to do something wrong—akin to my crude Mother's Day example. Still another point Young makes is that this brusque 'Mother's Day' approach too often ignores and throws away the powerful part of role-playing present in all hypnosis."

"How does all this apply to our case?"

"In the startling similarities we find here to Young's suggested procedure. Surely you recall Randall's testimony here this morning telling how he came gradually to feel himself a kind of daring folk hero who would be helping everyone, including this wayward creature herself, once he'd subdued her. Young has a powerfully resonant phrase that beautifully sums it up."

"Let's have the phrase, Doctor."

" 'The point,' Young writes, 'is that any method that stops short of the use of the full armamentarium of hypnosis should not be considered an adequate method.' " Doctor Hugh paused and widened his hands. "And that about sums up how Jason Spurrier succeeded here. He patiently built up his victim to dwell upon command in a topsy-turvy world of make-believe where violets were red and roses were blue, and when the time was ripe he simply shot the works."

Much of this testimony was speculative and probably objectionable, and as I saw my opponent rise and begin pacing beside his table I decided it was time to turn to the enigmatic paper bag Doctor Hugh was still holding on his lap.

"Doctor," I said, coming to the point, "are you now ready to divulge what it is you're holding in that paper bag?"

"I am."

"What?"

"Two law books."

"On what subject?" I said, gingerly feeling my way.

"On the same subject—they're duplicate copies."

"To whom do the books belong?" I said, trying another approach.

"One belongs to and is part of you and your law partner's own law library—I borrowed it from your conference room this noon to make sure of the matching."

"And the other?" I said, a dim light beginning to glow.

"The other was found during this noon hour on the bookshelves of Jason Spurrier at his fishing lodge on Lake Superior, among the several shelves in his library devoted to psychology and hypnosis."

Eugene Canda, once again seated, half-rose from his chair and again sank back, and my mind raced, trying to cope with the tangle of legal questions with which this new situation bristled.

"Doctor, who found Jason Spurrier's law book this noon in his house on Lake Superior?" I pushed on, hoping to get as much in as I could before the inevitable clash.

"Your young jailer friend, Gary what's-his-name."

"Kallio," I said. "And he did so at whose suggestion?" I added, already half-guessing.

"Mine, made just before they took off during this noon hour to go look for Jason Spurrier"—here the old boy paused, carefully choosing his words—"to inquire whether he planned to return and take part in this afternoon's court session."

"And did they see Jason Spurrier?"

"No, he wasn't there and evidently hadn't been—no fresh tire tracks, that sort of thing."

Much of this was possibly objectionable as hearsay, among other things, but my opponent still remained seated and silent, cagily not wanting to frustrate an absorbed jury. "How then did Gary Kallio gain entry to the Spurrier lodge if the owner wasn't home?" I pushed on, hoping it was not by a physical breaking and entering, which would be a droll touch indeed by the sheriff's own deputy.

"Because I'd earlier told Gary where Jason hid his spare key."

"And how did *you* know?"

"Randall Kirk told me last night—just as Jason had long ago told Randall."

"Will you please show and hand me our office copy of the law book in question?" I asked, still ducking a direct showdown.

Doctor Hugh uncoiled himself and reached in his paper bag and pulled out a heavy, leather-bound volume. He glanced at the flyleaf—"Wups, wrong one"—and then grabbed for and handed me another similar-looking book as I came forward.

"Doctor," I continued, after quickly examining the book and handing it back to him, "I show you a copy of Volume Forty of *Lawyers Reports Annotated,* dated 1898, with my name stamped on the flyleaf and ask if it is the copy you—ah—borrowed from my partner and me during this noon hour?"

"Yes, Frederic, it is."

"And I again ask you, is it an exact duplicate of the other book you are still holding?"

"Exactly, except the other book is signed by Jason Spurrier on the flyleaf, not stamped, and much of it is heavily underlined by someone, particularly the long annotation on hypnosis and the law and the several references to that old California Worthington case."

"Worthington?" I said, momentarily forgetting.

"The old murder case where the lady defendant unsuccessfully tried to show that her husband had put her up to murdering another man while she was in a state of hypnotic trance induced by the jealous husband."

"Ah, yes," I said, moving back to my table in search of a much-needed drink of water. I suddenly decided not to risk offering Jason's law book in evidence, at least not for now, thus avoiding what would almost surely be a prolonged wrangle, and instead leave it up to the prosecution and Jason to explain, if they could, its interesting presence in the latter's own library. I also fleetingly wondered if the paper bag was also Jason's.

I glanced at my notes and felt a tug and found my law

partner grinning up at me from the chair next to me and patting a thick manila folder on the table before him.

"May I please have a moment to confer with my associate, Your Honor?" I asked the judge.

"Confer away," the judge said.

"Where in hell you been?" I whispered to my partner.

"Working on these goddam further requested jury instructions that are needed on account of Kirk's testimony here this morning. Looks like we may need 'em today."

"Thanks, pard. While you're here, do you think of anything else I should ask Doc?"

"I sure do—main reason I'm here."

"What?"

"Ask him if he visited probate court this noon."

"But why? And how do you know he did?"

"Ask him and you'll bloody soon find out. I know he *did* because I sent him there so I could sneak up to the law library and work on these bloomin' instructions."

"Doctor," I said, still seated so I could more easily confer with my partner, "following our court recess this noon did you have occasion to visit the probate court in this building?"

"Yes, I did."

"For what purpose?"

"To see if Jason Spurrier was there."

"Was he?"

"He had been but had just left—after filing some documents for probate."

"Do you know what kind of documents?"

"Yes, the first was the latest last will and testament of his late wife, Constance Spurrier."

There was a rustle of excitement in the courtroom. "Were you able to get a look at it?"

"Yes," he said, reaching into his inner coat pocket. "I also ordered and have here a certified photocopy," he added, producing it.

"Were you able to determine who the beneficiaries are under her latest will?"

"Well," Doctor Hugh said, stroking his chin, "I am no lawyer but it seems plain she left Jason just about everything—

except for a modest allowance for the support and education of her young son."

"Do you recall when and where the will was made?"

"Earlier this summer in the city of New York."

I looked across at my opponent, who sat listening intently to this latest bombshell development in our case. "The defense offers the photocopy of the will of the late Constance Spurrier into evidence as its latest defense exhibit," I arose and said.

"Any objection?" the judge asked the prosecutor.

The prosecutor was on the spot and knew it: If he raised an objection the People would at least arguably appear to be joining in an attempted coverup; if he didn't, here was possibly additional motivation for Jason Spurrier having done precisely what the defendant had said he'd done. The bombshells were piling up; first an old law book and now a brand-new will.

"No objection," the prosecutor said, almost with a sigh.

"The exhibit is admitted," the judge said.

"What was the second document Jason Spurrier filed, Doctor?"

"The last will and testament of Jason Spurrier himself."

This time the judge had to grab for his gavel to restore sufficient order for me to proceed. "Were you able to get a look at that?" I asked, knowing that he probably couldn't.

"I was not, the clerk explaining that it was not open to public inspection until the testator's death." He lowered his voice and glanced left and right like a naughty boy. "However she told me in confidence that she'd taken a little peek and that Jason had left about everything to some lady in New York City and to her son Jason."

All this was probably objectionable for a variety of reasons and I all but ducked as I awaited the expected blast. None came and above the sudden courtroom din I could scarcely hear His Honor declaring a ten-minute recess.

Chapter 31

"It's my further hunch," my law partner continued as we three sat going over our case in the conference room during recess, "that our young prosecutor has now gotta concentrate his heaviest fire on Hugh here. Fact is, I wouldn't be surprised if he cut short or even skipped any cross-examination of Randall."

"What's your thinking, pard?" I asked, half-sharing his view but still wondering why.

"In order to win his goddam case, of course," he said. "Especially so if brother Jason doesn't show up to face the music."

"I don't quite follow," I said.

"Look, a smart prosecutor will want to avoid having the jury once again hear Randall's harrowing story from his own lips—it sounded so goddam real the first time, even to this detached observer. If it *is* true, repetition can only make it all the more impressive; if not, repeating it raises little hope that Randall will care or dare change it, for he's now stuck with his story, true or false. So our clever prosecutor probably already sees that his one big hope is in maybe cracking honest Hugh here."

"But how can he ever hope to do that?" I said.

"Because he already knows that good old honest Hugh will and can only tell the truth, the whole truth, and nothing else but

—and that from that very fact the same dependable Hugh could also become his last best chance to shatter our defense."

"I still don't get it," I said. "Shatter in what way?"

"By getting him to admit that Randall could have dreamed up his whole goddam defense and is lying by the courtroom clock."

"Impossible," I said, shaking my head.

"Possible or not, Hugh?" my finger-pointing partner turned and demanded. "Could Randall possibly have cooked up his defense, yes or no? No speeches."

"Of course he could have—however unlikely," Doctor Hugh said after a reflective, eye-blinking pause, turning to me. "In his partisan zeal Frederic here has simply momentarily forgotten our maxim that if you can dream it there'll be people who'll do it."

"And whether in bed or out," my partner added. "Just watch television or read the goddam newspapers."

"How else can the prosecutor get our truth-telling star witness, Doctor Hugh here, to help him convict our own client?" I sarcastically demanded.

"By showing, through Hugh, or at least raising some doubt, the unlikelihood that Jason ever possessed the know-how, patience, and psychological savvy to have pulled off such a brilliant stunt. Or maybe even getting honest Hugh here to more sweepingly admit that there are still plenty of doubting psychologists around ready to swear on a stack of Bibles that nobody can *ever*, by hypnosis, persuade another person to do what Randall claims Jason made him do. In short, that Jason couldn't possibly have done it because nobody can."

This time I turned and appealed directly to Doctor Hugh himself. "How about it, Doc?" I demanded.

"Again I'd have to agree, Frederic," the old boy conceded, shrugging and rolling up his eyes. "After all, psychologists are still people and tend to share one thing in common with politicians and the rest of us—they rarely agree wholeheartedly about much of anything."

"And while I'm about it I'll also predict one more thing," my partner added, glancing over at our closed door as he conspiratorially lowered his voice.

"Let's have it," I said, wondering what was coming next.

"I further predict that brother Jason will not be seen back on these hallowed premises again today," he said. "In fact I'll bet each of you ten bucks he won't."

"I'll take it," I said, picturing all those siren-sounding cops out there zealously scouring the county to round him up.

"What he's really betting, Frederic," Doctor Hugh explained with a smile, "is that something dreadful has already happened or surely will happen to brother Jason. But it's still a good gamble, considering the magnitude of Jason's ego, so I'll take the bet if I can be sure to get a crack at him in cribbage later this evening."

"Sold," my partner said, slapping our glass-covered mahogany table with his open palm, and it was only later that I recalled how eerily soon after our bets were made that we heard a peremptory knock on our mahogany door.

"Come in," I said.

"Judge wants to see all you guys pronto in chambers real bad," the sheriff popped his head in our door and said, and then disappeared.

"They got Jason!" I all but shouted, rising and making a knee-jerk grab for my briefcases, thinking not of ten-dollar bets but of the floods of questions I wanted to pelt at Jason once I had him facing me on the witness stand.

"My experience has been that whenever recessing judges want to see us lawyers real bad," my partner murmured dryly, "chances are real good that something real bad has already happened."

We found the judge and the others seated around his mahogany table in chambers, the judge's glasses resting upside down on the table before him and the judge himself wearily massaging the corners of his eyes at the bridge of his nose with his thumb and forefinger. He was sitting untypically in his shirt sleeves—a rare informal view of His Honor, as he usually donned one or the other of his impressive array of woolen jackets the moment he removed his robe. "Too damn hot out there wearing both," I'd often heard him say. Today his divested robe hung limply askew from a wire hanger on the wall behind him, though he usually carefully hung his things away in a narrow cubicle next to what he still called his "water closet." So it was increasingly plain that whatever His Honor wanted to see us about "real bad" must indeed be mighty pressing.

"Fellas," the sheriff said, hooking a thumb at the two city police officers sitting on the judge's right, "this is Officer Hartvigh and Officer Libby." Then to His Honor: "Looks like we're all here, Judge."

"Jason Spurrier is dead," the judge began at once in a low, recitative voice. "His body was recovered within the hour by these two city police officers from the harbor below," he continued, and I followed his glance out the window, down to the old, ore-stained loading dock stretching far out into the harbor. "The investigation and autopsy both proceed but it already seems apparent that he either fell or jumped from the old condemned dock itself. So far no known eyewitnesses have been found. A passing motorist saw a large object falling from the dock and notified the police but neglected to leave his name."

The judge leaned forward and poured and took a sip of the sheriff's water, again glancing out the window. I wondered whether he felt some sense of guilt for Jason's death for, after all, it had been he who'd earlier sent the officers out looking for him. Meanwhile my solemn-faced law partner quickly opened and closed both fists, flashing ten fingers twice, ever so subtly signaling Doctor Hugh and me of his latest betting triumph.

"Well, there you have it, men," the judge said, shrugging and putting his glasses back on. "Jason is dead, a champing jury awaits us out there, and we face at least two problems: What does all this do to our case, and where do we go from here? Any ideas?"

"What are some of the possibilities, Judge?" the prosecutor asked, shaking his head. "Never in my professional life have I faced anything like this."

"Nor I," I said. "Not even on television."

"That makes three of us," the judge said with a grim smile. "One obvious possibility would be to stop the trial and throw the case out," he continued. "That route might be more feasible if only Jason Spurrier had confessed his guilt and admitted his suicide—that's if he *was* guilty and *did* take his own life." The judge took a breath that sounded more like a sigh. "Instead he has left both questions shrouded in ambiguity and doubt." He sighed again. "But the more I think of it and of whatever part Jason may have played in this case, the more I think any such action by us would only raise more questions than it resolves. So it's my view that we forge ahead."

"Sort of like the trail of doubt left behind when too many of our Tom, Dick, and Gary politicians continue to whitewash their erring brethren before the whole blooming story comes out," my partner put in.

"Well spoken, Jeremiah," the judge said, once again blinking out at the lake and lowering his voice so he seemed to be musing aloud to himself. "Every criminal trial is—or should be—as much an exercise in public therapy and conscience-cleansing as anything, once again proving both to ourselves and to the whole world that we still have the guts to wash our dirty linen in public. Alas, it doesn't happen everywhere."

"Bravo, Judge," my partner again put in, off on another wave of declamation. "Might call every courtroom in the land a sort of public laundromat. Many places, any guy accused of crime is deemed convicted before he even warms up the witness chair; places where the winning politicians either hang or shoot their rivals, you takes your choice, or else clap them in the clink. As Sir Winston once removed his cigar and said, 'Democracy is the worst form of government ever invented—except all the others.' "

"Bravo to you, Jeremiah," the judge said, nodding soberly.

"By any chance are you suggesting, Judge," the prosecutor inquired, staring intently through his glasses, "that maybe the People should throw in the sponge?"

"Not even faintly, son, as I thought I'd just made clear. What I'm trying to say is that the longer I wear yonder black nightshirt the more I'm coming to think that a prosecutor's main job in every criminal case is to explore and expose and show the world what really happened, not merely to win, and that any other course not only weakens his chances of doing the latter but reduces his role to that of a bickering, adversary, civil litigant bent only on victory."

"Bravo, bravo," my partner repeated. "Should have fetched

my tape recorder—if only I owned one and knew how to run it—to make a recording of that pearl, to be played every morning in every cotton-pickin' court and law school across the land."

"I could call in the court reporter, Jeremiah," the judge suggested with a smile. "I might add that one further reason for going ahead with our case is that the defendant may by now have richly earned his chance at winning public vindication, if he can."

"Judge," I hastily put in, glancing at my watch, aware that the trial was going ahead, whatever I said or did, "I hate to interrupt but I think I should remind you that we're already running seven minutes late."

The strategy worked; the judge rapped his knuckles on his table in lieu of a gavel, abruptly arose, moved over and grabbed his black gown off the wall and began wrestling himself into it as he talked.

"I say we should all go back out there and continue to wash this latest batch of dirty linen," he ran on, "win, lose, or draw, no holds barred, and—let's see, seems I need another cliché—"

"How about letting the chips fall where they may?" I said. "And also, how about my getting Jason's old law book into evidence?" I looked at the prosecutor. "Will you agree, Eugene, or do we launch a new wrangle?"

"I'd like to hear the judge's views," my opponent said.

"I'd offhand say it should go in," the judge said, still having trouble finding the arms of his flouncing gown. "Look, there's been a violent homicide committed in this county and everybody knows it. Only question left is whether it's murder, who did it, and whether *this* particular defendant deserves to be punished for his admitted part in it. The questions are easy but the answers are mighty subtle and complicated, and add up to far more than a simple question of guilt or innocence. Our job is to go out there and not only wash our dirty linen but hang it all out on public display. . . . Damn, aren't there *any* sleeves in this bloody gown?"

"Let me give you a hand, Judge," the sheriff said, quickly moving over and grabbing the gown and flouncing it up and down like a matador twitting a bull—or maybe more like a janitor shaking out a rug—until, presto, victory was achieved. "There," the sheriff said, smoothing down the still billowing tails.

"Thanks, Sheriff," the judge said, striding purposefully over to his door and turning and facing us. "Thought occurs, we could save lots of time and wrangling if both sides agreed now to admit any possibly disputable items of evidence. Just a little suggestion, is all."

Both my opponent and I nodded as our hard-driving judge made still another small suggestion. "I also see a chance to end this case today—that's if you two harbor no ideological reservations about working overtime. Are you game?"

"My wife has a dinner meeting tonight, so I'm game," my opponent promptly answered, sensing, as did I, that the judge's question was less an inquiry than an edict.

"And *you?*" the judge challenged, turning to me.

"Me, too," I hastily answered. "I did have a date earlier but it seems she's come down with the Russian flu."

"Doubtless a communist plot," His Honor said, giving his gown a final flounce and resolutely turning away, then once again turning and facing us, reflectively rubbing his gleaming bald head as he spoke. "On second thought I think I'll join you out there shortly," he said with a sheepish smile. "Seems I've first got to go adjust my toupee."

Chapter 32

My opponent and I both got the judge's message, and on the way back to court quickly agreed to let Jason's old law book into evidence without further wrangle or fanfare. I wanted it in since it not only confirmed Jason's long interest in hypnosis but, containing as it did that old, underlined California murder case, lent added force to the argument that it could indeed have been his main source of inspiration. I guessed the prosecutor wanted it in so that he in turn could argue that my client had earlier found and read the same source of inspiration.

We also agreed to let in a copy of Jason's will, as both of us also saw that it would be difficult for the jury to be told of Jason's death without informing it of all the circumstances surrounding it. But above all, by then both of us were so weary from courtroom battle fatigue that we no longer coveted arming ourselves with any small tactical courtroom victories that might only mean winning the dubious right of trying the whole case over again, a prospect so chilling that it probably hastened our agreement.

Once back in the courtroom, I found the spectators and waiting jurors so expectantly hushed and tense that I wondered whether the word on Jason's death had already gotten out. My partner and Doctor Hugh were already seated at my table, breaking the news to my client, who sat listening in stoic silence. Meanwhile I finally spotted and appropriated a lone unoccupied mahogany chair in the section reserved for visiting brother lawyers, and joined our crowded table.

"Partner," I said, as much to ease the tension as anything, "are you sick or do you really plan to waste the rest of the afternoon slumming here in the courtroom?"

"Wouldn't miss it for a barrel of baboons," he came back, hudging his chair closer.

"I believe the correct idiom is barrel of monkeys," I said.

"Baboons," he said.

"Monkeys," I said.

"Betcha," he said, "once we settle any other small, outstanding bets we have."

"Baboons," I conceded, reaching for my wallet.

I'd barely paid him off when the judge swept in and mounted the bench and, after quickly reconvening court, turned and nodded at the sheriff. The latter lurched to his feet, peering down at what appeared to be a printed form he'd evidently lacked the time or fortitude to learn by heart. Squinting as he read, he delivered himself as follows: "His Honor is about to make an announcement to the jury and has asked me to warn all present that any untoward demonstration or disturbance during or following his announcement could result in an immediate clearing of the courtroom of all spectators, including the expulsion and possible further disciplining of any and all guilty parties."

"I've always interpreted that particular courtroom chant as fair warning to the multitude that goes as follows," my partner leaned and whispered: " 'Cut out the yackin', folks, lest thee be tossed out upon thy can.' "

"Hope it works," I answered.

The judge leaned forward in his chair, his hands folded and resting together before him on the bench, and spoke to the jury in a low voice. "Jason Spurrier is dead," he said, and the sharp, communal intake of breath I heard sounded for all the world like the sudden blowing of a startled deer. "His body was recovered by the city police within the hour from the waters of Lake

Superior in the harbor below this courthouse, floating near the old condemned ore dock, from which it appears he may either have jumped or fallen," the judge went on. "Further details will become available and be passed on to you as the investigation and this trial continue. We shall now get on with the latter."

That was all: The enigmatic Jason had met his death and his body recovered and the trial ordered to proceed all in four staccato sentences. I felt vaguely disappointed and let down; surely the occasion demanded at least one rolling and reverberant farewell Latin phrase. Aside from the occasional murmur and cheep of sibilants escaping from a few whispering spectators—sounding oddly like hesitant crickets on a cool summer evening—the courtroom seemed to grow even more hushed than before the judge had spoken.

"Mr. Prosecutor," I heard the judge saying to my opponent, "are you now ready to proceed with your delayed cross-examination of the defendant, Randall Kirk?"

My partner gave me a quick glance as my opponent arose to reply. "Your Honor," he said, looking up from a pad of notes, "I had rather planned and prepared to examine Dr. Salter next, if it's all the same."

"It's no longer the same because the main reason for allowing any earlier delay has now been resolved," the judge went on, plainly referring to the death of Jason Spurrier. "Therefore I'd prefer that you now proceed with your postponed examination of the defendant while his morning's testimony remains fresh in the jury's mind." The judge paused, and I wondered if he shared my partner's intuition that a *smart* prosecutor might now better turn his big guns on Doctor Hugh himself. "Or do the People wish to waive any cross-examination of the defendant?"

"One moment, Your Honor," the prosecutor said, shuffling the papers on his table and finally finding and poring over another pad of notes.

"Betcha five he'll waive," my partner leaned and whispered.

"No thank you," I whispered back, grown a little wary of *his* intuitions.

"The People will waive cross-examination of the defendant," the prosecutor looked up and said.

"Very well," said the judge, looking down at me. "When we recessed, Dr. Salter was on the stand and I now ask the defense whether it has any further questions to ask of him?"

I *had* planned on asking Doctor Hugh some further questions and still had a pad of unasked ones. But there still remained a chance of ending this trial today, I saw; and after all, wasn't it now only fair to give my opponent his chance to pry and probe? And wasn't there always the slim chance that he might even now be dabbling with the motion of tossing in the sponge?

"No further questions now, Your Honor," I said.

"Does the prosecution wish to examine Dr. Salter?" the judge pressed.

"It does indeed, Your Honor," my opponent said, rifling his files for still another batch of notes while an unshaven Doctor Hugh slowly made his way back to the witness stand to face the rhetorical bombardment my partner had predicted.

"Let's first get any lingering exhibits or whatever into evidence before we proceed," the judge said.

So before old Doctor Hugh had a decent chance to recross his legs a certified copy of Jason's will along with his old law book were offered and admitted into evidence without objection.

"Doctor," my opponent began briskly, rising and approaching the witness, holding his note pad out before like a collection tray, "please tell us, if you can, why such an intelligent person as Jason Spurrier would, if he were guilty, as the defendant has charged, have left behind that old law book touching on hypnosis and especially referring to an old California murder case suggesting the very defense being offered here—namely, that the defendant had been hypnotized by another into committing an act of murder?"

"You may now expunge," my partner leaned and whispered, "any dream that the People are throwing in the sponge."

"Dream duly expunged," I whispered back.

"Before I try to answer that question, young man," Doctor Hugh said after a pause, "may I remind you that the same California case also raises the possibility that such a feat may be accomplished in the first place—that is, that one person, while in a state of hypnosis imposed by another, might ever be persuaded to harm a third."

"What are you driving at, Doctor?"

"That it might also have suggested the possibility to Jason Spurrier himself."

"But you still haven't answered my question, Doctor. Why would a guilty man ever keep such a volume on his open shelves? Especially along with dozens of other volumes on the same subject?"

"I don't really know but I have some ideas."

"Please share them with us, Doctor."

"Maybe he clean forgot about his books. Or simply wanted to keep them. Or maybe he lacked an adequate chance to destroy or move them elsewhere. Or maybe he concluded, after his abrupt exposure and flight from court at eleven forty-seven today, that to try to do anything about them now would be tantamount to admitting his guilt."

"Doctor, I'm curious. How could you possibly remember the exact time of Jason Spurrier's—ah—departure this forenoon?"

"Because at the time I wrote it down in my notebook."

"But why did you?"

"I don't really know," the witness replied with a smile. "Perhaps largely to prove to myself that despite the larger languors of seniority I'm still capable of a few small efficiencies." He stole a glance at the judge. "And, since we're only young twice, perhaps also to prove that I'm still in the prime of my second childhood."

"Thank you, Doctor, and now that we've got all that clarified, do you think Jason Spurrier forgot his books or simply wanted to keep them or lacked the time to remove or destroy them, or that maybe he concluded that to do anything about them at all might only add to his posture of guilt?" the prosecutor asked as I sat up, sensing an attempt to confuse the weary witness and lure him down a blind alley of speculation and hairsplitting.

"I have no way of knowing, young man," the witness answered and I relaxed in my chair. "And while one or more of these things might have been factors, I'd guess that the one big reason he did nothing about his books was prompted largely by his ego."

"Ego, Doctor?"

"Ego, son. The same lardy brand of ego that keeps so many politicians and assorted bribe shovers and takers tumbling out of office, and occasionally their office windows, still writhing and entangled in their own guilty records and tapes—and now, it seems, even embalmed in sound films. The kind of ego that seems invariably to include a corrosive scorn of the capacities of others ever to outwit them. The kind of disdainful ego that so often ignores all mistakes and warning signs and scoffs at the idea of ever being caught—that is, until it's too late. In short, the kind of ego possessed, I'm afraid, by the late Jason Spurrier."

"Doctor," the prosecutor pushed, "so far your answers have assumed the guilt of Jason Spurrier. Hasn't the thought ever occurred to you that Randall Kirk himself could have dreamed up his entire defense?"

"The thought has occurred, yes," the witness answered as I held my breath.

"And isn't it possible that he did exactly that?"

"Possible, yes, but rather unlikely."

"Why?"

"Because the pieces don't quite fit."

"What do you mean?"

"Because if Randall *is* guilty—as your question assumes—then he's been lying to everybody—the police, his lawyers, this old country doctor, today to this jury, under oath. All I'm suggesting, young man, is that both his story and actions more nearly add up to a pattern of truth."

"Truth, Doctor?"

"Truth," Doctor Hugh repeated. "Because truth, like a suit of armor, stubbornly resists all attempts to penetrate it while the lie, under probing, almost invariably reveals some chinks and cracks. Surely you lawyers, who invented cross-examination, know all about that."

"Please, Doctor, spare the platitudes and just give us one reason why you think the defendant could not himself have made up the story he's told?"

"I'll give you several the minute I find the place in my

notebook," he said, fumbling in his coat for it and riffling its pages. "Ah, here they are. . . . Since I've just said that only the truth can resist probing, I've reduced my points to questions, if that's agreeable."

"On with the questions, *please.*"

"All right," the witness said, clearing his throat and frequently consulting his notebook as he spoke. "First, why did a guilty Randall ever leave any note on the island, especially one in his own handwriting, signed by him and bearing his fingerprints, and one that your own witness here earlier called his confession? And why did he leave the note pad it was written on in his home, confirming beyond any doubt that he'd written it? Why did he invent the sound of a little bell that so suddenly quit ringing just before his jail visitors were stopped? Why did he fake any loss of memory and then prolong it so far that its recovery would come almost too late? And why did he fire his own lawyer on the very eve he knew he had to tell the jury what you call his made-up story?" He looked up. "Those're only some of the highlights," he said, closing the notebook.

"Any more, Doctor?" the prosecutor asked with sarcastically feigned patience.

"Several, sir, including the interesting question of why, if the prosecutor honestly believes Randall is faking his defense, he didn't months ago grant Randall's repeated requests for a lie-detector test on his claimed loss of memory."

"I'm asking the questions, Doctor," the suddenly flushed prosecutor said. "But you do still admit that it's possible for the defendant to have made up his defense here?"

"Possible but unlikely."

"I think we'll take a five-minute recess here," the judge said, reflectively rubbing his bald head.

Chapter 33

"Doctor," Eugene Canda, now carrying a yellow pad of notes, began when our recess was over, "earlier you've testified here that quite a few respected psychologists and others flatly deny that any person can, by hypnosis, ever make another do what the defendant claims Jason Spurrier made him do. Will you now please tell us what reasons, if any, they give for taking this view?"

"The grand strategy has now shifted," my partner whispered, "from trying to show Jason didn't do it to showing he couldn't have done it if he'd tried."

"A nice question, son, and I'm glad you brought it up," Doctor Hugh began, blinking thoughtfully. "One of the main reasons most of these dissenters give—dissenters from Paul Young's view, I mean—is that no matter how clever the operator or deep the subject's state of hypnosis, the latter still retains a basic sense of decency and moral values and would simply be outraged and repelled into wakefulness by any suggestion that he commit an abhorent criminal act. All the more so, many add, if the suggested act involves violence against one near and dear to him—akin to the Mother's Day example I gave earlier."

"And what if the hypnotized subject nevertheless follows

orders," the prosecutor said, "what view do these dissenters then incline to take?"

"Generally that the subject is either a latent criminal type waiting to be unlocked or that all along he secretly wanted to do what he was ordered to do—motivated by jealousy or hate or covetousness or any other of the old biblical reliables. In short, when the hypnotist is successful, many say, he has merely uncovered and activated what was there all along."

"Like maybe the subject had been nursing a long-smoldering grudge, say, against a woman who'd twice rejected him for other men, along with a lurking, vengeful rancor against his latest successful rival?" the prosecutor softly asked.

"Many such dissenters might take that view, yes," Doctor Hugh said after a pause.

"Something possibly akin, say, Doctor," the prosecutor went on in a gently rising tone of voice, "to the real reason why Randall Kirk so swiftly fired his lawyer last night and yet so conveniently let you go ahead and recover his memory?"

"You make a point, son," Doctor Hugh conceded with a smile. "Something like that, yes."

As the prosecutor shot a quick look at the jury and consulted his notes I heard my partner whispering, "Lad's finally scoring on honest Hugh," and I nodded a grim assent.

"Doctor," the prosecutor continued, moving closer to the witness, "might not these same dissenters also take the view that any subject who admits to a lifelong penchant for mythological sirens and assorted watery creatures might be all the more ready to both ease his conscience and cloak his rancor against such a spurning woman by turning her into an unhappy siren who needed subduing?"

The question was loaded, cutting to the heart of our case, and I held my breath, awaiting the answer by Doctor Hugh, who sat staring sightlessly out across the courtroom.

"Did you hear the question, Doctor?" the prosecutor inquired, using an old courtroom ploy aimed at showing the jury how baffled and stumped the hesitant witness was by the sheer, unanswerable brilliance of the lawyer's question.

"Yes, I heard you, young man, and I guess the answer is yes, some dissenters might indeed take the view you speak of." A faint smile crossed his face. "While other more thoughtful dissenters, however set in their views, might well begin to wonder whether a clever operator mightn't have seized upon that very penchant to gain his own way, just as they might also wonder why such a guilt-laden subject would have consciously left behind a note so unmistakably linking himself with what took place."

"Doctor," the prosecutor pushed on as I again began to breathe easier, "turning now to—"

"I hadn't quite finished," the witness continued, "for it also seems to me that your recent questions imply a rather dramatic shift in the prosecution's position in this case."

"What *are* you driving at, Doctor?" the prosecutor said, casting an amused glance at the jury.

"One minute the prosecution seems to be claiming that Randall fabricated his whole story here, a proposition I've earlier conceded is possible and which is at least arguable."

"Yes?"

"Then in the next breath it not only seems to be at last conceding the existence of hypnosis—for which I congratulate it—but also implying that, while Jason may have attempted to hypnotize Randall, all he really succeeded in doing was unlocking a latent desire in Randall to do what he wanted to do all along—thus making them sort of uneasy fellow conspirators, as it were. Seems to me you can't have it both ways, son, can't you see?"

"I'm asking the questions here," the flushed prosecutor repeated, now almost shouting, stung by Doctor Hugh's answer. "And I'm sure the jury will see that the prosecution is not switching anything, but only buttressing its basic claim here by showing how and why so many of the world's top psychologists would in turn scoff at the defendant's phony story."

"Objection!" I arose and thundered. "Prosecution attempting to turn cross-examination into a premature jury argument."

"Gentlemen, gentlemen," the judge spoke soothingly from the bench. "Time's a-flying so suppose we move on to something else."

"Doctor," the flushed prosecutor pushed on after again consulting his notes, "you have already testified here at length, citing your folk hero Paul Young and others, how brilliantly Jason Spurrier succeeded. Will you now please try to explain, if you can, how such a brilliant performer came finally to fail?"

"See-saw, Margery Daw," I heard my partner whispering.

"Another good question, young man, and one that continues to puzzle me," Doctor Hugh said, nodding agreement. "But first I think we must define what you mean by failure, for if Randall is telling the truth here, Jason succeeded all too brilliantly, failing only in ultimately covering his tracks."

"But that's my very question, Doctor, for how could Jason possibly have succeeded in his main purpose if he couldn't block a retired country doctor, say, from now sitting up there calmly claiming to be showing up this brilliant operator?"

"Once again we're in the realm of speculation, young man, but since Jason is no longer around to explain it himself, I'll gladly give you my own views. First and foremost, the very arrogance and self-centered brilliance that made Jason scorn the conventional psychological wisdom that such a thing couldn't ever be done also appears to have made him scorn the petty, boring details that ultimately proved his undoing." The witness paused, blinking thoughtfully. "In a way Jason was like the popular picture of the deep thinker who, however brilliant, absentmindedly shuffled around in his carpet slippers and unzippered trousers, or like the daring gambler who breaks the bank at the main casino and then on the way out pauses to play the tourist slot machines and loses everything."

"Please, Doctor, let's forget deep thinkers and slot machines and try to explain how, if this scenario could ever have been enacted, as you claim, such a brilliant operator could possibly have failed in any important aspect of it—unless this whole fantastic defense story has been made up?"

"Very well," Doctor Hugh said, after a quick look at his trusty notebook. "First, it is not I who claim such a thing happened, as you've just said; the defendant did today, from this very witness stand, under oath, a story still undenied by the only other person who might have. All I claim is that psychologically it could have happened."

"*Please,* Doctor, on with the details."

"I've touched on some already, so I'll be brief," the witness began, holding his notebook out before him and continuing as though he were ticking off a shopping list. "First, the inadequately erased initial ring of the telephone on the fatal night, though the fact and import of the call itself were successfully erased; second, the abrupt erasure of its lingering ring following our summer courtroom session, coupled with the revealing violence of Randall's rejection of my earlier, lone attempts at hypnosis—here I'll skip a few—then yesterday's even more revealing emergency phone call by Jason, followed so swiftly by your opponent's firing; and above all, Jason's erroneous assumption that having Randall fire his lawyer would banish me, who had been appointed by the judge, when he should have concentrated everything on blocking me—just another irony added after everything he'd already accomplished."

"And what are some of these mysterious ironies, Doctor?" the prosecutor drilled away, evidently bent upon letting the witness talk himself into a trap.

"So many, son, I can only touch upon the more obvious ones. Having to live with a woman he didn't love and who, equally ironic, did not love the great Jason; having to pretend to be a pal and confidant—you heard him testify here—of the man he knew all along was busily cuckolding him and whom he must secretly have loathed."

"But why should he care about *that* if he didn't really care about his wife or she him, as you've just said?"

"Ego and pride, as I've been trying to say. Perhaps one of the biggest ironies is the note Jason persuaded Randall to write and leave behind on the island that fatal night. Damning and harmful as that note surely was and remains, perhaps everyone in this room is still wondering why Jason didn't make Randall come right out and flatly admit he'd killed Miss Connie."

"Suppose you enlighten us as to why?" the prosecutor continued in a sarcastic vein.

"Because that would be akin to the crude go-shoot-your-mother example I gave earlier and might well have ruined everything. It simply *had* to be ambiguous, as susceptible to being construed as a confession of guilt as to being a direction by a modest folk hero as to where he preferred to receive his hero's medal."

"But why any note at all, Doctor?" the prosecutor pressed. "Doesn't he still get rid of his wife without risking that?"

"True, but he was aiming for more. Without the note Randall might well have followed Jason's orders and safely returned to his cottage without anyone being the wiser, including Randall himself. But Jason not only wanted *that* from him but also to see him humiliated and punished for ever daring to wound the pride of the great Jason. That's why we're all here today, don't you see?"

"Quite frankly I don't," the prosecutor said. "But wouldn't Miss—ah—wouldn't Axholm's testimony have still taken care of all that without risking any note?"

"I repeat, her seeing and relating here what she saw that night was just a happy accident—I mean from Jason's point of view—a surprise dividend he never counted on."

"Are you suggesting that the note itself was a purposely ambiguous compromise to implicate Kirk and yet not risk scaring him off?"

"I am indeed. What else can one believe? In my view the note Jason persuaded Randall to write and leave at the scene is one of the fiendishly beautiful and subtle examples of his using the full hypnotic armamentarium that Paul Young spoke of. Ironically enough, he must have toiled over it for days."

"Why do you keep saying 'ironically,' Doctor?"

"Because, brilliant a stroke as that was and remains, almost alone compelling this long and exhausting and still uncertain public prosecution, the note still remains perhaps the most compelling single proof of Randall's innocence."

"Please tell us why, Doctor."

"Because of the screaming unlikelihood that any truly guilty person would have consciously left behind such damning proof of his own guilt."

I glanced over at the jury and thought I saw some of its members ever so faintly nodding. Meanwhile my opponent looked up from his notes and fired another question.

"Any more ironies, Doctor?" he inquired brightly, rather obviously determined to continue to draw out the witness and give him free rein in an effort to depict him as a fantasizing, biased, garrulous old man.

"Yes. Jason having to sit here and listen to a public exposure of his cuckoldom, Jason being exposed here today with the help of a retired country doctor, Jason being forced to flee this courtroom and file his precious wills before this trial was over, to name a few."

"Any lingering ironies, Doctor?"

"One minute, please," Doctor Hugh murmured, peering at his notebook and then removing and wiping his glasses, blinking mistily, again returning to his notebook and at the same time smiling faintly and murmuring, "Sorry, seems I didn't get too much sleep last night."

"Just one more irony, please," the waiting prosecutor begged, prayerfully clasping his hands together. "Surely there must be at least one more irony lurking in your notebook, mustn't there?" He glanced smilingly at the jury as he continued. "Or will you now concede that maybe poor defenseless Jason already has too many ironies in the fire?"

The courtroom tittered and Doctor Hugh managed a weary smile before he spoke. "There are indeed a few more ironies, yes, but I've just been thinking how sad it is that your 'poor defenseless Jason' isn't here to explain them himself. Most of them existed for quite a spell before his sudden death today."

"Are you now telling us he committed suicide, Doctor?" the prosecutor asked, gambling that the witness would take the bait and thus further expose his bias on a still baffling subject that none of us was prepared to prove.

"I don't know the answer to that any more than you do, young man, but since you raised the subject I must say that the climate for suicide was rather favorable."

"In what way?"

"Ironically enough, your poor defenseless Jason appeared here today to be possibly guilty of murder, forgery of a will, using undue influence, and contempt of court, not to mention possibly perjury by his earlier testimony."

"Ah, were you able to figure all this out either before or after you so magically recovered Kirk's memory last night, Doctor?"

"No, but my friend Jeremiah Dundee did today, including the idea that Jason may have also persuaded the deceased to change her will by hypnosis, which would be tantamount to forgery."

"My, my," the prosecutor pushed on, still bent on trying to reduce the doctor's testimony to an absurdity, "then please tell us why Jason wouldn't have thrown in the sponge long ago, hounded by all those baying ironies you've just unleashed?"

"Because of his invincible armor of ego of which I spoke earlier and will spare repeating. After all, only last night he still felt he had the upper hand—Randall had responded to his hypnosis and agreed to fire his lawyer and the trial was rapidly nearing its end."

"Until the great, infallible Dr. Salter suddenly appeared and, presto, made Jason's world crumble; is that what you're saying?"

"No, son, you just said it," the witness replied. "But I did help Randall recover his memory—which about then I think almost any competent operator might have managed. And then came this morning, perhaps the most humiliating irony of all, with Jason suddenly finding himself as exposed and helpless as a writhing beetle on its back. Ah, yes, son, your poor defenseless brilliant chameleon Jason reminds me of what Max Beerbohm once wrote about Beau Brummell. The Beau, he said, always 'looked life straight in the face out of the corners of his eyes.' "

"But Doctor, how come such a brilliant operator as Jason could perform all the dazzling things you say he did and then so suddenly and miserably fail, entangled in all those ironies?"

"*Randall* said," Doctor Hugh again corrected the prosecutor, pausing to blink reflectively before he continued. "First of all I'm not too sure he has failed, for not only did he rid himself of a woman he didn't want, but here we are still engaged in this public prosecution of the man he used to gain that end, the outcome of which still remains in doubt. Moreover his estate could still inherit most of Connie's money under her latest will—which apparently would now go to some lucky lady back in New York and to some lad with the fairly uncommon name of Jason, a most interesting coincidence."

"Ah, Doctor, so you're now also an expert on wills. May I be among the first to congratulate you?"

"Thanks, but my friend Jeremiah filled me in on that too, adding that Connie's latest will could also possibly be upset under the so-called New York rule holding that anyone who murders the maker of a will to hasten his own taking under it may instead be left holding the bag."

All this was probably objectionable but by now the prosecutor was gambling so heavily on cracking a key defense witness that he lowered his voice and quickly switched to a new subject.

"Doctor," he began quietly, "earlier here on direct examination I believe you admitted that it was you who asked the sheriff's deputy to look for a certain law book in Jason's private library, did you not?"

" 'Admitted' is a loaded word, young man, as I suspect you well know, but yes, I did testify here that I asked the young deputy to look for it."

"But how did *you* know about it, Doctor?" the prosecutor suavely continued, "or that such a book might even be there?"

As I awaited Doctor Hugh's answer I glanced at my partner and shrugged, recalling his earlier "Honest Hugh" prediction.

"Randall had earlier told me that Jason had numerous books and periodicals about psychology and hypnosis on his shelves."

"Ah, so *Randall* told you," the prosecutor purred along. "And might they include *this* very book, Doctor?"

"He thought that was possible, yes."

"Some of which books Randall had already read or glanced over, Doctor?"

"That is correct."

"Including *this* very book, Doctor?"

"He thought that was also possible, yes."

My opponent arose and walked toward the witness, stopping halfway. "Doctor, let me once again ask you this final question," he said. "Is it still possible that the defendant, Randall Kirk, could have invented the entire story he has told here today?"

"It is still possible, son," Doctor Hugh replied steadily, "but once again I must say, quite improbable."

"Thank you, Doctor," my opponent said, making a slight

bow like an opposing boxer in midring, abruptly turning and marching back to his table. "Your Honor," he said, "the People have no further questions."

"No further questions of this witness," I dutifully popped up and said. "Also no further witnesses and the defense rests."

"No witnesses in rebuttal," Eugène Canda said. "The People rest."

The judge turned and spoke to the jury. "Before the jury arguments, we'll take a fifteen-minute recess while counsel and I meet in chambers to go over any requested jury instructions. All right, Mr. Sheriff."

"Last clear chance," my partner murmured as he quickly arose and headed for the nearest door, "for all good students of crime to go adjust their toupees."

Chapter 34

Under the curling rhetorical lash of the judge our session in chambers was short and soon over. First my opponent submitted seven requested jury instructions, handing me copies.

"Anything new, Eugene?" I asked, hefting my pile. "Or are you still seeking a return to the law of the nineteenth century?"

"Pretty much the same old pitch, Fritz," he conceded, shrugging. "Guess it's not up to a backwoods prosecutor to change the prevailing criminal law of Michigan and most of the rest of the country."

Both he and the judge visibly winced as I in turn dug into my pregnant briefcase and withdrew and plopped down *two* fat manila folders of typewritten requests on the latter's table, handing my opponent his copies.

"Are these requests for instructions," the judge asked, smiling, pointing at the mound before him, "or the galley proofs of still another two-volume analysis of why Henry James never wore the monocle he secretly carried?"

I giggled and snorted appreciatively, explaining that most of the requests bore on our theory of impaired consciousness, while the others were additionally inspired in the light of Kirk's testimony that very morning.

"But where did you ever find the time to draft 'em?" he asked, plucking gingerly at one of the typewritten sheets.

"I didn't," I confessed. "Blame it on my partner. Fact is I've barely had time to read some of 'em myself."

The judge shook his head as he swept his hand out over the stacks of unread requests. "Court rule ordains I must pass on all these before you men can argue to the jury, as you know. Big question is, how the hell I'm ever gonna? Could well take me hours just to skim all this stuff, let alone decently make up my mind. Might have demanded 'em earlier, I know, but again how the hell *could* I in a case where the defendant claims he only recovered his wits last night."

"What we gonna do?" my opponent inquired, sliding as I had into His Honor's relaxed idiom.

"One thing would be either to recess or else to outright adjourn court until I have a chance to read and meditate over these mounds. How does that strike you?"

"Right through the heart, Judge," I said, thinking of that fishing expedition I'd planned for the next day, now approaching a major obsession with me.

"Or the thought just occurs," the judge ran on with a gleam in his eye, "that I might flatly turn down the entire batch in one swoop, thus appeasing the rule and giving me additional time during your jury arguments to read and ponder and maybe even change my mind. How about *that?*"

"Yes!" both of his listeners chorused without consultation or rehearsal.

"That way, too, I might be spared overexposure to some of your more extravagant rhetorical flights," His Honor added with a smile, turning to the bored and nodding court reporter. "Malcolm, please take this down."

"The People's opening argument to the jury may now proceed," the judge said, nodding down at the prosecutor from the bench.

The People, being the complainant, had the privilege of both opening and closing the jury arguments, and if I'd earlier hung up some sort of courtroom record for the brevity of my earlier opening statement to the jury, at the midpoint of the trial, my opponent seemed determined either to tie or beat me at it in his own opening argument to the jury. As I listened to him quietly talking along in a subdued and preoccupied fashion quite foreign to him, he seemed not so much to be discussing our case as musing aloud to himself while exploring and redefining his role in this and all future criminal prosecutions.

As his argument went on, uncharacteristically delivered in a low voice and without notes, I felt more and more that in many ways he was making one of the most powerful arguments I'd ever heard him deliver. For not only was he skillfully removing both himself and his office from the conventional adversary role, which often reduced a public prosecutor to the partisan level of a covetous bill collector, but was at the same time by his very neutrality and detachment making the jury all the more aware of its own large responsibilities in the outcome.

"This case has in many ways been a rare education to me," he went on. "For one thing it has taught me that, whatever may be your verdict, my job is not necessarily to win this or any criminal case but rather to act as a kind of public ombudsman to help bring before you all the relevant evidence, both good and bad, whenever our laws and the public peace may have been shattered. That they have been violently shattered in this case is all too evident, alas, so I shall not dwell on the bleak and gruesome details."

He turned and glanced back at the courtroom clock to time himself, and instead of raising his voice to his usual dramatic crescendo he seemed to lower it still more. "My main job is almost done while yours has only begun," he said. "And what *is* your job, you may ask. As I see it, it is to weigh and carefully explore all this tangled mass of evidence and, guided by the instructions of the judge, honestly tell us whether you think what has happened here is or is not a punishable crime against the public peace of this commonwealth. It is both that simple and that awesomely complex. And what your decision should be is not for me to say or for my opponent to say or even for the judge here to say, but only for *you* to say. That this is still so is one of the greater glories of that old dream called democracy."

Again the quick glance back at the clock, like a nervous shopper keeping tab on a dying parking meter. "For it is you alone, ladies and gentlemen, who are the sole judges of guilt or innocence here," he pushed on, "just as you alone are this commonwealth's sole link to seeing to it that no innocent person shall unjustly be convicted and no guilty person unjustly let go. In that exploration, then, I wish you good judgment, stout courage, and much good luck, along with my grateful thanks." With that he turned and headed back to his table.

"When and if the lad runs for Congress he has my vote," my partner whispered. "I swear he's making noises like a budding statesman about to bloom."

"My vote, too, if he really means it," I whispered, wondering as I gathered up my various pads of notes how I might best respond to his oddly moving argument. I wondered, too, if it truly represented the "new" Eugene Canda or was instead a final maneuver by a crafty opponent seeking to lure me away from my own carefully planned argument.

"You're up, Mr. Ludlow," the judge said, jolting me out of my reverie.

"Here, partner," I whispered to my table mate, suddenly shoving all my various pads of scribbled notes in front of him, "save these for the next used-paper drive."

"Dance lightly and fast, pard," my partner whispered as I arose empty-handed and made my way up and stood facing the jury.

"Ladies and gentlemen," I began in an equally low voice, "during this trial—from the very first gun in fact—it cannot have escaped you that my scribbling opponent and I have been jotting down dozens and scores of notes to use as ammunition during this trial and at this final moment of truth. At least, most of mine were, and while I cannot surely speak for him I suspect most of his were too, else he'd turned to scribbling poetry on the taxpayer's time. In any case mercifully you will shortly be reprieved from having to listen to either of us."

I stole my first look at the clock to mark my own time. "So today you may be witnessing an event unique in legal history anywhere: two lawyers actually arguing to a jury without a single note between them—though I swear I've just abandoned at least a satchelful. In legal circles I'm told this is akin to public nudity, a form of indecent exposure which I hope will not shock you into a state of indecision."

Several jurors smiled and I decided that for me now to launch upon the full-dress discourse I'd planned might not only bore but irritate an already weary jury. Instead I resolved to do a little friendly leveling on my own.

First I complimented my opponent on his argument and especially on his redefinition of the proper role of a public prosecutor in a criminal case as being one to bring out all the relevant evidence of guilt or innocence, both good and bad. "I couldn't agree more," I ran on, "as the usual, traditional—or should I say televisional?—role of a prosecutor envisioned by the general public seems rather to be one of a finger-pointing public avenger seeking only to convict any poor devil who ever dares cross his path."

I turned and looked back at my seated opponent surrounded by his battery of books and briefcases and manila folders and assorted tumblers and water pitchers, speculatively cupping and rubbing my chin as I appraised him. "While I welcome and embrace my opponent's public conversion to what I've long felt to be the true role of all public prosecutors in all their cases," I pushed on, "at the risk of sounding ungrateful I must say that my one big regret is that he failed to see the light far earlier in this case."

I blinked up at the skylight. "For think of all the time we might have saved here had I not had to fight every inch of the way, first to dare try to recover my client's lapsed memory and then, once it was recovered, to find a way to allow him to tell you what it was he recalled. Think of all the booming objections and flushed hagglings we all might have been spared here had his conversion only come before some venturesome soul in this room had dared utter aloud the one verboten word in his vocabulary—*hypnosis*—which, it wryly turns out, now appears to be the key to our case."

Again there were some fugitive smiles as I bore down to end my argument. "Again I agree with my opponent—if I dare any longer call him that—that you have as grave a duty and responsibility to the public as you have to the defendant himself.

But once again I must point out that neither of us invented this old democratic dream of public trials, which was already quite ancient—if the memory of my early course in English common law serves me—when the first Elizabeth was a child."

I paused to gather my racing thoughts and once again pushed on, deciding not to review the facts that Doctor Hugh had already so brilliantly done from the witness stand. "Time flies, weariness mounts, so I too shall refrain from dwelling on what my opponent so accurately calls 'the bleak and gruesome details' of our case," I said. "Instead I shall take the liberty of suggesting a few questions I urge you to ask yourselves when shortly you retire to your room."

Lacking notes I glanced up at the skylight for inspiration and again faced the jury. "What do you think your verdict might be were Jason Spurrier rather than Randall Kirk on trial here for the murder of Constance Spurrier? Who, at all times, was the planner and moving spirit in this whole, strange tragedy? Who among you does not believe she would be alive today if fate had not crossed her path with that of Jason Spurrier?"

I paused and took a few steps closer to the jury. "What would you say if Jason Spurrier were himself on trial here today for shooting his wife and sought to defend himself by blaming it on the innocent bullet he had aimed and fired? And has not Randall Kirk, rendered unconscious and helpless by this man, played the role of the innocent bullet in this strange case? Or, to bring the figure somewhat closer to our facts, was it not the obsessed and driven Jason Spurrier himself who reached out from distant New York that fatal night and drowned poor doomed Connie, using a helpless Randall Kirk as an extension of his own arms?"

I walked back to my table and stood facing the jury. "Two short questions and I am done," I said. "One, does an innocent man arise and flee his sworn accuser and, after filing two wills, retreat to the top of a towering old ore dock and do whatever in God's name he finally did? Two, does it strike you that any kind of justice anywhere demands that, as guardians of the public weal, you must now retire to find an already tormented

Randall Kirk guilty of murder, thus allowing the fled Jason Spurrier to hurl one final bolt of evil on his way to the grave? I thank you."

Chapter 35

The judge, pressing hard, moved on at once to give his instructions to the jury; this following the waiver by my opponent of his closing argument to the jury—some heartening clue that his recent professed conversation was not all cosmetic.

Speaking often without notes, since he'd long ago learned by heart most of what he had to say, the judge interspersed his instructions with some of the basic ones heard by all juries in all major felony cases—reasonable doubt, presumption of innocence, burden of proof—expressions of the ancient dreams of justice and fair play that for centuries men had fought kings and conquerors and each other to achieve, quaint-sounding chants I'd heard so often they'd taken on the nostalgic ring of old nursery rhymes.

"A reasonable doubt," I heard him saying, "is a fair doubt growing out of all the evidence in the case. It is not an imaginary doubt plucked out of thin air, or a possible doubt, but one based on reason and common sense; such a doubt as shall leave you, after a careful review of all the evidence, unable to lean back and say to yourselves that you have an abiding conviction to a moral certainty of the truth of the charges against the defendant, as I shall presently explain them."

As the judge droned on I listened for some clue to whether any of our own requested instructions might be given, but still none came. Doctor Hugh and Jeremiah had retired to the front row of benches—aided by a bustling, space-clearing sheriff—and my opponent and I sat at our respective tables, he alone, I with my client, our work finally done, both trying to hide our weariness and concern by absently rearranging our swollen briefcases or taking another swig of the sheriff's tepid water or occasionally appearing to be scrawling some by now obviously useless notes. One of mine instead emerged as a drawing of a primitive trout leaping up out of the water with all of the rigid grace of an arthritic porpoise.

"The People, in the information filed in this case, have charged the defendant with murder in the first degree," the judge went on. "That charge may be defined as one where a person of sound mind and memory and discretion willfully and intentionally kills another human being with malice aforethought," and he then further expanded on the meaning of these terms.

"In defense of the charge against him the defendant claims that at the time of the offense he was in a state of unconsciousness due in turn to a state of hallucination induced by his involuntary hypnosis at the hands of another," the judge went on. These words made me suddenly sit up, for I now knew I would soon learn whether he was going to accept or reject our novel theory of defense—novel in Michigan, that is.

He paused and glanced out at the clock and then reached for another batch of papers and placed them on a small stand we courtroom regulars knew he used during his instructions to avoid having to squint forward too obviously when he had to read. At this signal I grabbed for our own copies of our requested instructions to check whether His Honor was going to reject or keep alive any real chance of winning this case.

"This is a defense that is recognized under our law," he went on, proceeding to quote one of our major requests word for word, "for one of the important incidents of legal responsibility for crime in our society is that the defendant shall have his wits about him, that is, be aware of and intend to do what he is doing. Therefore I charge you that if you should find that the defendant, through no fault of his own, was unconscious at the time of the fatal encounter, as I shall presently further define that term, or if a reasonable doubt remains in your minds on that score, then, in either case, you should acquit him on the grounds of unconsciousness."

The judge deftly moistened a finger and flipped our first instruction aside and moved on to still another, while I sat in a state of suspended bliss listening to him, in a droning voice, read all of our requests, foggily noting he'd even improved on a few. When finally I heard him paraphrasing the provisions of the Model Penal Code on the subject of impaired consciousness, adding its specific proviso that crimes induced by hypnotic suggestion also came under its umbrella, I could not resist stealing a look back at my partner and Doctor Hugh, who both nodded and returned my smiling nod.

The judge looked up from his reading and spoke directly to the jury. "When you consider and weigh the defendant's story," he said, "I should also charge you that it has not been denied or rebutted here by any probative evidence at this trial that you are at liberty to consider." This was an obvious, if oblique, reference to Jason Spurrier's shouted courtroom denial of my client's testimony that forenoon, an instruction we had not, in the rush of events, even to think of, much less ask for.

The judge then proceeded to charge the jury from memory on some routinely necessary legal odds and ends and then pushed back his chair and heaved a prolonged sigh, a familiar warning to us courtroom regulars that he was heading into the homestretch. "Your first job when you get to your room will be to elect one of your number foreman," he said faintly smiling. "Since that event will pretty well coincide with your supper hour I trust you will not unduly prolong your campaigns for that office. Your foreman will announce your verdict." He glanced down at the waiting Clovis, already poised to croak again. "Swear an officer," he said.

Clovis popped up in his cubicle like a toy released from a box and faced the advancing jury matron to administer still another oath in words that were doubtless antiquated in the days of Sir Thomas Malory. "You do solemnly swear," he croaked in his French Canadian accent, his flypaper memory still disdaining all notes, "that you will, to the utmost of your ability, keep the persons sworn as jurors in this trial in some private and convenient place, without meat or drink, except water, unless ordered by the court; that you will suffer no communications, oral or otherwise, to be made to them; that you will not communicate with them yourself, orally or otherwise, unless ordered by the court; and that you will not, until they have rendered their verdict, communicate the state of their deliberations or the verdict they may have agreed upon, so 'elp you God."

"I do," the lady devoutly murmured and I stole a look at Doctor Hugh, who caught my glance and wagged his head and rolled his eyes that such an archaic chant could survive into our day—"Sounded more like a curse of eternal banishment," he told me moments later—while the jury matron, all aglow from her brief period in the sun, turned and solemnly beckoned the jurors to follow her out to their room.

When the last marching juror had filed out of sight, waves of fatigue suddenly swept over me and I fought an impulse to flop forward on my table with my head on my arms and fall asleep like any sensible barroom drunk. For trial fatigue was unlike any other, I'd early learned. It seemed to scale the very peaks of exhaustion, mental, physical and emotional. It was more than a matter of being always on one's toes, framing and hurling endless questions and objections, or resisting them, vital as these could be; there was also the business of chasing down and interviewing witnesses, taking statements, preparing subpoenas, looking up the law, and always the intriguing gamble of choosing a jury. In short, an unending procession of lightning guesses and spur-of-the-moment decisions that might at any moment make or break one's case; this accompanied by the steady pressure of forever trying to wed the chameleon facts of one's case to a body of law that one might, with luck, persuade a puzzled or skeptical judge and jury to adopt. One thing was sure: Trial fatigue made an all-day wade up a slippery trout stream seem but a casual summer stroll.

My partner predictably phrased the thing more colorfully. "A lawyer trying a tough case," he one day typically delivered himself, "is like an overworked juggler, tossing not balls and bottles in the air but whole whirling avalanches of questions, objections, citations, annotations, witnesses, jurors, mistresses, perjurers—as, hell—the poor bastard's busier than a hockey goalie with two of his pals in the penalty box. Alas, his poopti-tood knows no bounds."

A weary Doctor Hugh had already disappeared; an armed deputy had marched in and escorted my client back to his cell for what I groggily hoped was his last supper—there, I mean—and as I looked around for my partner in the thinning crowd he appeared out of nowhere and stood patting me on the shoulder —"dam nice jury argument, lad"—and then, hooking his thumb over his shoulder, virtually ordered me to join him and Doctor Hugh in our private conference room.

"C'mon, c'mon," he said, shaking me, "before you fall off your chair. Might look bad for the firm. Anyway I gotta little surprise for you."

"Could you please give a pooped pal a hand with these?" I said, plucking at one of my swollen briefcases. "Don't think I'm up to all of them right now."

The promised surprise was to find a darkened conference room with all the ancient wooden window shutters lowered and two canvas cots set up and a fully dressed Doctor Hugh already gently snoring away on one of them.

"Remembered them from the days when busy or blizzard-bound jurors used to bunk overnight in the courthouse instead of trekking out to a motel or way up to the old Northland Hotel, so had a couple fetched up from the basement," my partner explained, pointing. "Now crawl in that spare one, dammitt, or you won't feel up to fishin' tomorrow."

"But suppose the jury comes out early?" I feebly fought back.

"No way before it enjoys one final free meal on the county," he predicted. "Wanna make a friendly little bet? Anyway I'll keep the vigil. Now go lay down, dammitt."

"Maybe I will take just a little catnap," I murmured gratefully, flopping on the spare cot. I fatalistically mused that if the added tension of keeping a jury vigil of indeterminate length did little to ease my fatigue, at least what that body now did with our case was finally out of my hands. "Thanks, pard," I murmured.

Only once during the long jury vigil did I half wake up and lie there sleepily blinking across at, of all things, Doctor Hugh and my partner sitting at a corner of our conference table under a single light bulb, once again playing cribbage. During a lull I heard my partner ask Doctor Hugh in a low voice if Randall had been right when he'd earlier guessed that the doctor hadn't really tried to hypnotize him that first time in jail.

"Dead right," I heard Doctor Hugh answering, "but probably for the wrong reasons."

"Why then?"

"Because I was afraid I might succeed."

"But why afraid? Wouldn't it have saved lots of time and worry all around?" my partner asked.

"Sure would have, but when earlier on that same occasion Randall had told me he'd forgotten about the ringing of the little bell it suddenly swept over me that almost surely there had to be a rival hypnotist in the picture. Seemed a clear case of induced amnesia."

"You mean that was when you first suspected Jason?"

"Jason was then only one possible candidate."

"But why did you make a phony stab at hypnosis anyway?"

"So that any possible rival might not himself smell a rat if I failed to try. That and also to help him think that my own initial failure might remove me as any real threat to Randall's memory remaining lapsed."

"You mean you were afraid that Jason or whoever might have harmed Randall if you'd really tried and made it that first time?"

"Exactly, for if I *had* succeeded, the jig would have been up, Jason would have known it, and there mightn't have been any client left to defend. Which was one of the big reasons I asked Gary what's-his-name and the state policeman—without explaining—to sit a row behind Jason earlier today, don't you see?"

"Hm . . . I'm afraid I do. But how come you didn't clue me and my partner long ago about your rival-hypnotist hunch? Or did you feel you couldn't trust your old lawyer pals?"

"Never that, Jeremiah, but I figured you two had quite enough on your minds without *that*—especially if my hunch proved wrong."

"Modesty will get you nowhere, Hugh. . . . Who's turn to deal the cards?"

"Mine," I heard Doctor Hugh answer. "Maybe I was also afraid it might upset your cribbage game."

"Or shock me into playing a better game, you mean. . . . Why don't you deal the bloody cards? Or are you staging a goddam filibuster till the jury comes out?"

"Wake up, Frederic," I heard someone saying. "Wake up, wake up, lad, the jury's on its way out."

"Oh, it's you, Doc," I mumbled, sitting up. "Musta taken more than a little nap. What time is it?"

"Time to get moving, son. We'll see you out in court. Jeremiah's already there holding the fort. Better straighten your tie —it's got that hangover look."

"Thanks, Doc," I murmured, groggily sitting up on my creaking cot like an awakened drunk teetering on his bar stool. "Be out in a minute."

My client was already at our table when I joined him, looking like a man about to face a firing squad. The half-empty courtroom had grown as still as a midnight bus station, bathed in the wavering copper glow from the old serpent-headed brass chandeliers that the local historical society had rescued from the neon-lit march of progress. A myriad tiny feebly-lit light bulbs also encircled the courtroom skylight, lending the scene the unlikely air of a gala Christmas party.

The judge nodded; the sheriff arose and left; the jury door breathed open and the twelve tired jurors, led by the matron, filed into the silent courtroom like badly rehearsed mourners, forming a straggly half-circle between the judge's bench and our counsel tables.

"Mr. Clerk," the judge said.

Clovis arose and faced the jurors for his final big scene, his croaking voice seeming to echo back upon itself in the half-deserted chamber like the strum-plucked noises frogs sometimes made on certain ponds I fished.

"Membair of the jury," he rasped, "have you agreed upon a verdict and if so, who will speak for you?"

"We have," a lady juror said, taking a rehearsed step forward. "I am the forewoman." Small victory, I thought; at least she didn't say foreperson.

"What is your verdict?"

"We find the defendant not guilty by reason of unconsciousness," she announced in a firm voice.

A gasping communal sigh was quickly quelled by the judge's upraised gavel as Clovis delivered his final lines. "Membair of jury," he hoarsely sang, "listen to your verdict as recorded: You do say, upon your oaths, that you do find the defendant Randall Kirk not guilty of murder by reason of unconsciousness? So say you, Madame Foreman? So say you all, membair of the jury?"

There was a nodded rumble of assent from all twelve jurors and the judge lightly tapped his gavel for silence. "Ladies and gentlemen," he addressed the jurors, "I thank you for your loyal and attentive service in a difficult and unusual case. You have deported yourselves well in one of the highest privileges and gravest duties of citizens in a democracy." He smiled faintly. "As a reward for your diligence you will be reprieved from further duty until tomorrow morning at nine—sharp—when we'll take up a new criminal case." He squinted out at the courtroom clock. "Court is now adjourned until that time."

I, too, looked back at the courtroom clock. The time was 10:13.

The jurors turned and slowly began filing out through their mahogany door, the last juror now leading the way, the lady who had just announced the verdict turning and giving a smiling farewell nod back at my client just before she disappeared. Another victory for apple pie and motherhood and my partner's jury theories, I thought.

My client wordlessly grabbed and wrung my hand, followed by my partner and Doctor Hugh. Both of them hovered, watching the proceedings, while Eugene Canda came over and gamely congratulated my partner and me, and finally turning to Doctor Hugh.

"Congratulations to you too, Doctor Salter," he said, grasping and pumping his hand, "surely one of the toughest and most resourceful opponents I've ever met in or out of the courtroom, you—you magnificent old goat." He suddenly turned away and moved back to his table.

"Thank you, son," the old boy called after him, his eyes misting a little, I thought. Maybe it was only out of anticipation for cribbage, which the two gladiators shortly hurried back to the conference room to engage in.

Viola Axholm suddenly appeared out of nowhere and warmly hugged and kissed my client and then turned on me, but I warded her off with an upraised hand, managing to mutter "Strep throat" in a cawing croak, whereupon she grabbed my hand and kissed it, several times shrilly repeating, "I *knew* it, I *knew* it, just as I knew all along about his two-timing. . . . I never *did* trust that dreadful man!"

She apologized to my client for having to leave to clean his cottage, a chore she'd lacked the courage to face earlier, she explained, until she knew for sure he was free. "You'll also find a clean bed, darling," she added as she gave him a final embrace and turned and left, leaving me wondering vaguely whether he mightn't also find her in it.

I grabbed up my briefcases and moved away toward our conference room, motioning my client to follow, but he still remained standing by our table looking confused and uncertain.

"Follow me, Kirk," I called back to him. "We'll pick up your jail stuff later."

"Are you sure?" he said, glancing uncertainly about him. "You mean I'm really free to go?"

I returned to our table and handed him a couple of my briefcases and locked my free arm in his and firmly led him away, wrenched to see how imprisonment could so swiftly manacle and subdue the human spirit. "You're a free man, Kirk," I told him huskily, repeating it several times. "Come, let's go see and thank the two old boys who toiled so mightily to get you that way."

References

Part One

Page

56 William James, *Principles of Psychology* (1890).

59 James Esdaile, *Mesmerism in India* (1851).

66 See related article on police use of hypnosis by neurologist Richard M. Restak in "The Week in Review," *New York Times,* August 15, 1975, p. 6; and for a general discussion of hypnosis, see *Newsweek*, March 7, 1977, p. 54.

68 Joseph Breuer, and Sigmund Freud, *Studies in Hysteria* (1895; 957): 1957.

78 For early Michigan case on "irresistible impulse" see People v. Durfee, 62 Mich 487. Also see annotation on the subject in 70 ALR 659.

84 Sanford J. Fox, "Physical Disorder, Consciousness, and Criminal Liability," 63 *Columbia Law Review* 645.

84 For legal annotation of insane delusion as a criminal defense see 1917F LRA 650.

85 Fain v. Commonwealth, 78 Ky 183 (1879).

86 People v. Freeman, 61 Cal app 2d 110, 142 P2d435 (1943).
88 "Amnesia: A Case Study in the Limits of Particular Justice," 71 *Yale Law Journal* 109 (1961).
89 State v. Gooze, 14 NJ Sup 277, 81 A2d 811(1951).
94 For early annotation (1898) on hypnosis and the law, see 40LRA269.
97 Right of counsel in consulting with client to be accompanied by psychiatrist, psychologist, hypnotist, or similar practitioner, see Cornell v. Superior Court (1959), 52 Cal 2d 99, 338 Pac 2d 447, 72ALR2d 1116.

Part Two

Michigan has had occasion in two recent cases—apparently for the first time, at least at the appellate level—to consider the admissibility of testimony in criminal prosecutions in which the use of hypnosis was present. The facts are too complicated to review in a reference note, more than to say that the first case involved the testimony of a defendant allegedly stimulated by hypnosis on behalf of the defense and the second, that of a prosecution witness on its behalf. People v. Hangsleben (1978) 86 Mich App 718, 273NW 2d 539 and People v. Tait (1980) 99 Mich App 19, 297NW 2d 853.

Both opinions discuss some of the dangers present in the unrestricted admissibility of such testimony and suggest certain limitations. The opinion in *Tait* states "the courts that have dealt with the admissibility of hypnotically induced testimony are hopelessly split," an observation borne out by one of the few legal annotations found on the subject, which the opinion cites, appearing in 92ALR 3rd 442 (1979), where the relatively few American cases bearing on the question are cited and discussed.

230 William J. Bryan, *Legal Aspects of Hypnosis* (1962).
230 U.P.I. account of once secret document recently obtained by the weekly Washington newsletter *Science Trends* under the Freedom of Information Act and appearing in the *Detroit Free Press,* February 21, 1978.
231 See "Antisocial Uses of Hypnosis" by Paul C. Young in *Experimental*

Hypnosis by Leslie LeCron (1952); for contrary view see "Antisocial Behavior and Hypnosis" by Martin T. Orne in *Hypnosis: Current Problems,* ed. by George H. Estabrooks (1962); for a general review of the subject see Samuel Glasner's discussion in *Hypnodermic Psychology,* ed. by Milton V. Kline (1955).

236 For a Michigan case holding that a final divorce may impliedly revoke a will favoring a surviving former spouse, see In re McGraw's Estate, 228 Mich 1, 199 NW 686, cited in 95 Corpus Juris Secundum at Section 293.

259 For a leading American case on effect of murder of testator by a beneficiary under his will, see Riggs v. Palmer (1889), 115 NY 506, 22NE 188, 5 LRA 340; see also 36ALR 2nd 960.

262 See Michigan Circuit Court Rule No. 516 for requested instructions to the jury.

269 Section 2.01 of Article 2 of the Model Penal Code of the American Law Institute (1974 edition) provides in part as follows:

(1) A person is not guilty of an offense unless his liability is based on conduct which includes a voluntary act or the omission to perform an act of which he is physically capable.

(2) The following are not voluntary acts within the meaning of this Section:

(a) a reflex or convulsion;

(b) a bodily movement during unconsciousness or sleep;

(c) conduct during hypnosis or resulting from hypnotic suggestion;

(d) a bodily movement that otherwise is not a product of the effort or determination of the actor, either conscious or habitual.